# A Bit Of Fresh

Tabbie Browne

Copyright © 2015 Tabbie Browne

All rights reserved, including the right to reproduce this book, or portions thereof in any form. No part of this text may be reproduced, transmitted, downloaded, decompiled, reverse engineered, or stored, in any form or introduced into any information storage and retrieval system, in any form or by any means, whether electronic or mechanical without the express written permission of the author.

This is a work of fiction. Names and characters are the product of the author's imagination and any resemblance to actual persons, living or dead, is entirely coincidental.

The views expressed in this work are solely those of the author and do not necessarily reflect the views of the publisher, and the publisher hereby disclaims any responsibility for them.

ISBN: 978-1-326-47085-2

PublishNation, London
www.publishnation.co.uk

# Other Books by this author

*White Noise is Heavenly Blue* (Book One of The Jenny Trilogy)
*The Spiral* (Book Two of The Jenny Trilogy)
*Choler* (Book Three of The Jenny Trilogy)
*A Fair Collection*
*The Unforgiveable Error*
*No-Don't!*
*Above The Call*


Visit the author's website at:
www.tabbiebrowneauthor.com

"Tabbie's original and unusual plots and storylines make for a really intriguing read."
Dave Andrews, Presenter, BBC Radio Leicester

"The master of supernatural suspense." Peter J Bennett, Author

"The books are catching, they keep you thinking, and make you 'look outside the box'. I enjoy reading Tabbie's books in my limited down time."

Anne Royle and Spook (my four legged glasses). Founder Pathfinder Guide Dog Programme

# ACKNOWLEDGEMENTS

The author wishes to extend her grateful thanks
to all those who kindly offered alternative words
for parts of the male anatomy.
She tried to avoid the word 'penis' in case it lowered the tone.

Also special thanks to the gentleman friend
who offered to pose with her for the cover picture .
In your dreams!
Well, you have appeared in the story, so be satisfied.

# Chapter 1

The phone ringing made Danny jump. He had been relaxing on the sofa watching one of his favourite programmes on tv and hoped this wasn't another of those time wasting cold callers. He grabbed the remote, turned the volume down and picked up the handset which was lying on the side table. Still watching the screen he gave a short "Hello."

"Is that you Danny?" the voice sounded tense and not like his younger brother's normal manner, so something made him refrain from asking "Who else did you expect it to be?"

"Hey bro, what's up?"

"I… no I mean a friend of mine has a problem." Silence followed.

"Ok, what kind of problem?"

"Well, it's a bit awkward. Could we come over and see you?"

Everything was racing round Danny's head and he doubted if there was a friend at all but he was keen to know what was going on. Although they got on well, Joel wasn't one to bother him with his troubles and was happily married so he couldn't imagine there was a problem there.

"When were you thinking?" he asked but added "any time if it's that urgent."

There was a subdued whispering from the other end as if he was arranging something so maybe there was a friend after all.

"Oh Christ, I hope it's not a female!" Up to now Danny had imagined it was another man, a mate, but kept this thought to himself until he knew more.

"Could we come tomorrow evening?" The voice was almost a whisper now.

"No problem. Just turn up, with your friend."

The goodbyes were brief but Danny was intrigued now and he was actually looking forward to knowing what was going on because there had to be something serious to warrant all this cloak and dagger business.

Joel, his only brother had been through a few girl friends but when he met Zoe, he knew instantly she was the one for him. They had married in their early twenties and hadn't rushed to have a family, although recently both thought that if they were going to start, they had better get on with it as they were approaching thirty. They both had good jobs in management of a leading hotel chain and money wasn't a problem. They had a nice home, went on holidays, both had a car in fact all the practical things but the years had slipped by quicker than they realised.

Danny on the other hand was creeping up through his mid thirties but had never settled down. Not for the want of countless possible partners, but he enjoyed his life of freedom, to have whichever lady he wanted at the time and then part when things didn't run smoothly, but no ties. He was a very attractive man, had looked after his body and his mind and it was obvious he would retain his good looks into old age. He read a lot, his mind always cramming information in as though it would be lost if he didn't store it. He watched many documentaries but always wanted to know more than was being portrayed. His brain was like a sponge. But he was a very private person and although everyone assumed he had a good job he never divulged exactly what he did, passing it off by saying "Oh I work in logistics." In fact he ran a very successful internet company but under a totally different name, and not even his family knew the connection.

As he turned the sound back up, his mind was sifting all sorts of possibilities, but his sense told him to wait and see, then use his energy to be of whatever help was obviously needed.

The 'friend' was a young man of similar age and situation to Joel. They had met through work and at first it was thought that the two couples might strike up a combined friendship but it soon became obvious that Nick's marriage wasn't a happy one. His wife Emma seemed to lead a life of her own with her select group of female friends, always going to parties although he often wondered just where they went as she gave very few details. If he asked any questions she would just reply "You can always get me on my mobile." But that was useless because she never answered with some lame excuse that it was too noisy or she had switched it off by mistake. The distrust had now crept in and Nick found that he didn't believe anything she said and he was beginning to wonder what he had ever seen in her.

But now his own personal problem was taking over which is why he had confided in Joel, half expecting him to laugh it off, whereas he had offered a very understanding ear. Nick wasn't comfortable at the suggestion of bringing Danny into it, but he was assured that if anyone could come up with the answers he could, added to which he was the very soul of discretion, so somewhat reluctantly Nick agreed as he was getting to his wits end as to how to cope with it.

"Oh go on, we haven't done anything exciting for ages." Sam was coaxing her friend to go out the following evening. The subject of this phone call couldn't have been more different to the one shared by the brothers.

"I'm not sure. You know what happened the last time." Katie-Marie wasn't the gregarious type and often didn't feel comfortable at some of the places they frequented. Since her husband died a few years before, she'd never been interested in any other male company, whereas Sam, now divorced wanted to make up for lost time. They were both middle aged and had totally different views on life, one quite content to sit at home and watch films or house renovations, while the other wanted to enjoy all she could get before she 'went over' as she put it. Some thought she was well past it anyway but there were always men who would take whatever was offered, especially if it only cost them a few drinks.

Katie-Marie had been a pretty child and kept her innocent looks well into womanhood, and had she dressed with a little more flare could almost have been mistaken for Sam's daughter, but the older woman was content to let her tag along for company. She never wanted to go out alone but once at the event, even if it was for a drink at a pub, she scanned the area for talent, usually leaving Katie to get home on her own.

"Well, where were you thinking of going?" she added, knowing she wouldn't like wherever it was.

"Oh I don't know," Sam sounded unsure, then changed the tone to "there is one place I've been told about, but it's in the centre of town." She waited for the reaction knowing her friend didn't like night clubs or too much noise.

"I'm not sure, they're usually filled with teenagers, not our age."

"Ah well from what I've been told, this one caters for older people. Bit select like."

Katie-Marie really didn't like the sound of it but couldn't come up with a reasonable excuse so she played for time.

"And do you know these people well, the ones who told you?"

"Oh yes, known them for years. They work at our place."

She paused knowing this wasn't going to be easy. In fact she wasn't divulging the fact they she had been given the tip that you never left 'empty handed' and she knew very well what that meant. It didn't bother her that she would be dragging along an unwilling companion who would leave as soon as she had made her catch for the night, nor did it bother her that the woman would have to make her own way home usually paying for a taxi.

"Sounds like it could be expensive." Katie came up with another reason. "Like that other one you thought would be nice. Cost the earth when we got there."

"Oh well, if you want to stay at home all the time." The reply was curt and filled with disappointment.

"No, I like to go out only…." her voice trailed off.

"You don't like mixing."

"Yes, but I like going to the cinema, but you never come with me there."

Sam took a deep breath. Why she bothered with this creature was beyond her, but who else had she got? Her friends seemed to have drifted away and she couldn't see that they had summed her up and refused to be used as an acceptable companion then dropped like a hot brick when the time came. If Katie hadn't been so lonely and loyal, she would have done the same but something inside made her reluctant to upset her friend.

"Well I can't force you, I'll just have to go on my tod. Not the same though. Some of these places still don't think it right for a woman to go alone. I might not even be allowed in. Makes me wonder if it's worth it after all." She let the words drift slowly knowing the effect it would have.

"Um….maybe we could try it but if we don't like it could we go home?"

It had worked. Sam knew that Katie's weakness was her conscience and she wouldn't risk their friendship by refusing if she was pressured enough.

"Well of course we could, that goes without saying. We'll just go and check it out and if no good we can always go to the Eagles, you don't mind it there now do you?"

The Eagles Eyrie was a fairly local pub within a reasonable walking distance where they had the usual quiz nights or the odd special event evening. There was a small function room at the back and although the guests sometimes spilled into the bar or lounge area, it was never that noisy. Katie felt it was quite homely and sometimes the ladies had gone for lunch there as the food was good.

"Oh no, that would be alright, as long as that would be an option, if we don't like your new place." Katie should have said "if I don't like it" but that would have been futile because Sam would have agreed at the time, but once they were there any promises would have been forgotten once she had made her conquest.

Nick had been in bed some time before he heard Emma's key in the door. It had become the habit to feign sleep to save entering into any conversation. If she had been drinking she always hid it well but didn't seem to care what noise she made, almost as if he wasn't there. They had twin beds now and he wished he could move into the second bedroom but she had scoffed at the idea saying she hadn't time to sort it out and as they didn't use the main bedroom for the usual purposes apart from sleep, why waste energy?

She had been in bed about ten minutes and was snoring when Nick froze. Here it was again, that feeling creeping over his entire body. He daren't make a sound for fear of waking her but something was in bed with him. Knowing there was no way he could switch on the bedside light for fear of disturbing his wife, he had placed a small torch under his pillow. Now he would see what was causing this sensation that was making every inch of his body aroused, but as his hand reached for it something clamped down on his arm making him unable to grasp it. Gradually he could feel the whole length of the female form on top of him, her hands gently moving down his neck until they got to his chest. It took all his willpower not to groan or emit any sound as she explored every inch, working her way down his body. At his waist she stopped and he felt a gentle breeze blowing across every inch she had already covered and she had gone. He was almost crying as he gripped his groin unable to control the inevitable that always followed, but at least this time he was prepared for it and wouldn't have to explain the state of his nightwear, to put it politely.

As he lay there, his breathing slowing to a normal pace, he tried to understand what was now becoming a regular occurrence and he wished more than ever that he hadn't confided in Joel as it felt as though he was breaking a confidence by telling anyone. Even more he wished they weren't going to see his brother and made up his mind to cancel the visit when morning came.

After the initial shock of the sensations, he now found he was waiting for the next hoping it would be longer than the last, also he wanted to give the female a name to make it personal. Words were playing around in his mind but he felt as though he was hearing something like Fortune or Phantom and something in his inner self told him to be patent and he would learn the identity when it was the right time.

Emma hardly knew he existed now. She had her own circle of friends, male and female and she was living life to the full. When she wasn't at work she was usually out somewhere, did very little housework and barely cooked a meal saying "Oh I'm eating out, you just look after yourself." There had been a few nights when she didn't come home at all and Nick now would have valued these, had he known in advance because it was the only time he was truly relaxed. But she never bothered to phone, just turned up in time for work the next day, or if it was her weekend off, didn't even show up during the day. He would never report her missing, which meant that if she was attacked or worse, it could be ages before anyone realised, in fact her friends would probably realise before he did, whoever they were. She wasn't short of sexual partners, but some of these came and went, not even bothering to exchange names. She was playing a dangerous game, and would soon look much older than she was if she carried on living in this style.

Nick began to wonder if this state of affairs was playing with his mind, and he was hallucinating to keep himself sane but pushed that thought away. There was no way he could ever love her again and wished she would make the decision to move on and let him get on with his own life. He'd thought of leaving her but while she had her feet firmly in the house there was little he could do.

Joel was explaining to Zoe that he was taking his friend to see Danny but couldn't say too much.
"Why, what on earth's the matter?" She turned in bed to face him.
"Man's stuff. Can't embarrass him, and I promised I wouldn't say." he gave a nod as much as to say 'don't ask'.
"But you can tell me, I won't say a word." She moved nearer.
"Sorry I can't. There's some things men don't discuss."
"But we've never had any secrets." The tone was impatient.
"No, but this isn't to do with me, it's Nick's problem, and I wouldn't be much of a mate if I went blabbing about it."
Her mouth opened to speak but he jumped in "So please don't ask any more."
"You won't even say when you've been to Danny's?" This was her final shot at finding out for her curiosity was really peaking now.
"No, I won't even say when we've been to Danny's." He repeated for effect.
She turned away in a mild huff, so he slipped his arm round her pulling her towards him as he whispered "If it was anything to do with me you would be the first to know. I wouldn't ask if it was a girl friend of yours. Wouldn't be nice." He lightly kissed her hair, and they drifted off in that position.

Katie-Marie woke up and looked at the clock. Only 6am. As she groped for her slippers to go and make a cup of tea, she remembered she was due to go out that evening with Sam.
"Oh why do I let her talk me into these things?" she scolded herself but knew it was useless. Her friend had a way of arranging thing to suit herself and dragging people along with her plans whether they were willing or not. In the past, those who had stood up to her soon drifted away, and she was always left with the lonely

souls who just went along for company. But Katie wasn't lonely. Of course she missed her husband, but would rather sit in their home surrounded by his things than go out to an environment where she felt uncomfortable just to please the other woman.

"This is definitely the last time." She told herself as she came out of the bathroom and made her way downstairs. There was no good trying to put Sam off today because that wouldn't work and Katie wasn't one to feign illness. She made up her mind that tonight, as soon as she was left alone she would get up and go home without a word of explanation and see if that went in. It wouldn't. Sam would be so busy with her latest conquest to notice. That would be the start, and next time, if there was a next time, it would be even easier until there would be no point in her going at all.

This made her feel a lot better and she decided to fill her day with things to keep her busy and not worry about the evening until it happened. There was that box of her late husband's that she had been putting off going through, so today would be a good time to get it done.

Sam on the other hand woke up in fine spirits. Saturday was always a good night to be talent hunting. The week days were ok but the weekend was when people were out for a good time and she had made up her mind to try out the new club no matter what Katie thought. As long as she went in with her, it didn't matter after that, and the promise of going to the Eagles held no weight as she just used it as bait to get her to go out. There was never much talent in that place unless there was a special event on in the function room, then if you were in the right place at the right time you could get lucky. She flicked through her wardrobe for something to wear that would pull the type of men she usually attracted and took it as a compliment that they could spot her a mile off, whereas others would have been insulted even if their motives were the same.

"No. I need something new." she decided as she rummaged among the well used dresses, some with hardly enough material to cover her essentials. Slamming the door closed, she got ready to go into town and find something stunning, well as stunning as she could afford. Her shoes would have to do for now for who would see them at night anyway? She didn't realise it was the accessories that could let a person down, a lesson her mother would have known only too well. Had her mother been watching she would have been appalled at her daughter picking up the pants she had worn the day before, giving the crotch a sniff and putting them on, and even more shocked at the thought that she could have gone out without any on at all. Some things are better not seen, even from the other side.

Danny had been having a relaxing afternoon looking at gazebos. There was a corner of the garden that he thought would be a nice place to have somewhere to sit and read in the fresh air, but afford a little protection. He would get his gardener to clear the area in readiness at the first opportunity. Normally he would have sat at his computer, studying all the different options and prices but he felt he wanted to go out and look at the products before buying to get a better idea of the sizes. It had been a successful project and he ordered one to be delivered. While he was out he decided to pick up a few snacks for later, no need to replenish the drinks cupboard for it was always fully stocked.

As he drove home his mind slipped to Joel's phone call. Something wasn't ringing true. There had to be more to it than a friend who needed advice. It couldn't be that he had got some girl pregnant, not nowadays, it had to be something to do with finance and the lad had got himself into a pickle and didn't know what to do about it.

"Well, I shall know sooner or later," he mused as he turned into his driveway, but he was still curious and looked forward to hearing whatever would be revealed never guessing what he would be privy to.

"I'm going out tonight." Nick said quietly.
"So, what am I supposed to do about it? You please yourself." Emma's reply was curt. "I won't be here."
Nick was grateful that she wasn't interested enough to ask any questions, but he had been banking on this.
"What about dinner?" he asked quietly.
"What about it?"
"Are you having any?"
"Nope."

"Well I'll just fix myself something then."

"Whatever." She muttered as she went out of the room presumably for another sleep before she disappeared later.

It was getting on for five o'clock so Nick took a pizza from the freezer and put it in the oven. He was getting quite good at these one man meals now but missed the proper freshly cooked meals they used to have. Sometimes he would go to his parents but have to make some excuse as to why he was alone. They knew something wasn't right but his mother wouldn't ask, and his father thought that if their son needed to talk he would.

He was just closing the oven door when he felt a hand on his bottom and spun round in surprise wondering what Emma was doing. But there was nobody there. The feeling was now spreading until he felt both cheeks clenched in two invisible hands and they were massaging his buttocks with such force he couldn't imagine a woman having that much power. The thought that a male presence was taking advantage of him made him shudder and he thrashed about with his arms trying to drive the feeling away. As quickly as it had started, it stopped and he leant against the working surface for support, his heart pounding. As he compared the experience with the bed session, something was telling him it was coming from the same source but he was confused by the different approach.

His breathing slowed and he tried to clear his mind of everything believing that this was all his imagination due to his enforced celibacy, but then he began to wonder if it was affecting him mentally. For the first time he was almost relieved to be going to see Danny but was still apprehensive in case he was ridiculed. Joel had said what a good listener he was and how many times he had given people good advice, but he didn't know the man. Then the question jumped into his mind.

"Why is Joel so keen for me to go? It's almost as though he's pushing me."

He knew his friend cared, but come to think of it he had been adamant and arranged the whole thing. He stopped as he reached for a plate.

"No, that can't be it. But it must be. This Danny bloke must have had the same, that's why he knows what's going on." The thought made Nick feel much more relaxed now. "So that's why he was so keen. He was taking me to someone in the same boat."

It was a different man that enjoyed his meal and started to get himself ready for the evening, feeling he could face this – whatever it was – because he wasn't alone.

# Chapter 2

The sound of the doorbell startled Katie even though she was expecting Sam at any time. She never knew what to expect when her friend arrived and thought she was beyond being shocked, but she should have known better by now.

"Ta dah!" Sam stood arms up in a pose as the door opened. "What do you think?"

"Well, um, will you be warm enough?" It was tame but what else could she say politely to the vision facing her? Had it been her mother, the reply would have been more like "well I'm not going out with you looking like that."

"Who wants to be warm, eh?" Sam almost danced into the hallway nearly knocking Katie to one side, but she stopped as she saw what the other woman was wearing.

"Oh, right, good, want to be comfy as usual."

"What's wrong with it?" Katie looked down at her dress.

"Oh nothing if you want to….." her voice trailed off as she saw the expression on her friend's face then drew the attention back to her own. "Like it? Got it today, thought I'd show my tits off for a change."

Katie really wanted to say "but you always do." but kept it to herself and instead said quietly "I think you'll show more than that."

The reply was a playful punch in the arm with "Well that's what it's all about. Show 'em what's on the menu."

"Oh you'll do that alright."

Katie couldn't help feeling rather out of place before they even got to the club and wished she had the courage to back out, but there was always the fall back option of ending up at the Eagles. Most people would have realised by now that Sam had no intention of doing that, she was dressed to kill and she wouldn't come back disappointed. Her dress was red, what there was of it, for there were more straps than anything and the whole thing couldn't have used more than a square yard of material.

"No," Katie thought "somehow this has to be the very last time I do this."

They found the club, although Sam seemed to know exactly where it was and once inside she was scanning the place for talent although how she managed it in the gloom Katie couldn't imagine. It took her some time to adjust but as soon as she began to see better she wanted to leave there and then.

"Hello darling" a hand went round her waist and a male was breathing into her face.

"Get away." she pushed harder than she intended and he bumped into someone behind him who threatened to thump him. Katie was panicking now, she just had to get out, she felt stifled. Frantically she looked around for Sam but couldn't see her anywhere because apart from the lack of light, the place was heaving, and not everyone was dancing, far from it although they were in very intimate positions. The music was so loud she could feel her heart beating in her chest and she tried to head for the door, but which way? There should be an exit sign but everything was becoming a blur and she stumbled about until she could remember no more.

Some of the staff had managed to get her into a small area behind the bar where she was beginning to regain her senses, but her body was sore from the bruises where people had simply walked over her or kicked her as she had gone down. They were suggesting she go home, but that was already uppermost in her mind and it was agreed they call a cab for her.

"I came with a friend, she needs to know." she almost whispered.

"What's she look like?"

"She's wearing a red dress."

The staff would like to have pointed out that wasn't much help but said they would do their best. They gave it a few moments then said they couldn't find her so she was helped out to the taxi assuring the driver she wasn't drunk. Never had she been so glad to open her front door and fall onto her sofa, safe in her own place. This settled it, she would go to the Eagles any time, but clubs, never, and whether Sam liked it or not she would have to go alone, because this girl would not be joining her and she could think what she liked.

Sam was lost in her own world. She'd worked her way through several 'possibles' and was now in the arms of quite a muscular hunk who made no secret of why he was here. They were near one of the archways leading to the toilets and he had her up against the pillar. It was quite a dark corner and as everyone else seemed intent on their own conquests nobody paid attention to them. It didn't take long before they were locked in more ways than one and with the rhythm of the music, they soon reached the peak of their enjoyment. This was an added thrill for her, to be able to score in a crowded place and she was so intent on her own pleasures, Katie never came into her mind.

It was only when they went to get a drink the bar tender asked if she had come with a friend.

"Oh yes, I did come with someone," she slurred "I'd quite forgotten." and went into fits of laughter. "Why d'you fancy her?" she nearly fell face down on the bar finding it all very funny.

"She's been sent home in a taxi."

Sam looked up "Oh good. Saves me the trouble." and turned to hang onto her current escort but he'd gone off looking for a bit of fresh and she nearly fell onto another man.

"Oi you get your filthy hands off my bloke." a woman screamed.

"Wouldn't touch him with a barge pole you old cow. I'm very partic…tic…ular."

"She's with me." The voice was deep and the owner slid his arms round Sam and pulled her away.

"I don't know who you are, but thanks, I think." The booze, the noise and her recent jump had left her quite woozy.

"I'll look after you." He breathed in her ear as he led her though the crush.

And so her evening continued, although how much she would remember was anyone's guess. One thing that wasn't on her mind was what had happened to her friend as long as she was having fun. Little did she realise the kind of attention she was attracting, and it was not of this world.

Zoe was still a bit put out at not being told why Joel was taking his friend to see Danny. It wasn't as if she was a prude as she was about as broad minded as anyone so she felt she wouldn't be shocked at anything she heard. She even tried the approach that there must be something to hide and repeated that they never had any secrets but her husband wasn't being drawn saying it was Nick's business and he was just being a supportive mate.

"Well don't be late." she called after him as he was about to leave.

"I'll try not to love, trust me, I'll be glad when this is over." and he gave her a loving kiss and left thinking it was a good job she didn't know just how much.

Nick was waiting just inside the door and as Joel pulled up he almost ran to the car.

"I didn't expect you to be in that much of a hurry," Joel almost laughed then seeing the man's face added "won't be long, soon be there."

"Can we get going?" Nick seemed very agitated and was looking around as if he didn't want to be seen.

"Ok." Joel drove off but cast a few glances to the passenger seat.

"Don't want the neighbours to see me."

"What?"

"Well they might know something was the matter."

Joel took a deep breath. "Look, it probably doesn't matter a toss to them what you are doing, probably too busy minding their own business and it's not as if you were going out with a woman is it? Come on man, two blokes, we could be going anywhere."

"I'm just edgy, that's all."

"I can see that. Would it help if I told you I feel the same?"

"How could you? You haven't got my problems have you?"

Joel didn't answer and the two travelled in silence both in their own thoughts until they reached Danny's house. As soon as the car was parked in the drive, the front door opened and Danny was welcoming them in. Nick was relieved as he still didn't want to be on view, whether he knew the people or not. They went into the lounge and for a moment the atmosphere was very tense. Joel introduced Nick and even the formalities seemed very wooden.

"Well," Danny smiled, sensing this wasn't going to be easy "let's have a drink then we can put the world to rights eh?"

He beckoned them to sit on the sofa while he filled the glasses then positioned himself in the armchair opposite where he could observe them both, not only while they spoke but watching their body language. His brother seemed a bit screwed up whereas the other one was a nervous wreck so the sooner he could find out what this was all about the better.

"Right," he began looking straight at Nick "I accept you don't know me but be assured that anything you want to say goes no further than this room. Ok?"

Nick nodded but barely raised his eyes although he could feel this man almost looking into his soul.

"Do you want to start?" Danny looked from him to Joel then back.

Joel gave him a nudge and said "Go on. It can only help."

"Well...." Nick couldn't seem to get started and looked at his friend. "Could you say?"

"Might be a good idea." Danny was thinking that they would be sitting here all night at this rate if one of them didn't start things off but he didn't show any impatience.

Joel coughed. "He's been having these experiences."

"What kind exactly?"

"Um, personal ones, I mean, um, well, its as though someone, I mean something is touching him."

Danny nodded trying to put them both at ease if that was possible.

"Could you say where they are touching you?" He was looking at Nick now.

"All over, only not at the same time."

It was time for straightforward talk, even shock tactics.

"Ah so it's sexual, they're trying to get you aroused, probably succeeding. I'm right aren't I?" He had to hide the smile that threatened when he saw the look on both their faces.

"How did you know?" Joel blurted out.

"Well, I wasn't certain but I guessed. It's quite common you know."

"What, not just me?" Nick was brightening by the minute.

"Hell no. Even had bit of it myself."

Both the younger men were relaxing finding this much easier now.

"What did you do?" Joel asked.

Danny shrugged "Oh just let them get on with it for a while, then the novelty must have worn off and they just stopped." This wasn't strictly true but it was working and this man knew how to handle people.

"So it might go away, they might I mean?"

"They?" Danny looked questioningly straight at him. "There's more than one?"

"Well, no, but I'm not sure now, perhaps there are different ones. I don't really know."

"Does the person always do the same things?"

"Sometimes, but not always."

"Female?" Danny was firing the questions now while he had him talking.

"Oh yes. But wait. Oh yes definitely female."

"And you are sure of this because….."

"I could feel her form, not a physical body but definitely a female form."

Shock treatment time. "And you touched her breasts." This was not a question.

"I didn't but I could feel ……

"Why not?" Danny cut in. "It would be the natural thing for a full blooded male like yourself to respond."

"I think I was too shocked. I didn't know what was going on."

Joel cut in with a laugh. "You're a married man, course you knew what was going on."

Danny held up his hand for silence. "Is this always in your bed?"

"Yes. No wait. It felt me in the kitchen."

"I wondered what you were going to say then, certainly not kitchen!" Joel was almost enjoying this which didn't go unnoticed by his brother.

Danny let the humour die down then came in for the kill. "Has she tossed you off yet?"

Nick's jaw dropped open. This had caught him by surprise and he wasn't ready with an answer.

"Well?"

"Um not quite."

"Don't worry she will." Danny's offhanded reply surprised both men. He let the thought sink in looking from one to the other.

"What do I do about it?" Nick asked slowly.

"Don't you like it?"

"Well, yes, if I'm honest I suppose I do, but I hadn't looked at it that way." Then turning to Joel said "That's why you brought me, you knew he'd had the same."

"I didn't actually, I just knew he was a good person to talk to. You had to get it out to someone the way you were going."

Danny let them finish then leaned forward and said very clearly "But that's not all is it?" His gaze was now on Joel.

Nick noticed and looked at his mate. "What's he on about?"

Joel was looking decidedly uncomfortable now and Danny smiled, sat back and said "Your turn I think bro."

You could have cut the air with a knife, twice, but Joel knew there was no way out.

"It isn't just you." he whispered.

"What? You as well? You never said." Nick had turned until he was sitting sideways.

"I've had it, and it's difficult for me because I sleep with my wife, sorry Nick but you know what I mean."

His friend understood only too well. "You mean yours comes to you in your bed, with Zoe lying there!"

"Now you see the problem. And she's been trying to get it out of me why we were coming here and I told her it was men's problems but how could I have told her the truth?"

Danny said quietly "If you are close, do you think she would understand if you explained?"

"Hell No. She'd go ballistic. She'd think I'd gone weird."

"Hang on." Nick was in full swing now. "If this woman is in your bed, why doesn't Zoe feel her there as well?"

"Look mate," Joel faced him now "You're lying there right, and this thing is getting you stiff, how can you have your wife at the same time. It's like two separate people man!"

"Oh I see." Nick looked towards Danny. "He's got more of a problem than I have, hasn't he?"

"Yes he has, but we need to face up to the fact that something is at work here...." He paused for a moment "......that may not be from a good source."

"What?" Both looked at him.

"Another drink?" Danny stood up to refill his glass

"I think I need one." Nick spoke first.

"Better not, unless you've got something non alchi." Joel looked more worried than he had done all night.

"Tell you what, I'll make a coffee." Danny headed for the kitchen allowing them time for his previous remark to sink in. He came back with a tray of nibbles and told them to help themselves then returned with the coffee and sat down.

"Now, I don't know what your beliefs are, or your thoughts on things that can't always be explained." He handed the cups round then continued. "There's a lot of things that go on that people put down to their imagination, possession, all sorts of reasons, but there are also events that affect us very personally. We don't know why. But they can be as real as our everyday tangible happenings. Some are just playful entities that come and go, but some concentrate on one particular emotion, fantasy, habit, preference, call it what you will."

"And this is one of those?" Nick asked.

"I'm not confirming anything. I only know what you've said and I can see the effect it is having on you both with your different circumstances."

"So what do you suggest?" Joel was expecting an answer to the problem.

"I think there are three ways of dealing with it. Let's say you both have exactly the same problem for now. One. Do you go along with it and get full enjoyment out of it?

Now that might be easy for you Nick but not for you." He looked at this brother. "Two. Do you try and find out what it is? Three. Do you want to fight it and send it packing?"

All sat very quietly for some time, each one weighing the odds against the choices. Then Joel asked "Have you ever been in this position yourself?"

"Aha, I was wondering when you would ask that." Danny smiled and said "Not in a sexual way. Seems like you are the lucky ones."

If he hoped he could fob them off with that, they were having none of it.

"So what way? You've never said, but you did go out of touch for a while and we never did know why."

"There's no need to worry about that now, it's in the past. But I just want to warn you both that we may be up against something quite strong that wants to take hold, so my advice would be to try and calm it as much as possible."

"Sounds good to me." Joel was nodding "But how?"

"I'll stick by you of course but if it comes to the really technical stuff, I can bring in someone with a lot more experience to help."

"Do we know him?" Nick wanted to know.

"Did I say him?" Danny gave him a hard look. "It is, but don't assume anything. That's why I asked if you were sure these are female visitors, they can play all sorts of tricks by appearing to be what you want them to be."

"Well if a bloke tries it on, he'll get a boot up the bollocks." Joel was adamant.

"Me too." Nick added.

"That may be just the attitude to get rid of them if they are only the playful sprites, but don't loose sight of other possibilities."

"Christ Almighty!" Joel suddenly gasped. "What am I going to tell Zoe? I've got to say something."

"There's always the truth, that is if you don't want this kind of attention."

Everyone was quiet for a moment then Joel ventured "I don't suppose you'd……"

"Sorry, this is something you have to decide, then do whatever it takes. I don't think she'd appreciate it coming from someone other than her husband, do you?"

"Well no but…"

There were a few general comments before the two left and after seeing them off Danny returned to the lounge.

"Oh not again," was his thought. He sat relaxed in his chair letting his whole being become weightless as he built up the protective shield around him to ward off any unwelcome visitors that may have entered his home along with the lads. He may need all his strength to keep himself safe, but couldn't turn his back on the two now driving home.

Zoe was watching something on the television although she wasn't concentrating on what it was but it was better than sitting waiting in silence. She had thought about putting a cd on but dismissed that idea. She had been on edge ever since Joel left and although she couldn't quite work out why, something was niggling at her. She had taken a shower and was sitting in a dressing gown in the lounge which was where she intended to be, and when he came in she would want a few answers. They had a perfect marriage and she wasn't about to let anything drive a wedge between them, so secret or not, she wouldn't go to bed until he had given her some idea of what was going on with Nick.

The sound of the car pulling into the driveway alerted her so she turned off the tv and waited for him to come in, her stomach churning.

"Hello, sorry I'm a bit late." Joel came into the room slowly.

Zoe looked at the clock. "It's not that late. Would you like a hot chocolate?"

Her husband looked almost relieved but at the same time guilty.

"No thanks, been drinking coffee. Must just go for a pee." and he disappeared across the hall. After a few moments he was back.

"Um, there's something I must tell you love."

"Well, I'm glad you've said that, but I don't know whether I will be pleased until I know what it is." She was still very apprehensive but tried to appear calm.

He moved to the sofa and beckoned her to join him taking her hand as she sat down.

"It's this thing with Nick. He's got this problem you see and, well there's more to it than that."

Zoe turned until she was looking straight at him. She squeezed his hand.

"Suppose you just tell me everything, don't bother how you say it. I know it's been getting to you and I can't bear to see you taking on someone else's problems when it's having this effect."

"You may not like it all."

"Let me be the judge of that."

He took a deep breath and relayed the discussion the three men had shared until he got to the point of his own involvement.

"Oo sounds a bit weird doesn't it? Do you think it's because Nick isn't getting anything, it's sending his brain a bit wonky. Frustration most likely." She was relaxing now.

"That's not all."

"Why? What else has he done?"

Joel paused for a moment before dealing the final blow. "It isn't just him."

"Excuse me?" she looked puzzled now.

"I couldn't bear to tell you before but the same thing has been happening to me. I hoped it would go away but it hasn't and it's been driving me mad."

For a long moment she sat there looking at him, sifting everything he had said through her mind, then without warning she took him into her arms and hugged him as though she would never let him go.

"No wonder you've been screwed up. But you could have said."

"Oh I wanted to, believe me," he was almost in tears at the relief of her reaction. "But how would you have felt, if it had happened to you?"

He didn't expect what she said next. "Well, it wouldn't have been the first time."

"What?"

"Oh it was a long time ago, I was only a teenager. I started to act a bit odd and my father called in the local priest thinking I was possessed or something, but it stopped and nothing more was said about it. They thought it was just growing up stuff but it wasn't polite to talk about it and I was never allowed to bring it up, not that I wanted to."

They were sitting holding hands again and made the agreement they would never hide anything from each other, now matter how bad it was. It seemed a good time to have a cleansing session where they could both be totally open and speak freely. It was as though a huge weight had been lifted from them and their combined love would act as a double protection for the future.

"So how long has this been going on?" she asked quietly.

"Well not long with me, but Nick's had it for some time it seems. Made him a nervous wreck but of course sleeping on his own, Emma doesn't have to know about it."

"She wouldn't care anyway. But getting back to you. What happens?"

"I get this feeling as though someone is touching me, just gently to start with and if I say not unpleasant, do you know what I mean?"

"Yes, go on."

"But then it gets personal until it's trying to take me off and I have to hold myself in an effort to get it to stop."

She looked thoughtful. "This thing, is it just hands or do you feel a whole body?"

"Up to now it's only been hands, no wait there was a mouth as well but that's when I tried to push it away."

"Do you think it is a woman?"

"Oh yes by the softness, I'd have known if it had been a man and you'd have heard the scream!" He tried to make light of it but knew this was no laughing matter.

"What did Danny have to say about it?"

"Gave us options." he tried to relate what had been said then asked "What would you do?"

She took a deep breath. "Get rid ASAP."

"That's what I thought, but how do I do it?" Then as an afterthought "Tell me it's not just in my mind."

"No love, I don't believe for one minute it is. It just bothers me that it's playing with you both at the same time unless……"

"What?" he was curious.

"……it isn't the same one."

"Oh Christ!"

They both sat in silence their minds churning, then Joel asked "Do you mind saying what happened to you?"

"Of course not, not to you anyway."

They were cuddled up now as though that strengthened their protection.

"Like I say I was young and just finding out the different feelings that go on in a girls' body when it changes but something used to feel as though it was taking me over, yes, possessing me for a while. No that doesn't sound right."

"How do you mean?"

"Well, in a possession you think of something controlling what that person does, but this was something other than me doing things to my body I'd never experienced before."

"Not going inside you?" he was horrified at the thought.

"Oh yes, well and truly. My breasts were starting to sprout and they got plenty of pummelling but when it started going right inside me I didn't know what to do. The trouble was it felt nice, but I'm ashamed to say that. Obviously I didn't tell my parents any of this, but they noticed I was becoming withdrawn but would throw a tantrum for no reason. But I only did it if a man tried to put his arms round me, so I was rebelling against it I suppose."

"It must have been frightening." Joel felt he had to console her for all those years ago.

"The worst thing was that, being rather old fashioned and very religious they called in the local priest and I went at him."

"No!"

Although this was serious it caused a light relief and they both ended up laughing at the thought of it. After a moment Joel asked "Did you hit him?"

"I swore at him and told him he was just like all other men, or something like that."

"Do you know? I would have paid to see your parents' faces."

She looked pensive. "Sad thing is they haven't changed much over the years have they?"

"No, you're right there. Hey how on earth did they ever conceive you?"

"In the dark I should think."

They sat for a while then both went to speak at once.

"No you go first." Joel said.

"We will be ready for when madam starts her dirty tricks next time. Boy is she in for a shock?"

"I was just going to say, be a right threesome," then he ducked before she hit him, playfully but there was a bond of love here that could repel anything, or so they thought.

Nick had gone into the empty house, grateful that Emma wasn't there. He felt much better for his visit and had decided his course of action. He would take from this spirit all that was lacking in his marriage and he would enjoy every moment to the full. It seemed a pity that he couldn't see her but he wouldn't let that stop his enjoyment. He also made another decision. Whether Emma was in agreement or not, he would move into the spare bedroom where he would be alone with his new love without interruption. That would be his job the next morning, but for now he was needed in his own bed.

He took a quick shower then lay naked under the covers waiting for his visitor.

For some time he thought she wasn't coming but suddenly he felt the presence and this time imagined he could even smell her perfume. Her hands were caressing his ankles, moving slowly up his legs, pausing around his knees as though tormenting with the threat of stopping there. He felt a pressure moving up on the inside of his thighs and he was panting with anticipation as the feeling approached his groin, but just as he was awaiting the final moment it moved outwards on both sides creeping up the top of his legs until it was giving the impression it was tangled in his pubic hair. He was reaching bursting point, his juices threatening to explode any minute when the unseen hands suddenly grasped his purple headed bed snake and took him soaring to another place.

How long he lay there clutching his equipment he didn't know, but one thing was certain, there was no way he could ever let this out of his life for it was the best sexual experience he had ever known and he knew nothing would ever come up to this in the realms of erotic enjoyment.

Whilst there is no need for names in the spirit world, they have to be used for those in body to identify them, as most earthly souls haven't yet learned to associate another being with memory without having to use a tag. It is often explained simply. If you see someone you know you recognise that person without necessarily bringing the name to mind. Of course names are used because that's how habit has dictated. A child will run to a parent shouting 'Mummy' or 'Daddy' but they have already accepted who the person is. If you are waiting for someone who is arriving by train, there will be dozens of passengers milling about but you instantly recognise your relative or friend with out thinking 'there is John Jones', it is more likely you will think there he/she is, as the case may by.

In the case of spirit identification where no form is seen only felt, it becomes necessary to have some way of being sure you know with whom you are interacting. So when Nick was getting the faint suggestion of Fortune or Phantom he was almost right.

Phantom, or Fortuna as she often called herself had targeted him as a challenge. She and her friend Phelia were in constant battle as to who could beat the other in their conquests and would set up pairs or even groups of men as their next objectives. The larger the group, the more they had to hump to win, but if they set their sights on a couple, it was how far they could take each one. The more hurdles the better.

They had been watching the two friends for some time and, weighing up all the factors, they thought they had an even fight on their hands. Joel seemed the more sexually charged, but there was the problem of his wife and as Nick didn't look as though he'd seen any part of a woman from the outside let alone in, he would be quite an interesting subject. They agreed it wouldn't be first past the post, but would set a time limit of three weeks and whoever had achieved the most in that time would be the reigning champion. At the moment Fortuna held the title but her mate was determined to seize it. Between themselves they shortened their names just for the fun of it and Fortuna shortened Phantom to Phani (pronounced Fanny) and Phelia called herself Pheel (Feel).

They were discussing their antics to date before moving onto the next stage.

"Well mine will be a pushover. He's gasping for it." Phani was boasting.

"That's doubtful with that wife of his. She's put a block up, I'm telling you."

"And you think your lanky streak of piss will perform? No chance! He'll fall at the first climax."

Pheel was angry. "You didn't see him. He was there, spurting all over the place."

"Premature E. That's all." Phani laughed, "That's all you'll get out of him, no experiments, just the same old shake shake, coming, finished."

"You think you know it all."

"I know men and I'm telling you, you're on a loser."

"So why didn't you take him on if you're such an expert?"

Phani was enjoying this. She always used psychological warfare the break down the opposition to try and make them feel useless before they even started and Pheel should have known by now what her little game was, but she always took the bait and got annoyed which only made her all the more intent on winning the next round.

"Right, time to go to work." Phani was raring to be off.

"Oh, have you seen Cela lately," Pheel asked. Cela was short for Celestial who often seemed to appear just as they were in full battle, with the intention of trying to take over when they had done the groundwork.

"You've not heard. She only does virgins now."

"What! Nothing else?"

"Nope. Sniffing round all the young men who need to get their feet wet."

"But why?"

"Reckons she got more chance, with us hardened souls looking for more satisfaction she's got the monopoly."

"But there's always plenty that will take anything, and a virgin can be a pleasant change." Pheel was pondering.

"We know that." Phani was off, her laughter echoing through the night skies.

Danny had been in touch with his contact for some time although his partner in this field existed only in spirit at the moment. They had worked alongside each other through several lives but always preferred to both be free of the physical if they had a choice. Sometimes it would be Abe in body but in the end it made no difference to their close friendship.

Danny knew he didn't have to explain the problem. "Guess you know."

"Been watching. I've been trying to push Joel your way so that you could deal with it better."

Danny agreed. "If I'd found out just by you alerting me, it would have still been a shock but at least it's in the open and I'll get their side of things. Oh, is it any of our old faithfuls?"

"No, a new bunch to this area, must have exhausted their previous haunts."

"Just female?"

Abe laughed. "No, there's a wave sweeping across here, everything male, female, straight, gay, you name it, we've got it." But then his tone grew serious. "It's not just the erotic side like the lads you've been talking to."

"Oh what?" Danny sensed this was only the tip.

"There's a male wave operating, going for pros, slags, all the common tarts. They start with the sex whetting their appetites to keep them going back for more but then, when they have them in their clutches, they pounce."

"Soul snatchers."

"You got it."

They were both quiet for a moment then Danny whispered "Hoped we'd got rid of them for now."

"Only moved them on friend." Abe then added what they both knew "Our work will never be finished. This is one of the hardest fights against evil because the victims don't want to give up their pleasures."

They agreed that Abe would watch discreetly and glean as much information as possible and pass it on during Danny's waking time but when he was asleep they could work together and then they were a force to be feared.

# Chapter 3

Sam was in someone's bed. She couldn't have said who's to save her life, as she was so far out of her mind but seemed to be enjoying it so didn't fight this new feeling. It was as though she had no body one minute, but the next was feeling the familiar rhythm of some male organ playing his tune in her inside, then she would float again. This was repeating itself until she just relaxed completely and carried on with no more excitement than if she'd been eating her dinner.

Her body's defences suddenly took over as she was aware of something stuffed in her mouth, the to and fro movement still going but there was also something over the rest of her face and it was stopping the air going into her nose. Frantically she tried to fight but seemed to be held by more than one person. Somehow she managed to get a hand free, almost as if something had pulled it away for her and she dug her painted nails into the hard stick of human rock that was chocking her.

The howl of pain that went up seemed to bring her back to her senses a little and in the gloom she saw images that looked like men leaning over her but one was clutching himself in agony which was turning to anger. Suddenly any light there was faded and in the blackness Sam felt a hand grab her and pull her out through the men who tried to grab her back but the force pulling her was too strong and soon she was outside leaning up against the wall in a dark alley. At first fear filled her but something was telling her she was safe here for a moment as long as she was quiet.

There seemed to be a breath of cool air caressing her body and a calming hand moving her hair from her face, then she was gently guided onto the street and eventually near to a main road. A taxi seemed to appear from nowhere and the driver asked if she needed a lift. She would never remember the journey or how she paid the fare, if in fact she did, but some good force made sure she was back home without being followed.

The helper spirits reported back to Abe that she had been rescued this time, and they all hoped it would teach her a lesson, but sadly they already knew the answer.

Had Katie known that these events had occurred after she had arrived home, she would have been not only shocked, but extremely relieved that she had left the place when she did, whether it was by accident or not. The whole atmosphere was unsavoury and she wished she had never set foot in the place, but it was too late for regrets although it reinforced her resolve to keep her distance. Little did she know she had received help from another source to get her out and they would also be protecting her from Sam in the future.

Now she rolled over, still in the same bed she had shared with her husband and imagined him being there making love to her in the most beautiful and loving way until everything else drifted away and she entered her own world where there were only the two of them walking under the cool trees, listening to the birds and feeling as much in love as ever.

But she was being observed. One of the spirits that had frequented the club had followed her home and was now enjoying the innocent picture beneath him. As he glided down to wrap himself around her sleeping form, he felt a rush of air and he was swept away at force with a distinct warning never to approach her again. So great was the power, he had been transported to a place which was unknown to him and was left to find his own way back to his 'working area' as he called it. But that would take some time and for now Katie-Marie was being guarded by the best group possible, the one containing her husband.

Joel and Zoe had made love on the floor of the lounge. It had started with the hugs and kisses after their talk but far from causing any wedge, it had brought them closer together and they had rolled off the sofa and continued where there was plenty of room until both were exhausted, but totally fulfilled. They knew that their love and solidarity would ward off any intruder and were determined to keep their guard up at all times.

As they were succumbing to the exhilaration when it is possible to loose self control for a moment, Phani was hovering over Joel trying to squeeze herself between the man and his wife, and when that failed she tried to enter Zoe's body to get the full impact of his thrusts, but something was holding her back.

"Who the hell are you?" she screamed facing the force that had her in its control.

"You're in my way rookie." The voice was definitely male but she wasn't aware of any spiritual presence apart from herself.

"Sod off, I was here first. You want him for yourself do you?"

She wasn't ready for what came next. There were no hands, no muscles or anything that resembled the physical, but the strength lifted her and threw her away from the house, but it didn't stop there. The being came after her and held her down and when it spoke it sent a shiver through her entire being.

"Don't play with what you don't understand. I am a protector and you will never outwit me. You are but a child playing with your little toys. Now go and amuse yourself somewhere else or your will regret it, for eternity."

As soon as the thought transmitted into her soul was finished, she had the feeling of being totally alone. Carefully she started to scan the area around her but the thing had gone. The place was full of the normal entities either wandering about or intent on some mission but nobody bothered with her so she pulled herself up and drifted off to gather herself into a state that could plan what to do next. She jumped as Pheel came into her mind. This was a great setback in the challenge, but she mustn't give any clue of it away and must make out she was scoring big time.

The spirit that had warned her away was not what he had led her to believe. Abe and Danny suspected Tule was in the area but had not surfaced enough for them to put a trace on him. He was a predator of the most evil and sadistic kind and he had been watching Zoe for a short time waiting to pounce, so when the juvenile got in his way in her attempt to seduce Joel, he had to remove her. He always liked the spiritual area to himself and wasn't one of those who went around in pairs, one taking the male, whilst the other helped themselves to the female of the couple. There were those who didn't care which they had and would swap amongst themselves and ironically he despised that kind. He was totally male and was only interested in female prey. It hadn't bothered him that she was already well into the sex act, in fact he often enjoyed watching for a while before he moved in for the kill.

But the next step was to make her his, and he would have to work on her when her husband wasn't there until nothing would match the thrill only he could give her, then she would be in his power. He wouldn't be looking elsewhere, he didn't flit about like most just satisfying their sexual lust, he wanted it all, he wanted her mind and of course her very soul. There would be no second best, it must be total possession.

Katie-Marie woke up slowly. She had a lovely calm feeling that had almost wiped out last night's unpleasantness, but this was no accident. Her guardian force had remained with her throughout the night and her husband lay beside her most of the time. They were aware that through her contact with Sam, she could have attracted the unwelcome predators that were just waiting to snap up any unprotected person and although the likes of her friend were easy meat if they must satisfy their lust, there were those who liked the chase and the kill of a good challenge.

She stretched now letting her hand stroke the pillow beside her before she sat up and swung her legs out of bed. As she sat for a moment, flashes of last night came into her mind and she was reassured she was perfectly alright now, but then she wondered about Sam. But it was nothing new for Sam to leave her to get home and when the woman finally woke up, she would be on the phone probably related details of how many times she had scored. This was the bit Katie couldn't stand. Sex should be a personal thing between two people who loved each other, not something to be announced on social media, to friends or anyone for that matter. It was private.

"I'll tell her simply I don't want to know." she thought as she popped on her slippers and went down to make a cup of tea. There was a new determination taking over and even if it meant Sam didn't want her company any more, that was fine, in fact she would rather be without it now as there was something very unwholesome about the other's life style. But whether she would listen would be another matter for she had the annoying way of only hearing what she wanted or if it suited her purpose.

The kettle had boiled and Katie was about to pour the water in the cup when she felt strong arms surrounding her from behind. It was such a beautiful feeling and could only be one person, so she closed her eyes and put her hands up to caress the strong arms that were enveloping her.

"Stefan" she breathed and was rewarded by the breath on her neck. They stayed like that for several minutes then slowly he was gone.

In the past she had put these feelings down to grief or imagination, but recently they had become so real that she knew there had to be more to it than that. She never spoke of it to anyone for fear they would think she was losing it. Smiling to herself she made the tea and took it back to bed to relax and ooze into Sunday gently. This was a new beginning and she knew she could cope. Everyone would see a new Katie-Marie and they could put it down to whatever they liked, because what they thought didn't matter a bit.

Nick also woke with a new resolve. Emma wasn't home of course, nothing new there, but he would get up and start straight away with moving everything of his into the spare room. As usual he was sporting an erection you could have hoisted a flag on and knew he had to take care of that first, but someone was beating him to it. Help was at hand. Pheel was already down there, her mouth seemed to be exploring every inch of his tackle while her hands were searching for his nipples, but if they were on his chest, how could he feel two more hands caressing his balls? But the feeling was so erotic that at this point he wasn't asking any questions, he just lay back groaning so loudly as every inch of his body seemed to be getting attention, that when the final thrust came he was yelling as though he had won the lottery! Any onlooker would probably have been crying with laughter at his antics, especially if they couldn't see the spirit presence, but those with greater insight would probably have been moved in a similar way just watching.

This may not have been the way some religious people would consider as being the proper way to start a Sunday, but Pheel wasn't religious, and Nick certainly wasn't thinking on those lines. His resolve now was to make his love nest which would be for him and his unseen lover. The door would be constantly locked and nobody must enter his world. He was thinking physically, but he forgot to put up a guard against any other unseen willing participants, a fact he may later regret.

Pheel sought out Phani and was surprised yet delighted to notice the drop in her energy.

"What's happened to you?" she asked with a laugh.

Phani didn't want to admit to the interference and replied "I don't always rush in like you do, I like to take my time, after all I am a connoisseur."

"A what? You? Never. Hang on, you didn't get it on did you?" Pheel was enjoying this. "Keep that up for another three weeks and I've won."

"Don't be so sure, anyway who says I've only had my attention in one place?"

"Ha! Don't give me that. When we have a challenge you go for it firing on both barrels until you've shagged the life out of some poor bloke."

"No, not always. There's such a thing as finesse you know."

"You? You don't even know the meaning of the word." She studied her for a moment "Well, aren't you going to tell me?"

Phani was feeling very uncomfortable but was trying not to show it.

"We aren't in that kind of race, are we? It's how far, how much we achieve, not just how many bangs we notch up."

"Hmm. You're not telling me, but I'll find out. I'm going to enjoy this one, and let me tell you now madam, your reign is over. I'm winning this."

They parted leaving quite an atmosphere in their wake, but Pheel knew that with Nick she couldn't possibly loose. The thought came into her mind that usually they had to witness each other's triumphs in order to win the crown, but she didn't feel too comfortable with that because knowing her opposition like she did, it wouldn't be the first time that Phani had moved in on a good catch and taken it for herself after leaving Pheel alone.

"Like hell," she decided, "winner or not, that bitch isn't getting her claws into my plaything this time." And so the gloves were off.

It was midday before Sam even remotely came to. Everything ached and as she moved, her lady parts felt as though a herd of wildebeest had trampled them which wasn't that far from the truth. She groaned. Her head throbbed and everything was so much in a haze she daren't sit up. Slowly she realised at least she was in her own bed and tried to recount the events of the night before but it was all a jumble. The caring spirits that had organised her return home had blocked most of the unpleasant knowledge until now so that she could have enough mental power to understand what they would try and get through to her.

Slowly they fed bits of information in the hopes the sordid side of it would act as a deterrent to future escapades but they knew that as soon as she had got over this instalment, she would be up and raring to go again. Added to that was the fact that she had been a beacon to all unsavoury characters in the neighbourhood and the word would have gone out by now attracting others from far and wide. She certainly wouldn't be putting up her own defences so the caring spirits would have to do it for her, but she couldn't rest on that, for much has to come from the inner self. She would be totally unaware of the helpers, such was her earthly attitude and it would take a lot to open her inner eyes.

Danny was awake but still in contact with Abe. They had spent most of the night scanning the area for all signs of activity, but concentrating on the sexual trend which seemed to be targeting the 20 – 40 age group.

"At least it not children." Danny was relieved, recalling some of the horrible things they had been forced to overcome in the past.

"They don't want the middle aged or elderly either." Abe added, "which makes me think its those that weren't satisfied in their earth lives, or were taken in their prime and still need to make up for what they feel they were deprived of."

"Looking very much that way, but why now, and why this part of the country?"

Abe thought for a moment. "We need to check if there was some sort of accident, or disaster round here that took a group of young people."

"That's a possibility, but it doesn't answer all the questions."

"Like why is there an evil element involved, because there is, it's not just sexual satisfaction in its basic sense, there's the soul seekers that are the real threat."

Danny agreed and both were silent for a moment.

"I think we still need to do more homework." Abe suggested then added "I think it would be better if I monitored your brother and you took his friend. Might be less embarrassing."

"We've had to swallow our personal feelings before now, but yes I would appreciate that."

They discussed the Sam situation and Abe confirmed that some of the female guardians were keeping a close watch there. Although there is no sex difference in spirit, the image is often used so that earth dwellers can relate and understand if they are being helped. It would add to confusion if a sexless being was floating around and some people wouldn't feel they couldn't trust them, because humans know that everything, even plants, have both male and female sides to them.

Fortunately Abe and Danny weren't alone and at times like this other workers of a similar standing were brought in to help until the threat has been dispersed. Like many emotions, the sex drive can be very powerful and in physical ways has often led to murder, and torture both mental and physical. For this reason, when this kind of epidemic starts to spread it has to be diffused as soon as possible.

There was still no sign of Emma and Nick realised that she wasn't due back at work until Tuesday, so there was a good chance she wouldn't show her face until Monday, possible in the evening so he had a couple of days to sort out his move without rushing it. He stood in the spare bedroom looking around. The double bed they had once occupied was here along with a fitted wardrobe and drawers. A small table and chair stood by the window and he seemed to have everything for his needs. It wasn't en suite but the bathroom was just across the landing and as the master bedroom had its own, he would have sole use of the main one.

He eyed the bed. Fortunately it didn't hold any fond memories of their early married life and it would do very nicely for his new found activities. Pulling open a few drawers he soon found the bedding and in no time the bed was freshly made. He speeded up now as if this had given him the urge to get finished so that he could leave himself available for his new partner's attentions. He left the doors open to both rooms and in no time moved all his clothes and personal belongings into his new den. He went back to the master bedroom and cast his eyes around to make sure there was no trace of anything belonging to him and shut the door with a satisfied click. Now his new life would begin and when once his door was shut, he would always be in his own world with his new love. Next he went to the local DIY and bought a lock for the door which he fitted himself. Now he didn't care if Emma came back today, tomorrow or at all.

He lay on the bed for a moment tired after his activities and wondered how long it would be before she showed her presence. Then a thought hit him. What if she couldn't find him in here now he had moved but just as quickly he realised that she would find him wherever he was. But Nick in his new found euphoria was making a big mistake, for he imagined that as she was becoming everything he needed, she was returning the favour and keeping herself just for him. Although he was her challenge, Pheel was spreading her affections all over the area and had previously had a go at Joel and Danny, although there was such a block there she had given up. Now she had to win her crown so would give him as much attention as was needed for three weeks then would probably be off to pastures new.

She had watched his activities and was raring to go, so as soon as his mind was solely on the matter in hand, she was ready for action. This time there was no gentle build up. She literally threw herself on top of him pulling at his clothes until he was forced to rip them off until he was completely naked. If he was about to explode with desire, she was way ahead of him and didn't bother with any foreplay but just went straight into action on his groin area. Even a periscope couldn't have produced a better result! It must have been the quickest he had ever shot it and it even took him by surprise, but as he lay gasping, there was a slight disappointment that it was over.

If he expected any aftercare he wasn't going to get it. He knew she had left as the room held no presence at all and he felt very deflated as he still needed to be loved. But then he became aware of a gentle soothing feeling working its way down his neck and arms like tiny little fingers all working together then changing to a stroking sensation and he realised he was becoming erect again. How long this session lasted he didn't know but he was just glad she was back and he gave himself to her to do as she pleased.

He was drained, almost lifeless. Every limb seemed like a ton weight. Never before had he had the life sucked out of him like this. If only he could have had the spiritual vision to witness the departing spirit, he would have been confused, for taking her leave with a sadistic laugh was Phani. After waiting a few moments for Pheel to leave, she had taken her place and enjoyed her own delights as well as weigh up the opposition.

"Hmm, I may have a challenge on my hands after all" she smirked. Then consoled herself with the thought "She'll never have the sense to try the same with Joel, and even if she did, she'd never get past his misses."

The reminder of her rapid departure from the pair made her shudder but gave her an idea. It would be fun to watch her try and then get ousted by the power that was hovering, then while he was chasing her off, she could get in and do her dirty deed with Joel. Well, it was worth a try, all in the game, and she set off to lay her trap.

If Phani thought she was clever, she was unaware that she had now come into contact with one of the most evil powerful sources possible who would use anything to get his way, and anything or anyone who stood in his way would be crushed.

Tule had been summing up the events when he had removed her from his scene but, being aware of her low status knew she was just the kind of pawn to help his objective. He could have set her to keep Joel busy while he moved in on Zoe, but this just wasn't his way, so he would use her to get Joel out of the way completely leaving him free private access to his prey.

As she left Nick she felt the presence behind her but was ordered not to turn round. It didn't take her long to recognise the entity and although she would have liked to have replied with one of her acid retorts, something made her obey for now.

"Do as you are told and you will be not be harmed. Disobey, and take the consequences."

Something wasn't ringing true so she had to choose her reply carefully.

"Are you the protector?"

"So you do pay attention, good."

She was wondering why the harsh approach if this was a good spirit and was about to ask more questions but something seemed to stop her.

"I have a job for you, if you think you are up to it rookie."

She was about to say "Depends on what it is" but again was stopped. The reply that came out was "I'm up."

"You will be informed when the time comes. Be available."

The silence and still air showed the thing had left and Phani was again left feeling very uneasy. Perhaps this was one of those mercenary spirits that used hard tactics to get results and were never liked but had to be respected. If that was the case, then she should feel honoured at being asked, but somehow a great feeling of caution was enveloping her but she felt trapped by this unknown force. She had every reason for the apprehension for on her level of spiritual awareness there was no hiding place from those such as this predator.

It was almost dinner time and Katie had cooked her usual Sunday lunch but today she had an extra spring in her step and was looking forward to a relaxing afternoon pottering about in the garden. Although it was summer, the temperatures were below average but at least it was dry and she could do a bit of dead heading and there were always weeds to pull up. She was just checking the meat when the phone rang.

"Hello." Her tone was happy.

There was a pause for a moment and she wondered if it was one of those annoying cold callers and was about to put the handset down.

"Katie?"

"Who's this?" She didn't recognise the slurred voice.

"It's Sam of course."

"Oh."

"I don't know where you got to last night but I ended up being brought home ….I think."

Katie wasn't amused and felt she had little time for this woman who obviously had the stinker of a hangover.

"I'm not surprised."

"Well, where were you?" The tone was accusing as if it was Katie's fault.

"As if you cared. You were having a good time I imagine."

"You'd gone."

"Sam, I've always gone when you decide you've finally had enough."

This wasn't what she expected to hear, and as she felt so ill her temper rose. "You didn't give a shit about me, just looked after number one as usual. Well let me tell you I got attacked."

Katie felt almost guilty that she felt no remorse, because whatever had occurred Sam would have left herself wide open, in more ways than one.

"And do you remember what happened to you by any chance?" the question was cutting.

"I think I was raped." This was supposed to be the shock treatment.

"No Sam, I don't think so, it's not rape if you go out begging for it."

"You heartless cow," she screamed, "acting as though butter wouldn't melt but you're as bad."

"I think you had better have a good wash and pull yourself together, then we can talk." Then as an afterthought "Later."

With that she ended the call and a smug smile of satisfaction crept over her face.

"There! They say the first step is always the most difficult and I've done it."

As she put the phone on the working surface she made up her mind that if Sam rang again soon she wouldn't answer. Let her stew for a bit.

Sam may have felt very alone when she woke, but it didn't last long. She had the horrible feeling that she was being watched, not just from one part of the room but which ever way she turned. As glimpses of the previous night flashed through her brain, images of leering faces kept appearing and try as she might she couldn't get rid of them. Her body was still sore from the physical abuse and she collapsed onto the bed sobbing. There was no one to turn to. Katie had been most offhanded which upset her and she blamed her for being so selfish.

"She needs me more than I need her," she thought, "she'll soon come running when she wants to go out somewhere." which proved that this woman had never listened or paid attention to anything her friend had said or she would have known that Katie went out mainly to please her.

She lay there for some time, then seemed to be aware of a presence but not unpleasant like the previous one. Arms slipped round her and guided her to the bathroom where she caught sight of herself for the first time. She was a mess. Her face was full of bruises, her lip split, and one eye was almost closed. What on earth had caused this, and more importantly, who had done it? She ran some water and eased herself into the bath almost screaming as the water went between her legs and the pain that shot up her inside. After a while the calming presence guided her to a bath towel and she dried herself very gently.

Her mind was in turmoil now. Instead of chastising herself with the knowledge that she had put herself in the firing line, she started to blame her attackers for preventing her from having her sexual pleasures until her body had healed. The guardian spirits knew they had a big job on their hands because they would be trying to get her to go against her own desires, and much as they would try to protect her she would always be attempting to break out of the cage like a female cat on heat. It was a bit like trying to confine a werewolf at full moon.

The sexual predators weren't put off by these guards for they strongly believed they could take whatever they wanted, as last night had proved. And there were plenty more like her once they had been fed drink or the right kind of pills, they could be picked off like berries. It was a case of who would win in the end.

Danny and Abe had been aware of this episode along with many others in the area.

"Sad to say, she's her own worst enemy." Abc could see the possible outcome only too well.

"Trouble is...." Danny agreed "....by the time she realises she's chosen the wrong path, it'll be too late."

"And she's only one. Did you see the amount of it going on in that club, and all the others we visited?"

"It's a drug in itself."

Abe was serious was he said "We need the antidote."

"Could do with some good old fashioned bromide."

Although Danny was joking, Abe suddenly said "You may have got something there."

"What? I was only....."

"Never mind. Let me chew it over."

They both went their own ways agreeing to meet later but Danny was wondering why that casual remark had triggered such a reaction.

Although the majority of sexual advances were being performed by female orientated spirits seeking out men for their fulfilment, there was a concentration of male operatives, some solely needing female prey, but a few not minding which as long as the person had a beautiful body, and some intent on taking young Adonis males. The number may have been smaller but it was much more intense and sadistic even lethal if they failed in a conquest. These were not amateurs and had been around for some time, not working as a team, but if the word went out that there was good 'fishing' in one lake, they would all congregate hoping to take the best pickings before the others.

Abe and Danny had agreed that they didn't think it was any of this band that had taken Sam, as the type of attack didn't bear their hallmark. These were merely a group of gang bangers who would pick up anything as long as it was willing, whereas the professional lot were much more choosy. Quality not quantity ruled but that didn't stop them helping themselves to as much as they could get while it was available.

If only it was possible to work out the next move but they seemed to strike at random and in several places at once which proved it had to be planned in some way. Then word came in from one of the scouts that two well known ones were about to enter the space which would cause an upset amongst the other predators, for these were of the highest calibre. This was good news as Abe and Danny had already had run ins with these although there would be fireworks.

Bollik and Vanke didn't work together as such when taking their enjoyment and possession, but they did have an agreement that the first to secure their catch took it. The other couldn't come in and help himself. Both liked to be in sole charge when servicing their goods and would preferably keep well away from the other. But it had been known from time to time that they would overlap then all hell was let loose and all the lesser sex fiends tended to back off as things got really nasty.

"Wonder what they have in their sights this time." Abe was going through previous operations knowing it was difficult to forecast.

"It was young widows last time as I remember."

"They must have homed in on the activity."

Danny was thoughtful. "You know that's what puzzles me. It's usually the flock that follows them, not this way round."

"You've got a point there." Abe jumped at the thought. "So what's so special about here?"

Danny was still turning things around in his mind. "I just can't see them having a load of others in the same field. They're bound to see them off."

"Should be interesting to watch."

"Can we get more guardians in?" Danny asked.

"Sounds the obvious, but for which ones? I think we'd better put the standing guards to be on high alert and if we realise who's going to be in the firing line we then bring the backup in there."

"We'll have to move quickly," Danny said, "you know what they're like."

"Only too well unfortunately."

Tule always did his homework. He would weigh up a situation and often tailor it to his needs. He liked a bit of class, nothing too high brow but he certainly didn't stoop to the scum that was available everywhere, he left that to the crowds of frustrated beings who would have anything if it was willing, and even if it wasn't. His ego refused to believe that there was a female in any form who would spurn his advances.

Bollik and Vanke on the other hand thrived on a challenge especially Vanke who would seek out the most unlikely candidate, work on her for some time until he had worn her down completely, take her for his pleasure then discard her like an old dishcloth and look for his next victim. His partner in crime however only homed in on the more experienced mortals, not necessarily in years, but as long as they were well honed in the art, they would do for a while until they had exhausted all possible ways of pleasing him. He didn't appear selfish and made sure they were more than satisfied but that was his means to an end, for while they felt special and he was being very attentive, they kept coming back for more. Many had been crushed when he threw them to one side, but they were yesterday's news as far as he was concerned.

So they would be scanning this area for their next encounters and as Tule already had Zoe in his line of fire, woe betide either of them if they tried to muscle in on his act, out of innocence or otherwise.

# Chapter 4

Joel and Zoe were about to go to bed. The mood was relaxing and very loving and as they lay on the sofa together watching television, neither suspected how many times they had been observed by the various entities in the area.

"What can we do up there that we haven't already done down here?" Joel kissed his wife affectionately.

"We can always have afters." she laughed.

"Greedy girl."

She pretended to tickle him and they both rolled onto the floor and were locked in each other's love.

These are the times that the spirits wait for, when all defences are down and the concentration is lacking. The protective shield is not being powered up and in they go.

Bollik was quick to take advantage of this moment and entered Joel's body to sample the wares. But he often made the mistake of diving in before testing the water and soon was roughly spreading Zoe's legs and shoving himself into her as though he would loose the chance if he didn't take it. The horror on her face as she gasped, yelling her husband's name begging him to stop alerted Joel's inner spirit and he tried to fight the power that was taking over his body.

"Get away from her, go in the name of God." he ordered, not sure if these were the words he should be using, then he yelled in her face "tell it to leave, force it away Zoe."

Their combined will must have worked for they both lay frightened and panting locked in each other's arms almost in tears, but the presence had gone.

"I didn't think it would be that soon, and not to you." he whispered.

She stroked his hair. "It's ok we will fight it together."

"Do you think we need some help?" he wondered as the extent of this power had unnerved him. "It was pretty strong."

"Let's see how it goes. If it comes back and we can't overcome it, then perhaps we should."

He brightened a bit "But it did go didn't it, I felt it leave me."

"Oh yes, me too."

They lay for a few moments then, hand in hand checked the house, turned out the lights and went to their bedroom, consciously strengthening their force field, and asking their guardians to protect them through sleep.

Although they did all the right things, it wasn't their efforts that had removed Bollik so unceremoniously. Tule had been keeping watch on his 'property' and as soon as the intruder spirit made his move, had homed in and snatched his entire being from the scene and transported it away. The action had caused waves of anger which affected the entire area and stretched far into the distance so everyone knew the master had been crossed for you didn't mess with his possession. He was also angry at the setback. All his homework was for nothing because as soon as he was ready to take her, the pair would be ready, and although he was a powerful spirit, the damage was done.

When he moved in, he always chose exactly the right moment and the recipient was in a receptive mood and gave in willingly, such was his technique, all planned with precision. So for an upstart to cause this disruption, it would not go without just punishment. Oh, he would still have this woman, but not for now.

Much to Nick's pleasure, Emma still hadn't come home but that wasn't a surprise. He had taken a bath and made his way to his new love nest. There was no need to lock the door but he felt he had to somehow, and he would always be doing that now as this room was private. He slipped under the duvet and waited.

Soon he felt the movement, but it was confusing. This wasn't his normal visitor because he had got to know her movements and she felt soft, so who was this? Instinctively his hand went down to protect his parts until he knew who this was. Suddenly he realised this wasn't female and shuddered in horror, his arms trying to ward off whatever this was.

"Don't you like me like this?" The words were implanted in his brain.

"What? Who are you?"

Suddenly the softness took over and he felt the usual caressing movements.

"That was you? Why?"

"You do ask a lot of questions."

He could feel the lips exploring everywhere. "I don't understand."

"I can be anything you want. I was finding out just what you do like, now I know."

He was being overcome by the treatment now and barely whispered "Tell me who you are really."

"You can call me Pheel, and you like me being female. So that's what I am to you."

"But – wait – I thought you were only a woman."

"Oh I am. But I also give people what they want, and some want some very different things you know."

He was getting to the desperate stage with the treatment he was receiving and just when he thought he couldn't wait any longer she stopped and he felt a cool breeze blowing across his little feller causing him to be in control. His hands went up to his head as though he couldn't control his thoughts or emotions, then he felt her turn him onto his side as she slid down in front of him until he was curled round her back. It was so easy to slide in from here and he knew that there would be no turning back this time.

If he expected her to remain after this session he was disappointed, for he lay there feeling very alone now. This spirit business was alright but he didn't like to be deserted and left to lie there wondering if he'd imagined it all. Another thought hit him. What if she had moved on to the next waiting male? That made it all seem so impersonal, but he also realised he didn't know what she looked like. Even in that world they must have some sort of image. What he felt had been good but she could have a face like a  - he didn't know quite what but he now had this urge to know.

He had to get to the bathroom and grabbing some tissues held onto his bits as he unlocked the door and made his way the short distance across the landing. As he stood having a pee he thought he heard a noise behind him and half turned to see Emma smirking at him. As he jumped he missed his aim and nearly wet the floor.

"Well, well, well. You filthy little wanker." The voice was slightly slurred but still weighted with disgust. "So that's what you've been getting up to. Where is she?" And she stormed out and made for his new room.

Shaking the drips, he galloped after her.

"You can't go in there."

She stood in the doorway motionless her mouth open. As he caught up with her he followed her gaze to the bed which was just as he had left it.

"Yes, do you want to join in?" the bell like tones drifted up from the apparition lying on the bed, one leg in the air, the other moving too and fro outwards.

Nick almost pushed Emma out of the way. "What are you looking at?"

"That…that slut." she was pointing in disbelief.

"What?" Nick was screaming. "There's nobody there you stupid bitch."

"Look for yourself, you call that nothing." Emma had grabbed his arm and was pushing his head nearly down on the bed.

He pulled free and ran his hand down the sheet, picked up the duvet and shook it then threw it back onto the bed.

"You are either drunk or hallucinating," he yelled then coming within inches of her face said quietly but menacingly "get your arse out of my room, and stay out. You are not wanted in here."

Her mouth was still open. She had seen the woman. She had heard the woman. So where was she? But it left her no option but to slowly walk to the front bedroom and flop onto the bed.

"I'm going mad," she whispered to herself, "or else I've had some bad stuff."

Pheel had enjoyed this little episode, it had been worth popping back for, but you couldn't leave it at that could you? Oh, she would get some mileage of enjoyment tormenting this woman, what a bonus.

All this activity hadn't gone unnoticed by Abe and Danny. The Nick incident seemed harmless enough for now but the Joel/Zoe one was a bit more serious for if Tule had decided he would be back, than nothing would stop him, Sam needed plenty of protection for her own good but she was her own worst enemy and would soon be off again, falling at the next fence. Katie-Marie seemed pretty safe, but that could be a downfall for she could already be in someone's sights so could not be dismissed. As regards the spirit side, there was obviously going to be an upheaval with Bollik and Vanke on the scene as they always upset the localised inhabitants, and Tule wouldn't be crushed by any power. Phani and Pheel were harmless enough for now, just taking their own pleasures but the experts knew this was how a lot of things started before evolving into the deeper darker rituals and had to be nipped in the bud.

They also had their eyes, not only on the club visited by the two women, but other such venues that seemed to be springing up, not only in this little town but other neighbouring ones and especially in the cities. There was an unwholesome taste to it all and the lads were aware such places were not always what they seemed, and could be a gateway for undesirable entities to use for their comings and goings and therefore made them difficult to trace. Extra help was needed to monitor them without being detected but that wasn't easy as these were used by the very experienced powers, but where there was evil there was also good.

It was late August and the weather had been quite warm lately so Sam would liked to have put on something fairly skimpy to wear under her garden centre uniform. It was only when she looked at herself she realised the extent of her bruises and she didn't want to be seen like that. She normally only put her overall on when she got to work and didn't fancy travelling in it. Her face was still a mess and much as she wanted to get on with her life, she didn't see how she could serve customers looking that bad. She picked up the phone and spoke to the manager explaining she had had a fall and could she work out of sight today. He seemed pleased she was making the effort to go in and said he'd find something for her as there was always help needed in all areas.

Mondays were never busy first thing and she was able to creep in without too much fuss but as soon as the rest of the staff saw her, a few whispers went round that she'd been out on the town again as they knew her only too well.

"Bill's not in, you can help with the watering today," the manager looked at her as he spoke. "Good god what did the other one look like?"

"I had a fall." she muttered.

"More likely pushed," he thought but kept it to himself. "Go and see Bill, he'll tell you what he wants doing."

Equipped with her hose, Sam found it refreshing to start with but wondered how anyone could do this day in and day out.

"Hello dear." the voice made her jump.

She turned and nearly wet the owner of the voice.

"Oh Hello Annie, you're early."

This elderly lady was a regular and quite a character and the staff put up with her wandering around as she didn't get in the way and seemed rather lonely. She also cheered them up with her friendly manner.

"I've come for me cuppa tea." Then looking at Sam said "Who did that to you lass? I'll hit 'em with me handbag I will."

"Oh Annie, you're lovely. No, I fell down, nothing really."

"Hmm, I know falling down when I see it and that ain't falling down."

"The café isn't open till ten Annie." Sam tried to change the subject but this wily one wasn't having any of it.

"You put anything on that lip?"

"Yes Annie, now do you want me to give you a shower?" she pointed to the hose in her other hand.

"You naughty girl." Annie laughed then said "Did you see that programme last night on the telly? It was a wildlife thing and this giraffe, well I don't know what he'd just been doing to the other one but he couldn't stand up, his legs didn't seem to want to hold him. Now what about that then?"

"Annie, you get worse, now off you go." Sam had to laugh even though it hurt.

"I'm going." She turned "Just reminded me of you that's all."

All the events of the weekend seemed to disappear as this little old lady waved her hand without turning and walked slowly away. It was the best tonic she could have had at that moment, but how long would it last?

Although Joel and Zoe worked for the same company they were usually at different hotels which they didn't mind, as they had the opinion that to see each other all day at work and then at home could be too much, whereas they both looked forward to catching up at the end of a shift. Emma would sometimes be working alongside one of them but Nick was permanently at head office and had to travel quite a bit further. It was becoming no secret as to Emma's lifestyle and more than once a manager had to take her to task for her lack of attention to detail.

Previously she had won the receptionist of the year award but the way she was going, she would soon be lucky to even be cleaning the bathrooms. Nobody wanted to work with her and when Joel found that she would be joining their staff the following day, his heart sank. He had always set his own high standards and had worked his way up to the position of deputy manager, often being in charge of training newcomers, such was his reputation. But he carried no passengers and if a new staff member didn't make the grade, he knew they would be out within two weeks, not by anything he did, but just by letting them dig their own hole. Everyone was on a probationary period, had to pass a first aid at work course and take a written test before being permanently accepted onto the staff.

He had the gut feeling therefore that top management were sending this woman as a final resort, knowing full well that if anyone could legally kick her out, he could. But that was tomorrow. Today there was the normal work to do.

Zoe also covered reception work if there was a staff shortage but usually was out of sight in the offices. Like her husband she had very high standards and was most critical of her own work, let alone anyone else's.

Phani and Pheel were having a banter, each one boasting they would win this challenge hands down and with the latter also setting her sights at playing Emma into the ground, she welcomed the chance of getting her and Joel under the same roof. While she was entertaining herself she could also keep an eye on the opposition

"What are you planning?" Phani was very suspicious. Why was she elated? It wasn't as if Nick would be there and she could show off what she had achieved in full view.

"Me? Why should I be planning anything? I'm home and dry I can tell you."

After her rogue visit, Phani realised that Nick could easily come up trumps as he had more to learn than Joel and that would make Pheel the winner, especially if, when having tasted the wine he couldn't wait to get drunk.

"I wouldn't be too sure on that point if I were you." the tone was smug.

"You may be in for a surprise. I'm saying no more." Pheel closed the subject but couldn't wait for tomorrow, then she would really have some fun.

They left to go their own ways, Phani seeking out Joel as she wasn't going to miss any opportunity that may arise and she didn't have to wait long. He was sorting out a problem in one of the rooms and had sent one of the staff to fetch something, so he was alone. In a second she was in front of him massaging his sausage until he became flustered and fidgeted around trying to get it to behave, but there was no chance of that while she was still working on him. Before he knew where he was he was pinned up against the wall of the shower but what happened next came as a surprise to both of them. A tremendous force seemed to emit from his chest pushing Phani away at speed whilst other presences reduced him back to normal and helped him out of the bathroom so that when he was rejoined by the staff he appeared as though nothing had happened.

He didn't know just who had come to his aid but he said a silent 'Thank you' to whoever it was, knowing that there were more forces at work here than he ever imagined, but relieved that the one protecting him was good. He hoped that Zoe too had her shield up as you never knew when then next onslaught would be. As soon as he could he sent her a text warning her to be on guard at all times.

She wasn't on duty until noon so got the message at home, but knew that he meant her to protect herself wherever she was. She wondered if something had happened but maybe he was only being cautious and she wouldn't bother him while he was working, but would find out later when she got home.

Phani was angry. How dare anyone remove her from her working place, and what was so special about this man that he had to have divine intervention. There could only be one answer, Pheel. She must have got someone to step in for her, but she wasn't that clever unless…..they owed her one. She hovered a safe distance from the hotel trying to piece things together.

"She said I may be in for a surprise" she mused. "Is this what she was on about?"

This made her even more angry. To think this upstart could try and get the better of her, and succeed. That was the annoying part. Well if she was going to play those games, she was in for a fight, but she wouldn't win, she was nothing and Phani would soon prove it to her. Time for a test.

She slowly inched her way back into the building and hovered at a safe distance from Joel.

"Now let's see what you're up to." she thought.

She needed to know how near she could get without being pushed away again, in other words how big was the force field. Another few inches, a few feet, nothing happened.

"So, it left when it had done its job did it? Not very professional dear." She sneered.

Thinking she was in the clear she went to move forward at a quicker pace but was stopped as if by an unseen wall about three yards from Joel. When he moved, she did and if he came towards her, she was pushed back but always at the same distance. Not only was there a strong field around him but it was also controlling her movements. Frantically she tried to pull away but was held flat against this wall, but it was lifting her and throwing her about as if she was a ball until she was almost begging it to let her go. Now she felt as if she was being tossed between this wall and another unseen one, then another. All of a sudden everything came to a halt. Joel was nowhere in sight and she was conscious of activity going on around her until something pressed itself to her from all sides.

"Let's see how well you perform after that!" The message was clear although there were no actual words but the mocking laughter rang all about her. As she tried to move away something picked her up and threw her, somewhere, anywhere, even in spirit it is possible to be disorientated and it would take a while before Phani would regain her faculties.

Pheel on the other hand was in high spirits. She was making progress with Nick, was going to use Emma as a plaything and knew she had rocked Phani's boat. She may not have always had the capabilities as her friend, but she had something which always drove her forward. She had to get even. For every knock she took, she didn't rest until she had evened the score and it was now her objective to put a time limit on it. Through experience she was learning just what could rattle somebody's cage and she would use it to her advantage at every possible chance.

When she left Phani, she had no idea what kind of surprise could be in store, but she did know that the very thought was enough to get the other one going. Now she could hone the skill to perfection and use it, not only to get back at anyone but during her sexual activities which could only enhance her standing. Soon everyone would want her and she could take her pick instead of other people's left offs which she had been given up to now. Nick? Oh he'd do for her to practise on, but she would soon move on to bigger and better things, and see how smug Phani would look then. These silly little challenges of hers would be fish food.

Danny was still wondering why, out of all the antics the playful spirits got up to, there should be this surge of sexual activity. He and Abe had come up with nothing to suggest there had been any kind of mass passing over leaving the souls hankering after their physical pleasures.

"It's something in the mind." he suggested.

Abe agreed "It keeps coming back to being like a drug, but instead of a mortal requirement, it's the spirit that has to be satisfied."

"But the evil is so attracted to it. Look at the attention that girl is drawing towards her."

"Sam? Yes don't like what's hovering there."

"If they only knew what danger they were putting themselves in, but they still come back for more." Danny was struggling to put all the pieces together.

"Even with all that protection round her, she will still try and break out not realising its there to protect her." Abe was still thinking of Sam.

"That's the bad force willing her on. She wants more and yet look at the state of her this time."

"Aah, it's just a battle between them and us, never been any different. I don't care what they say about good overcoming evil, it's no better than it was centuries ago, even worse but possibly in a different way."

Danny shrugged. "It moves with progress. It infects every good invention and turns it into something sour."

"How's that Katie doing?" Abe suddenly asked.

"Seems ok. They're giving her the boost."

"Oh good. Still plenty of protection?"

"Yes and more standing by especially with those two mavericks in the area."

Abe paused then said "I expected that Vanke to have had a dip there by now. Wonder what's keeping him?"

"Likewise. Unless he's on to us."

"Probably found a few others on the way."

They fell into deep silent conference planning the placement of certain top guardians to strengthen the area and monitoring those already in situ but undetected by any lesser entities.

It was about 2pm before Emma dragged herself out of bed. She lay there for a moment trying to remember what had happened when she had come home. Nick had moved into the spare room. She sat up with a start.

"He had a woman in there." she actually shouted. "And they'd just had it off."

Why she should feel so affronted considering her own lifestyle was a joke. She must have had at least three or four different partners over the weekend with never a thought of sexual health matters, and yet the thought that Nick had entertained one hit her.

"Hang on," she thought "he said there was nobody there, and she didn't leave."

She struggled up and made her way to his door but it was locked.

"Who's there?" the female voice was muffled.

Emma hammered on the door. "Come out here you shitbag. Show your face or whatever else is on view."

"Why, you want some?" the mocking tone was getting to her.

"Get your filthy arse out here NOW." she screamed.

"Sorry no can do."

"Unlock this door." Emma was still beating on it until her hand was sore.

"Can't."

"Why not?"

"I think you need a little bit of metal which you put in that hole near your nose and then your turn it and……."

"Shut up!" she was screaming with rage and her head was pounding as though it would burst.

All was silent for a moment then Emma said very precisely "Then you can stay in there until you rot."

She turned to go back to her room but a movement made her look towards the backroom. There was the image of the girl giving a cheeky little wave as she closed the door behind her. Emma rushed towards her but it was slammed in her face. She was about to hammer on there but stopped.

"Something's not right." she thought and shuffled back to the bedroom. Again the thought came to her that she had used some drugs, or the alcohol, or both must be causing this and she was hallucinating. For the first time she was frightened and as she caught sight of herself in the dressing table mirror she shuddered for she didn't know the woman staring back at her, but that wasn't all. She wasn't alone. The other woman dressed in skimpy underwear with beautiful hair falling over her shoulders was behind her, laughing at her. Whether it was the shock or the effects of her lifestyle she would never know for she passed out, sliding off the bed and landing on the floor.

When she came to, she stumbled into her own bathroom and splashed cold water onto her face. She was alone and had never felt so ill in all her life. But she felt it would pass and was just a one off. This had never happened before and she would have to be careful who she mixed with. There seemed to have been a lot of people she didn't know this time so perhaps she should just stay with those she trusted then everything would be all right and she could continue having the kind of fun she enjoyed, not the dull life she had with Nick.

Tule had been aware of Joel's warning to Zoe, and out of experience he knew he didn't have to rush in to take the spoils, but plan carefully. Time was no object, for when he had secured this catch she would be his forever, and nothing would take her away from him. He had made several visits in the past undetected by using other forms, but he knew that soon she could associate her previous experiences with him, so he had to play an even better part now to let her think he was new on the scene. He was extremely possessive, and what bore his mark had to remain untouched until he took command. Most knew this, but there were always those who through ignorance, or were just too foolhardy to know when to exit, that soon realised the extent of his wrath and power. He was still angry at Bollik's ham handed assault and although it had cost him a little time, had now regrouped his plans but if the under spirit thought he had seen the last of him, he was very much mistaken.

He watched her from afar as she planned to go to work knowing she would not be home until late and would be driving herself, Joel having finished earlier would be at home. Tule made his way to the hotel ahead of her and familiarised himself with the layout, staff and general day to day routines. He was adopting a bodily form and was planning to be checking in when she would be on the desk, standing in for staff on holiday.

Letting her get established, he arrived with a small case and made his way to the counter.

"Good afternoon sir, may I help you?" she was looking straight at him which stirred his spiritual desires immediately.

"Yes, I have a reservation. The name is Tully, Jude Tully."

She found his name and asked him to sign in. After the usual welcoming spiel, she directed him to his room and he settled himself to play his next move.

Katie-Marie seemed to have a new spring in her step but didn't know why.

"It must be because I've taken charge of my own life and not let it be influenced by others," she thought as she sat at her desk in the accounts department. It seemed as though the events of the weekend had been her turning point and she had found new strength of purpose. Even work didn't seem so bad and some of her colleagues had asked what she was on, and could they have some!

Although she wasn't looking for a new man in her life, she did feel that maybe she should now get out a bit more and meet people socially, but not at clubs or the places Sam seemed to prefer. There was no one at work that she had bonded with but got on well with everyone on a day to day basis. But where would be the best place to go? She wasn't one to be attracted towards agencies because you never knew who you would meet and she was still a little vulnerable and she didn't want actual dating.

It had always been her belief that fate took its own course and you didn't have to give it a shove, but at the moment it felt as though it could do with just a little push.

When she had met Stefan they knew they were made for each other and she never imagined they wouldn't be together until old age and that had been a major upheaval in her life. Although she still spoke to him as if he was alive, there were many times when the aching void seemed too much to bear. But she had come to terms with it and found comfort in having his belongings around her. Nobody could every take his place, but she would like a good friend, whether male or female.

When lunchtime came, she grabbed her bag and went to sit in the small park alongside the offices. There she would eat her sandwiches and watch the birds flitting about the trees and sometimes would spot a squirrel that was always on the lookout for food. It was quite mild and she felt at peace with the world. The hum of the nearby traffic seemed to melt away and this was like a little haven where she could feel happy. Little did she know she was far from being alone.

Vanke had been scouring the area, and true to Danny and Abe's supposition had spotted Katie and followed her to this place. He positioned himself behind her and gently massaged the back of her neck letting a cool breeze caress her ears.

"Stefan" she whispered.

The answer was a stronger pressure on her neck but it wasn't stopping there, it was going down the front of her chest until it was almost on her breasts.

"What are you doing?" she almost said aloud, then "Wait, you're not Stefan."

The feeling had gone and she looked around wondering if anyone had noticed but other workers were too absorbed in their phones or tablets to pay any attention to her.

Although she felt that the presence had left her and started to relax, Vanke was only a few feet from her.

"Perfect." He thought. "You will do very nicely." But he didn't realise that he was being watched just as closely but with spirits that were skilled enough to remain unnoticed. The group containing her husband were on all sides and would have intervened had the fiend continued, but they knew this was only the beginning and she would have to be constantly monitored even more now.

Vanke settled back quite content with his catch. He would travel with her to her home and then he would take up residence so that she would belong to him until he tired of her, then he could go and find another innocent creature that needed breaking in. The beings of his level never believed that anything would stand in their way because in their eyes they were doing no harm, just having a playful time, albeit sexual, but that didn't hurt anyone so why didn't others mind their own business and go and find someone else to pester. When they did get taken down a peg or two, it always came as a shock.

Katie went back to work but the incident was being soothed from her mind by her guardian whilst the others monitored Vanke which wasn't difficult but they had to be one step ahead all the time, not only with him but what he could attract.

# Chapter 5

Tuesday was going to be an eventful day, not only in earthly terms but the spirit guardians knew something was building. They could always tell because it was like the stillness before the storm and while the sexual predators were intent on being totally satisfied the protectors were equally determined they wouldn't succeed. As they kept being reminded, it wasn't how a simple situation started, it was how it could finish and they had often witnessed lives, earthly and spiritually being ruined and it was their job to prevent it happening as much as possible.

Joel was very apprehensive knowing that Emma was being sent to him on a loan basis as they put it and he prayed that no long term harm would stem from it. He wondered what had changed her. Both he and Zoe had liked the couple at first but always felt Nick was a bit down trodden and wished he would stand up for himself more. But this was work and he must put aside any personal thoughts and concentrate on the fact that this was an employee who had not come up to scratch recently and was in danger of being dismissed. His loyalty to Nick couldn't come into it although he realised that their marriage was irreparable and if she did end up loosing her job it may not have any ongoing effect. She would have to change her ways drastically to be any good in any area of her life the way she was going.

He alerted Megan Clarke the head receptionist to the situation and said he would be available if there was any trouble. Fortunately she was also a stickler for professionalism and would stand no nonsense from anyone.

At two minutes to ten Emma arrived looking flustered and blamed the traffic.

"At least I'm not late." She announced looking at the clock.

"As I am sure you are well aware, all staff are expected to be at the desk ten minutes before their shift to hand over. Therefore you are already eight minutes late so I suggest you deposit your things in the lockers in the staff area and report back here."

This greeting didn't go down well at all and Emma took her time moving asking everyone on the way where the staff room was.

When she returned, Megan looked her up and down.

"Well before you can even think of dealing with our guests, you can go and tidy your hair and give your uniform a brush. It looks as though you have slept in it."

"Maybe I have." Emma muttered as she left again.

Megan was on the phone to Joel. "How long do we have to suffer this creature?"

Joel asked "Already?"

"She's a disgrace to the company. Not a good image for first impressions."

"I'll come down."

Emma returned looking a little better than before just as Joel appeared.

"Ah, this is my friend, aren't you Joelly?" She gave Megan a smug sniff.

Joel stood motionless for a moment then, looking round to make sure no guests were in earshot said very precisely "For one thing I am not your friend, and while you are at work you will treat everyone with respect. Do you understand?"

"Oh yes boss." She tried to snuggle up to him but he was too quick for her.

"You are on duty until 7pm today and you will be under Megan's instruction. Is that clear?"

"I'd rather be under you." It was clear what she meant.

Joel turned to Megan and said "Excuse us for a moment." He indicated for Emma to follow him and marched her into the staff room, but left the door open where they could be seen by other staff. He turned sharply holding his hand up in front of him so that she couldn't make any advances.

"Now listen to me and listen well. You are skating on thin ice lady, today will decide whether you have a job or not. Do I make myself clear?"

"Ooo, aren't we the Mr high and mighty now? You can prance around with all your airs and graces, but you're just the same as the rest. If I dropped my knickers, you'd be in there before I could cough."

He looked her straight in the eye. "You are insulting a senior member of this company. Take this as an official warning." As he finished speaking he looked over her shoulder making her turn suddenly.

"I witness that." Megan stood in the doorway and Emma swung between her and Joel feeling like a trapped animal.

"Now perhaps you would like to take your position at the desk and try to behave in a ladylike manner for the rest of your shift." Joel nodded to Megan who escorted the unwilling woman out of the room. But Emma hadn't finished with him yet and wouldn't be leaving until she had brought him down to her level. Then they would see who was without a job.

Although the towns in the surrounding area were not very large, none of them were many miles from the nearest city and as there was a connecting train line, many commuted there on a daily basis. Abe had been scouting around trying to find a link between the unsavoury clubs and found that the ones in the towns were often placed down a passage between shops with only the simplest name to identify them, but the city ones were positioned behind existing larger clubs which gave a front of respectability but hid the depravity behind the scenes. You could only gain entry by invitation and there seemed to be a presence of heavily built bouncers in attendance. But it wasn't the physical aspect that was the interest. He and Danny knew that these places were linked in some way to a gateway to another dimension, or maybe each had its own entrance, but that was what they must find out. Also where did it lead and was it two way? It could be the answer to the influx of sordid sex entities but also posed the question as to whether they returned, if indeed they wanted to. Also they may have no choice but could be pawns in a bigger plan. It was becoming increasingly essential to find the answers and be sure of the facts before they could call on higher powers to help fight this. There had been many jobs of this kind over the centuries and the two friends were well aware of the tremendous power that the need for sexual satisfaction could produce, which was why evil entities always harnessed it, knowing it wouldn't be stopped.

They had often come up against the question "Why would spirits need sex?" The answer always came by means of a lengthy explanation.

When in earthly form, memories of everything encountered are stored in the memory banks of the mind and carried permanently in the soul's knowledge. Therefore if anything is upsetting or enjoyable it will be forever there. Many people enjoy sex much more than others and there are those to whom it becomes a necessity, something they cannot do without. Although some say they never experience it, ask anyone who thrives on the 'brain surge', which they describe as a much more in depth thrill for them. This is what the spiritual side is seeking once they have discarded their bodies. They must have that 'pow' and if they are deprived of it will either go into withdrawal or become violent in their search for their next fix.

It is this sector that the likes of Danny and Abe are always fighting, even now and for all time, however long it may be.

Zoe had been quite busy since she arrived but now there was a bit of a lull and she was joined by the deputy manager who thanked her for stepping in. The lady always liked having her on board as she was always so smart and very efficient. Although this hotel was smaller than the one where Joel was stationed, it was never short of customers so there was always plenty to do and high standards were always maintained. Emma had worked there, as well as at one in the next town, and the management were sad to see how she had dropped, not only in appearance but in her attitude to work.

"I see your husband has Emma with him today," she said almost apologetically.

"Yes. But I expect he'll cope." Zoe wasn't going to be drawn although the woman was only offering sympathy.

"We had her last week. I don't envy him, but fortunately he won't stand for any nonsense."

Something made Zoe's ears prick up. "Oh?"

Realising she may have said too much the deputy quickly covered herself with "Oh just how she is, you know sloppy."

"Oh, right." Zoe relaxed a little.

If the woman had continued with the fact that Emma had been almost assaulting the male staff but no complaints had been made so no action had been taken, she may have had more cause to worry, especially as her husband was now in the firing line. But she trusted Joel and had no worries that he would stray anywhere, let alone with this trollop. All the same it wasn't pleasant to think she may try if the opportunity arose, and if it didn't she would make one.

The deputy suggested that Zoe take her break while it was quiet, so she went off to the staff area which was deserted. Making a cup of tea she took it to the small table and went to place it down when it seemed to shake. It was as if something had enclosed her entire hand and was moving it against her will. She fought against it and finally managed to put the cup down but instinctively her defences came up as she remembered Joel's words about keeping their protective shield up at all times. Since she had arrived at work she had completely forgotten this because she was concentrating on what she was doing. What could be with her now?

It never occurred to her that she had made contact with the guests in some way, and one in particular had made the connection when he arrived. Now Tule was holding both her hands leading her away from the table. She could feel his arms encompassing her whole body, yet they weren't arms, they were a power without shape and she was feeling as though she was drowning, fighting for air, but she didn't recognise who it was. The terror made her fight back and suddenly there seemed to be a power lifting her up and up then just as quickly she was lowered gently and placed on the chair, her hand resting on the table near her drink.

She shook herself, looked at the tea, and wondered what had happened. Two questions were foremost. One, who had enveloped her, and two, who had rescued her? The latter proved that the initial source was up to no good and she felt very vulnerable and frightened. This was so different to what Joel had described and to her previous experiences which both seemed to be purely sexual, but this was a controlling power and she didn't understand it. She needed to speak to her husband and glancing at her watch, realised he wouldn't be home for a least an hour and they never contacted each other at work unless it was absolutely essential. She decided to text him and he could read it when he could but knew he would immediately warn her to keep her shield up. She sat for a moment mentally strengthening her force field and rejecting any unwelcome visitors, but also thanking those who had come to her aid.

When she had finished her break she went to the washroom to make sure her appearance was immaculate before returning to the desk. She was just applying her lipstick when she felt she saw a shape in the mirror behind her, nothing solid but more than a mist. She swung round to face whatever it was but there was nothing there. It was only when she realised she had be pointing her lipstick at nothing she was forced to smile.

"A fat lot of good that would have done," she thought but there was still an air of uncertainly hovering about the place "Oh go away and play somewhere else." She said aloud this time at which point the door opened and the cleaner came in.

"You talking to me?" The man asked giving her a quizzical look. "I did knock but you didn't answer."

Zoe had to think quickly. "No, I'm sorry, I was just going through some lines, you know practising on my own."

"Oh, what's that for then?"

Again she must come up with an excuse. "Oh nothing, I probably won't get it. There's lots better than I am."

He seemed satisfied with the answers and said that if she'd finished he'd like to get on with his work. His manner broke the unpleasant feeling that she was being watched and she began to see the funny side, which then made her wonder if she had imagined the other thing.

She returned to the desk and within minutes 'Mr Tully' walked up to her.

"I wonder if you could help me please?" His tone was rather intoxicating and she couldn't remember that he had spoken like this when he arrived.

"Of course sir. How may I be of assistance?" she was drawn to his eyes of deep blue.

"I am not familiar with the area and have to meet someone at….." he took a card from his pocket and gave the name of a road not far from where she lived.

"Oh that's on the other side of town sir. About half an hour's drive at the most."

"Ah thank you." He started fumbling in his wallet. "I did have the name of the taxi firm that brought me here but I seem to have mislaid it."

"Would you like me to give you the numbers of some reliable ones?"

He leaned forward and looked her straight in the eyes. "I need to go at nine o'clock."

Her mind was floating under his gaze. "I'm off at nine."

"Good. That will be perfect."

Suddenly she was looking at him wondering what had happened. He seemed to speak in normal tones now.

"That is extremely kind of you. I will see you by your car when you have signed off." He gave a little bow before turning and going back to his room.

She stood wondering what on earth had happened. Never in this world would she have offered a lift to a perfect stranger, guest or otherwise, and it was against company policy. It was obviously a mistake and she couldn't work out how it had happened but one thing was for sure, she must cancel it. That wouldn't be easy as she couldn't tell another member of staff, and how could she just go up to his room and says she wasn't going to give him a lift? Ring him! Of course.

She waited until the foyer was empty then buzzed his number. No reply. She tried several times but he didn't answer, almost as if he knew the reason for the call.

As Joel drove home he felt something wasn't quite right. It wasn't anything to do with Emma, she was on the way out anyway. He couldn't get Zoe out of his mind but thought everything must be alright or he would have heard. He checked his phone but it was dead, the battery had run down completely.

"Strange" he thought "it was ok last time I looked." As soon as he got home he quickly plugged in the charger and waited until some power was indicated. It was then he saw that there was an unread message. As soon as he saw the contents he knew by the tone something was wrong and sent a reply straight back, whether she was working or not. This was more important with the current events. There was no reply as she must have it on silent. He checked the time she had sent hers and guessed she must be on break then. He read it again.

"Joel. I need my shield up. Do the same, please."

The thought of food went out of his mind as he paced up and down wondering what to do. He could drive over, have a drink in the bar and hang about until she left just as a show of support, but unless they could speak in private he stood little chance of learning why she would alert him.

After a few moments, his curiosity and worry got the better of him and he decided he would change out of his work attire and go over. He had just stripped down to his underwear when a familiar feeling came over him.

"Oh not now for Christ's sake." He yelled.

But Phani wasn't taking 'No' for an answer and wrapped herself round him then slid inside his boxers. He felt both hands grasp him and get to work straight away as though she was hungry for him. Her mouth was seeking his and he frantically tried to push her away but she seemed to draw on his strength and the more he fought the stronger she got. It came as a surprise to her, for never before had she felt this tremendous force working with her almost leading her on.

Joel was on the floor now, naked from the waist down and although he wanted to push away this creature, the effect she was having on him was taking over his physical reactions and he was trying to hold everything back without much success so he tried another tactic.

"Zoe." He yelled.

"If you want Zoe, I'll be Zoe. Now what does she do that you like best?"

"Get away from me. Zoe come in." He was yelling but Phani was riding him like a horse winning the Derby and his self control couldn't cope with the rush of the inevitable as he gasped with anger yet relief as he emptied himself.

Phani knew she wouldn't be welcome as soon as he had shot his bolt and made to leave but something was holding her there, urging her to go for more. The battle that ensued between man and spirit was ferocious and it wasn't the female that was in charge, but the force driving her from afar.

Tule had broken the contact between man and wife, and the seed he had planted in Phani would keep working until he turned it off, leaving him free access to Zoe. He knew his previous warning wouldn't stop this stupid young spirit keeping her distance and she thought that as long as Joel was on his own and Zoe nowhere in the vicinity she could get away with it, after all she still had her challenge and her crown to protect. Little did she realise this was just the way Tule was playing her and she still felt she was calling the shots, even putting her added power down to her own skills.

Zoe handed over to the night shift and, gathering up her things quickly made her way to her car, praying she could leave before Mr Tully appeared.

"Oh thank goodness," she thought, "no sign of him."

She unlocked the car when she was only a few feet from it and as her hand touched the door handle a voice behind her whispered "I like punctuality."

Although startled, she swung round to face him. It was time for her back up plan.

"I'm sorry, I've been trying to ring you to say I'm not going straight home and I've ordered a taxi for you. It should be here any moment now."

His hand came past her in a flash and held the door shut preventing her from getting in the car.

"Mr Tully, I have to warn you that there are cameras covering every inch of this car park and you are being filmed, now please remove your hand, and yourself and wait in the foyer."

He gave a sickly smile and breathed "There is no taxi."

"But I ordered one." she was feeling really trapped wondering how he knew.

"And I cancelled it."

"But….." she trembled

"How did I know? Oh my dear, I know all about you, and now it is time for you to get to know me."

She reached for her personal alarm that all staff carried but he pre-empted her movement and, taking her arm he pushed her instructing her to get in. When she resisted he moved closer to her ear and the words came out hot and sinister.

"If you value your husband's safety, you will do exactly as I say."

The temptation to run back to the hotel, knowing she would be picked up on camera was very strong, but the threat of Joel being in danger made her stop for a moment which was just long enough for Tule to get into the passenger seat.

"Drive." he ordered.

Zoe wasn't one to get frightened easily, but the power of this person was very threatening and she was beginning to fear for her life. It flashed through her mind that the man didn't know Joel and was using him to get her under his control. He hadn't used his Christian name but would guess she was married by her wedding ring. So she tried another ruse.

"Jack will be wondering where I am."

"Who's Jack?"

"You just said if I valued his safety."

They had turned out of the entrance and were heading out towards the open country on his direction.

"No I didn't, and don't try to be clever young lady."

Suddenly she did something either very brave or very foolhardy. She stopped the car.

"What are you doing? I said drive." He was becoming frustrated and angry.

"And I said that Jack will be wondering where I am." She repeated, turning to face him.

If he had expected an easy ride, he was somewhat taken aback at this show of strength, but it seemed to have a stimulating effect on him and he was becoming aroused by it. He tried to turn off the engine but as he leaned over she suddenly took off again and he was caught off guard. Fortunately she knew these roads and soon took a round about route until they were heading towards the hotel they had just left.

Tule wasn't a power that anyone took on and won. He always got what he wanted. The fact that he now had a fight on his hands forced him employ his skills for he wasn't going to be beaten especially in the early stages.

The car suddenly spluttered and came to a halt near a field gateway. Zoe tried in vain to get it started but Tule sat back saying smugly "You don't think that's going to work do you?"

Now he had her alone and it was simply a matter of programming her mind and soul to his ways and by the time he had finished she would want no one but him, ever.

Abe had alerted Danny to Joel's area as something fishy seemed to be going on. Although it was quite normal for Phani to be seducing this man, they knew there was a greater being at work here. This may be the lead they had been waiting for so Abe went to locate Zoe and traced her just as the car came to a halt. He immediately recognised her passenger and sent the thought wave back for Danny to remove Phani at once leaving Joel's connections free.

He knew he was up against a strong force so didn't try to remove him, which was what one would have expected. Instead he sent Zoe into an unconscious state, removed her spirit to a safe place and put a temporary placement in her body to keep it alive until she returned to it. It all happened in a fraction of a second and by the time Tule had realised he had lost his catch she was far away. He knew there was a placement and as his anger took over, he began to plan that if he could remove the resident and leave the body empty for long enough, Zoe would not be able to be returned to it. But that meant she would be safe elsewhere and he would never possess her. For now it was a setback, but it would not stop him.

Danny was having quite a fight with Phani at first but when he realised she was being controlled, he worked on that, and although found it difficult to remove the programme altogether he did manage to water it down just enough to send her packing under the guard of some of his backup.

Now Abe and Danny could reunite the bond between the husband and wife which had almost been severed. It was also the time for a bit of manoeuvring.

Sometimes people take a wrong turning or miss a train and find they have escaped an accident or similar and say a 'thank you' for being spared, but equally guardians use their powers for the opposite. They will direct help to an incident. In this case a helper spirit was told to direct a patrol car down the road where Zoe's body was now alone in the car. The officer could never have explained what made him take that route and could only put it down to his gut feeling, but he soon saw the car which looked as though it had veered off the road at a strange angle.

"Can't be that dogging lot" he thought, "they wouldn't be doing it in a gateway."

He approached cautiously switching on his body cam and shining his torch into the car. As soon as he saw Zoe's body he checked she was still alive then called in for an ambulance but didn't move her. He thought it strange that she appeared to have no injuries and was sitting quite normally in her seat and the idea of a whiplash crossed his mind. He checked she was breathing alright and as he waited he went to the passenger side and felt the seat with the back of his hand. Although not warm, it wasn't as cold as he expected and he felt the rear seats also. There was a very slight difference and he suspected there had been a passenger who may have gone for help, but why not use a mobile? Then something attracted him and he sniffed near the seat.

It wasn't so much a smell as a strong feeling, but he knew from experience it wasn't something he could put in his report as there was nothing physical to go on.

Abe was working on this officer trying to alert his instincts that something wasn't right, and in bodily terms it would come to nothing, but in his subconscious would warn him to keep his protective shield in play as he was on dangerous territory. Everyone had to be protected when dealing with evil forces.

The paramedics took Zoe to the city hospital as it was the nearest with an A & E department. Although they could find no apparent injuries, she was still unconscious and would obviously have to be detained, the officer saying he would inform her husband, the details having been found in her bag. Abe had strengthened the guard on her, and although knew her soul was not on board needed to protect the body ready for her return. They would have to keep her in this state while the temporary occupant was there and bring her round when she had returned and could answer all the relevant questions. The cause of the accident would probably never been known and she would have to undergo tests to see why she had passed out. She must have felt unwell as she appeared to have parked rather than just run off the road, but that was for the humans to decide. Abe needed to know the truth and would visit Zoe at the first opportunity.

Joel was recovering from Phani's onslaught with mixed feelings. At first it was anger at her insistent advances and the fact that she had made him perform against his will, annoyance that he hadn't managed to rid himself of her even with trying to protect his shield and calling out for Zoe. Then it all turned to guilt. It felt as though he had physically had sex, you couldn't describe it as love, with another woman, and yet this wasn't a woman as such, just a ghost. He felt grateful that his wife could understand but somehow it didn't make him feel that much better.

He looked at his watch, she should be home soon. It was strange that she hadn't texted him before she left, but perhaps she was in a hurry to get home. As the minutes ticked by he became more and more worried and toyed with the idea of ringing the hotel to check if she'd actually left. But if she had been held up, she would have let him know. He wasn't keen to alert anyone there that they were on edge because of the recent happenings, but then he thought about talking to Nick. He was about to call him when the door bell rang.

"Must have forgotten her key." he thought as he hurried to let her in.

The sight of the police officer made him jump. There must have been an accident.

After the preliminaries of checking who he was, the PC asked if he may come in. He picked up Joel's nervous manner and realised the man must have been wondering as to his wife's whereabouts, and then when a policeman appears at the door, one always fears the worst. So he got straight to the point and answered as many questions as he could.

"Where is she now?" Joel knew he had to get to her. "I have to see her."

The officer explained and also told him where her car had been taken, then questioned if he was in a fit state to drive but Joel explained that he would have to call his brother to tell him and he would most likely take him.

Left on his own, he somehow knew that this had to have a bearing on the recent visitations and he blamed Phani, thinking she had somehow got his wife out of the way so that she had a clear run on him. But this was evil and he would muster all the fight he had to be rid of her and her kind.

# Chapter 6

Sam was starting to feel a bit more like her old self and with a bit of extra make up was covering her bruises quite well. It was Wednesday already and she was wondering where to go the coming week end. The manager felt she was recovered enough to go back on the checkout and she was just wiping away some moisture that had dropped from a plant and splattered over the working surface when she was aware of a familiar voice.

"Hello dear. You're better today aren't you?"

"Oh hi Annie, you come for your tea?" She put the paper towel in the bin.

"I have, fair parched I am. Hey, there was this programme on last night….."

"Annie, you're not going to tell me about the giraffe again are you?" Sam had to laugh. This lady always lifted her spirits and made her feel as though everything in the world was a laugh.

"Giraffe? Now don't you go flustering me." She looked around to make sure she wouldn't get the girl into trouble, she always called her a girl, and sidled round until she was almost hidden behind a display.

"There was this horse and the woman on it was being interviewed, stuffy cow she was too. Well, I don't know if anyone else noticed but the animal had got one hell of a parsnip on him, if you know what I mean." She paused to make sure Sam knew what she was on about.

"Oh, I get it, Annie, what you like?"

"Ah well, this snooty bit carries on talking, all posh like, and this blooming thing, well I tell you, I never knew they was mottled like that."

"Mottled Annie?"

"Yes, that's what I'm saying. You know the piebald ponies, well it was all patterned like that. Couldn't take my eyes off it I can tell you."

"Didn't the reporter notice?"

"Wasn't looking at him. Bet he'd have liked one that size. Eh? Eh?" she was giggling now but her eyes were alight.

"Beats me how you find them Annie. You must watch all the right programmes."

"Aha, can't do better than a good old parsnip, now my old man, God rest his soul…"

"Annie, I've got customers, sorry." Sam turned towards where the old lady had been hiding but she must have made a hasty exit and gone for her tea.

The incident had started her day off well and she imagined this little ray of sunshine would have many tales to tell if she only had time to listen. The morning got busier, but more people seemed to be inside than out due to the constant showers. The café was busy and Sam hoped that Annie would find another ear to bend as she obviously needed to have an audience.

"Probably using the giraffe one again," she thought but then decided "no, I reckon she saves those for me." Little did she guess just how right she was in more ways than one. When it was time for her break, she half expected the manager to remind her not to get into lengthy conversations with her as it could give the wrong image, but he never mentioned her at all which came as a relief.

Eating her lunch, her mind turned to Katie-Marie. If only she could remember all that had been said when she spoke to her. She had a feeling that her friend had been a bit on the cool side, but it was probably nothing and she needed her to be in tow if there was going to be any action on Saturday night.

"Ah glad I've caught you, feeling better now?" The manager's voice broke into her reverie.

"Much, ta." She carried on eating.

"Only I need you in on Saturday, we're very short with holidays and the like."

"Saturday, what all day?" she spluttered.

"Well yes. Will be busy, but you can go off at five instead of six."

Sam thought of the overtime which wasn't to be sneezed at, and she would still have plenty of time to get dolled up as they didn't go out before eight at the earliest.

"Go on then." She finished her sandwich.

"Good girl. Knew I could count on you." and he breezed off to find another 'volunteer'.

She was still wondering where to go and, not being sure of Katie's attitude until she spoke to her, thought she would play it safe and stay close to home.

"Oh well, better find out what mood she's in."

Sam soon recovered from any upset, although this last episode had left her a bit shaken. Rather than ring her, she would send a message to feel the water. Quickly she tapped it on her mobile and sent it before she could change her mind. Katie had told her never to contact her at work unless it was an emergency, but a message could be read at any time, so Sam reckoned it didn't count. There was no immediate answer but that didn't concern her for now.

"See what that brings forth." She said to herself as she got ready to go back on the till. Walking back through the shop area, she nearly bumped into Annie.

"I thought you'd gone ages ago." Sam smiled.

"I did, but I had this idea that a spot of dinner wouldn't go amiss."

"You coming or going?"

"Oh just off dear. It was very nice. Now you be sure and take care, don't want you having any more falls do we?" She gave a very knowing look then went to walk away, but stopped turned and said "Did I tell you the one about the elephants?"

"Not yet Annie, but I expect you will, only another time. I've got to work now."

Annie waved over her shoulder as she left and Sam shook her head in amusement, but when she looked up the old dear had gone.

"Bloody hell, she's sprightly for her age, whatever it is." she thought.

Katie had seen the message but was in no hurry to answer guessing what lay behind it. It had been a bit too chilly to sit in the little park today and she had been flicking through a magazine at lunchtime.

"I may give her a ring later." she decided but her mind was on finding someone on whom she could trust and who would share her tastes in her leisure time, not keep going off to seedy clubs for the next catch, leaving her to her own devices. If the last club was anything to go by, she'd rather stay at home. But she did need to be hugged and genuinely cared for and she knew that although she still loved her husband, she was not being unfaithful to him now.

Aware of her thoughts, one of the guardian team reassured Stefan that she would be guided on the right path and although he knew this would be what she needed, his soul was heavy that it wouldn't be him.

Vanke believed he could move in and have his pleasure with her whenever he wanted. His level were not always aware of the guardian presence in any situation as they could remain cloaked from lesser spirits, so it was always a surprise when such as he came up against obstacles.

He knew where she lived, where she worked and he was tracing all her movements, even to where she did her shopping, but he never seemed to be able to get as near to her as he wanted as there was always this barrier stopping him getting to the final goal. But he wasn't giving up this easily. He found it difficult to find his fresh flowers, as he called them. By the time he had scored, so had many more before him which sort of took the edge off it somehow. He wanted them totally untouched but old enough to know what they were doing.

"OK she's been married," he mused "but she's not tasted the wine, well not the good stuff. Bet she doesn't even know all the names of my equipment." He was getting quite frustrated just thinking about it which was always a bad move as it meant he was pushed out of frustration to go for it which is why he always got caught by the good forces, and despatched with undignified haste plus a warning not to return to that source.

"This one's mine." He gloated, "Been waiting too long. Got to have her."

If he possessed a body just then he would have had no choice but to go and shake hands with his best friend, but being in spirit there was no chance unless...... The thought came to him that if he could used someone else's body he could get his satisfaction but then there was a problem. Who would she let do that?

He thought for a moment then chastised himself for not having worked it out sooner. He would put someone in her path. A man she couldn't resist, then he would take over at the right moment and soar in ecstasy, so now all he had to do was find the right one. Pity he hadn't got Bollik's intelligence, he'd have done that long ago.

"Let him play," the guardians were amused "while he's busy here we know where he is and he's not causing trouble anywhere else."

"Bit of a waste of energy when you think he has no chance of succeeding."

"He should have learnt that by now."

And so they let him live in his dream world until the time came to move him on.

Katie finally answered Sam's text saying she had been extra busy at work, which the other woman took as an invitation to talk so rang her straight away.

"How are you?" She asked.

Katie drew breath before saying "I'm quite good as it happens. How are you now?"

Sam wanted to say "As if you've cared" but bit her tongue.

"Not too bad. The bruises are going and my lip's better."

"Well I hope you've learned something from it." Katie's tone was far from warm.

"Look it won't happen again." Sam sounded sincere.

"Well, that's up to you, because I won't be going."

There was a silence.

"I wouldn't dream of going to that place again." Sam was right about that.

"That's entirely up to you where you go, because Sam, I won't be coming with you. I've made up my mind. A turning point if you like."

"What, not even to the Eagles?"

"Well maybe occasionally but nothing on a regular basis. I want to be free."

Sam hooked onto the 'occasionally' bit.

"That's absolutely fine with me. But hey, couldn't we just go this Saturday, have a drink, put this behind us. We've been friends for a long time, seems a pity not to go out at all."

Katie took a deep breath. Was this the thin edge of the wedge to get back into old ways? Only if she allowed it. She must keep a tight hold of the reins to stay in control of her own life.

"Well, alright. I'll go for a drink with you, but I will tell you now Sam, the first move you make to get off with anyone, I'm gone. Do you understand what I'm saying?"

There was a tone of relief in the answer. "Too right. A drink it is and thanks Katie, you won't regret it I promise."

As she put the phone down Katie stood for a moment.

"I must be off my rocker," she said to herself "but it sounds innocent enough, although I mean it, the minute she starts, I'm back here."

Phani and Pheel were having a quick catch-up session.

"I don't think we're going to need the three weeks, I'm home and dry already." Phani didn't liked the way things were going and was getting very uneasy about being either blocked from Joel at work, or rejected by him at home. Now she wished she had taken Nick on because she had realised when she followed her opponent into his bed, he was the most likely candidate. Also the memory of Tule was lingering in the back of her thoughts, little realising he was playing her like a puppet without her knowledge.

"Oh, I don't agree with that, it's only a few days into it, how can we possibly know what will happen, anyway I'm fine thank you very much." Then after a pause added "I've never known you to give in."

"Who says I'm giving in?" Phani was on the defensive. "As I said, mine's a push over, I'll get bored and I've noticed more interesting action going on. Don't want to miss out on something better."

"I don't believe you." Pheel said very slowly. "You're up to something."

"Oh please yourself, but we'll see who has the most fun." She tried to leave but the other one followed.

"Let me remind you, the challenge is still on. You can't just walk away. It's not in the rules."

Phani stopped and faced her. "Rules? Who made the frigging rules in the first place? It was always just a bit of fun."

Pheel knew that winning the crown was always important to Phani's ego, even if it was only her she was beating. But let's face it, where else could she find someone she felt was beneath her and she could beat every time? There had been one occasion when Pheel won easily, but so many excuses had been made and the atmosphere was electric for some time after, so another challenge had been arranged as quickly as possible so that 'madam' could regain her crown. These thoughts were racing through Pheel's mind but when Phani was in this mood, she felt it better not to add fuel to the fire, she wasn't that brave.

"Perhaps you're right." she said, then with a laugh "I win as you have backed out."

That did it.

"I never said I had backed out, backed off, or backed away, so don't put words into my mouth, if I had one."

Pheel could see the funny side, and if her friend hadn't been so wound up she would have told her how silly she looked, but she knew better and so let her play queen bee.

They parted fairly amicably but Pheel was the only one looking forward to her next session.

Danny had been a tower of strength, both on the physical and mental planes. When Abe had updated him about Zoe's outcome, he had to return to his body to wait for Joel to call him with the news. It seemed only minutes before he arrived to take his brother to the hospital, but that was because he was part way there already waiting. It was obvious Joel would be in a very worried state and would not notice the time it had taken which was what Danny had played on. He did a quick scan to make sure Phani hadn't returned and Joel was under extra protection, then drove him to the hospital.

Zoe was half aware that she was in a lovely place, floating with caring people at her side. She was trying to piece together what had happened but the guardians were keeping her under a mental sedation so that she would be in a fit state to return, fully restored.

Abe, having rechecked her body was still being protected, was in presence and gently eased her through the happenings, explaining the forces were not good and she must follow his instructions in order to beat them. She was asking about Joel and was reassured he too was under the highest protective force and they would be reunited shortly. The guard would remain in place, but he emphasised that she must always be aware and keep her own protective field strong at all times because it had to come from within to be most effective and ward off the undesirables.

She asked about Jude Tully as she felt he had been instrumental in this. Abe explained that he was certainly not a good spirit and would be angry at being thwarted, hence everyone must be on full alert. He tried not to frighten her, but felt the need to make sure she knew that everyone concerned knew this was not a minor playful sprite but one to be acknowledged for what he was. It was little consolation that the surrounding protectors were ignorant of just how powerful this evil being was, but they didn't need to know any more for now as it could weaken the defences. The likes of him would pick up in an instant any fear or anxiety.

Danny stood back while Joel was ushered into the room where his wife lay unconscious, then went and sat in a side room in silent conversation with Abe.

"Are you ready?"

Danny nodded slightly "Everyone in position?"

"Yes. Got them ready to take out the stand-in as I bring Zoe in. You leave your body here and guard Joel at the swap, he'll be emotional."

"Let's do it."

Angels of this calibre had carried out this task many times but still kept up their defences on each new case, for it only took the fraction of a second for it all to go wrong. In an instant Zoe was back and stirred slightly as Joel stroked her hand. She opened her eyes.

"Joel." she whispered.

"Yes my love, I'm here." To see her look at him and know she recognised him wiped any warnings from his mind for a moment as only the earthly happenings seemed important. Danny was waiting for this knowing it was the usual reaction and so strengthened the force field on his behalf.

The doctors took over and Joel found himself with Danny in the corridor.

"She's ok. Danny." The voice was trembling with relief.

"I know. She'll be ok, believe me." As he guided him to a seat he said quietly "Not a good time I know, but I have to warn you to keep that shield up."

"You mean this has something to do with what's been going on, but why? I don't see…."

"Look, you're upset and confused right now, and I will explain it all later, but for now, please, please keep your guard up. It really is that important."

Joel felt weak. "You did say she will be alright?"

"Yes she will. She hasn't been harmed physically, but they will have to do the necessary tests as to why she was unconscious for so long, and they won't find any injuries."

"But how do you know this?"

Danny lowered his head into his hands for a moment.

"When you and Nick came to see me, it was because you knew I could help. Well sometimes, I can't explain things to you but I do know more of what is going on …shall we say….in other dimensions than most people."

"You're psychic. I always knew you had something different."

"A bit more than that, but can you just accept that if I tell you something, you'll trust me."

"Course, but I'm not sure I quite get it."

Danny smiled now. "You don't have to bro, not sure I always understand, and sometimes I wish I didn't."

They sat there for a moment then Joel asked "Hey, this hasn't got anything to do with the sex thing has it? Only……"

"Go on."

"Well there's been more going on than I thought and…..um…."

Danny stood up "Look take care of what's going on here for now, then when you can, we'll have a talk. I'd really like to know everything, and I mean everything. Get it from your perspective, that kind of thing."

"Ok if you think it will help."

Danny agreed to stay until Joel was ready to go back home but kept a low profile so that he could be in constant touch with Abe. It was the early hours before the doctors assured them that she would be alright to be left as she had made a remarkable recovery so far, but they could ring in the morning to find out what ward she was on and take it from there.

As he said his goodbyes she whispered "I could do with a cup of tea, I'm parched."

"You behave yourself," he kissed her as though he didn't want to let her go and as he went they were blowing kisses to each other. One of the nurses had tears in her eyes. She was so glad this lady had made it, as she had dealt with too many deaths this shift and this one made her job worth while.

The overkill on spiritual guards was essential as was soon proved. One of Abe's helpers reported that Tule had been hovering around but they had been able to stop him getting near to Zoe.

"He won't give up." he thought as he thanked his informer "quite the reverse for this thing thrives on how difficult the obstacles are. Had it been an walkover, he would have discarded it and sought a new one. Well he will have a fight on his hands for he will never get her." He vowed.

Then another plan came into his thoughts, an old trick though and Tule would surely not fall for it again. But he would toss it around with Danny and get his opinion.

Tule had been nowhere near the hospital, but had merely projected his spirit to the vicinity knowing it would be picked up and would draw attention, while he was elsewhere. He scanned the pair's home and picked up the wake of Phani's antics. He wasn't pleased at the result because it was only what he had secretly ordered her to do, so knew it would work. But now everything seemed to be getting the couple back together, he must be one step ahead and the best place to start was in their love nest.

He summoned Phani and she was there in an instant, thinking she had come of her own free will. Joel had pushed her away but she thought she had the power to get him under her spell again. As she entered the lounge he was standing there as though he was waiting for her. He raised his hand and beckoned her, his towel falling to the floor showing himself in all his glory. She never stopped to realise this could be a trap, such was the bait and she was panting for him.

Her level couldn't possibly understand the ways of such a mighty power. Never in her existence had she known such sexual exhilaration as she encountered there. His body was exquisite, much better than it had been up to now but she wasn't asking any questions. They did things she had never dreamed of but at the time never gave it a thought, she only imagined he had been holding back and now something had made him want her and she wasn't about to refuse. They covered every room in the house, each climax greater than the last until even she was almost relieved when he beckoned for her to go, but making her promise to come back. Had she been in bodily form, she would have found it difficult to walk and certainly not sit down for every intimate part had been explored, invaded and abused. But she was one happy lady and couldn't realise the part she had played in Tule's masquerade.

When the news spread through the hotel chain that Zoe had been almost abducted there was great concern as she was a well respected and liked member of staff and was known at most of the establishments. But rumours grow and soon the various tales that were flying around became amusing but thoughts also were for Joel who would not be at work for the next day or so as his place was with his wife as often as possible.

Emma was elated. Now she wouldn't have to put up with his high handedness and wouldn't get the push after all, but little did she know that she was being put under the direct control of Megan Clarke, which meant she stood no chance of proving herself and when she realised this, then the sparks would fly, guests or no guests, for what had she got to lose?

But she didn't know she was no longer working alone. Her recent nocturnal activities had unleashed such a vile set of entities that had attached themselves to her spirit, that soon the old Emma wouldn't be recognisable. Now it was time for them to really have fun and it would go way beyond mischievous for they meant business.

It had been noticed that Mr Tully hadn't been back to his room and his key was at reception so the deputy manager assumed that he had already checked out but on going through the accounts found there was no record of payment. She wondered how long he had planned to stay so went back to the page where he had checked in but there was no entry. She thought for a moment then spoke to the domestics. They knew someone had taken the room as the 'Do not disturb' sign was there but hadn't actually seen him. After speaking to the manager, it was decided to use the pass key and check the room if nobody answered.

The two stood at the door and the manager knocked gently calling out 'Mr Tully, are you alright?"

No answer.

He tried a couple more times then said "I'm going in."

Slowly he unlocked the door and peeped round.

"Well?" asked the deputy.

"Nothing." He said as he entered the room. "Look."

They both saw an untouched room, the bed still made. They checked the wardrobe and drawers but there was of sign of any clothing.

"No toiletries have been touched." She was looking in the shower. "It's as if no one has entered this room since it was cleaned after the last guest."

"Well someone has to explain this." he closed the door. "It seems Zoe may be the only one who can shed any light on it."

Then he stopped mid step. "Oh my God."

"What is it?"

"Seems too coincidental to have this at the same time as she was, you know attacked."

The deputy thought for a moment before they moved off again. "If someone did come, and then tried to take her, they wouldn't come back here would they?"

The manager stared at her but had the same uneasy feeling.

"Let's go through the footage." he almost shouted.

"Shall we start with when Zoe came on? I was there then, and we could go from that point."

They soon reached the office and told staff that unless it was very urgent, they weren't to be disturbed.

There were a couple of bona fide minor problems which called one of them away at a time, but when they reached the point where Zoe went off duty, both pairs of eyes were fixed on the screen.

"She's alone when she leaves, and she's going over to her car." the deputy was tracing each movement. "Damn, she's off my shot."

"Got her on the car park cameras!" the manager said, and she turned her attention to where he was looking until he said "Keep watching the desk"

After a moment he said "Now that is strange."

"What?" the deputy was back on his screen.

"Well see for yourself, she seems to be talking to herself, but she's agitated. Wonder if she's lost her key."

"Oh that must be it. No look she's almost thrown herself in the car and driven off."

They sat for a moment then re-ran the sequence.

The manager sighed. "There's something not quite right."

"I know but what? It's not like her at all, she's so calm and efficient all the time."

"That's it." he thumped the desk. "She is calm normally, so what made her act like that?" then as an afterthought "Anything on the reception shots."

She shook her head. "Nothing, but I was just looking along the corridor on level one and...."

"What is it?" he joined her.

"Not sure, let me play it again."

As they both stared mouths open, he told her to run it frame by frame and what they saw left them speechless. The corridor was empty but slowly the door of the room they had checked opened and the sign was hung on the handle. They played it several times but it remained unchanged. There was no physical hand placing the sign and the door closed.

She didn't know why but she continued to run frame by frame following this, and on one shot only, there appeared to be a disturbance in the air as though someone had moved in the corridor. The frames either side were perfectly still.

"What time is that?" the manager asked.

"8.59pm." they both chorused. One minute before Zoe had ended her shift.

They checked all footage through the night but there had been no movement near the door and the sign remained where they had found it. But what could they say? It was if nobody had been there at all and the door key was hanging on its hook as though it had never been moved.

Sam was looking forward to going out on Saturday and even more pleased that she'd talked Katie into it as she felt her friend was really trying to get out of going out with her at all. It was her turn to set out one of the displays in the shop area and was arranging a stand of potpourri when a familiar voice whispered at her side.

"Ladyboys."

She swung round nearly knocking Annie over. "What do you know about that? You naughty woman?"

"Oh it's always on. Some good looking ones I can tell you."

"Bet they didn't have such things in your day Annie?"

"What? Never. Much easier to understand then."

Sam waved a bag under her nose. "Ever smelt anything like that?"

"Poo, no, they make me sneeze." Annie laughed and had somehow inserted herself between the displays so she could hardly be seen.

"Come for your tea?" Sam carried on as though she wasn't there.

"Ah well, I might have one."

"That's not like you Annie, you normally guzzle them down you."

There was a little smile creeping over the lady's face. "Have to ration myself."

"Oh." Sam didn't like to ask as she could guess the reply would be colourful.

"I been dribbling."

There it was. It had to be an Annie-ism and she never disappointed.

Sam felt a bit sorry for her. "Perhaps you need some of these love," she waved a spray of leaves at her "you don't want to stink do you?"

"Oh I won't do that dear, I've got three pairs on. It's when I cough you see, which reminds me, did you see that hippo on telly last night?" without waiting for a reply she continued but lowered her voice "when they farts, they wag their tails backwards and forwards so quick like, that when the turds come out they get spread all over the place. They go on for a long time. Longer than I could."

That did it. Sam couldn't contain herself and let out the biggest laugh attracting attention from all around.

"Oh sorry," she called out, "just looking at one of these little ornaments." Some smiled back at her but one or two gave her a strange look.

"Now look what you've made me do," she giggled towards Annie, but she had gone.

Annie always left a presence when she had been, which made Sam feel she could cope with anything, but today it wasn't like that. She could only describe it as an interference for something was hovering for one minute then going the next, then it would come back but she didn't like it and tried to push the thought away.

Having finished her display she took the old stuff to the storeroom and as soon as she was on her own she felt the unpleasantness creeping over her. It made her want to ask who was there but there was something else going on. But what was it?

With a deeper insight she would have been in for a shock for the most ferocious battle was going on, fighting for control. Bollik had been watching her and decided it was time to move in but he hadn't bargained on what came at him from all sides. Just as he was about to familiarise himself with her intimate places he was pushed to one side. Back he came like a snarling animal after its prey and again he was thrown, this time further back. But the battle was not twofold. Many of the entities she had attracted at the club were homing in on Bollik's target to grab it for themselves, but none of them had bargained for the protective force which was always in presence waiting for such an onslaught, and it never slept.

For some reason Annie's jokes were flying through her mind. "Did you see the telly last night?" then "There was this animal…" followed by "Never seen a parsnip like it." And so they kept coming, filling her mind with laughter and the love that little Annie seemed to have for her.

This attempt by Bollik had failed but he put it down to the venue. He must choose the next one more carefully and it would have to be in a place where it was sex ridden and full of debauchery, this place was too 'clean'. He must aim where the goody goodies couldn't get in because there was always an excess of heavy security to protect his kind. He wouldn't stay there for his pleasure, but it would be a good hunting ground then he could make off with his catch and there would be no opposition from Vanke as he had his sights set elsewhere. So he had no option but to leave this place and make his plans for when she would be out on the pull again.

Pheel's confidence was building by the moment. She had always felt she was in Phani's shadow and quite often had selected a target only to have the other spirit jump in ahead of her, but now it was due to the bad planning that the position had almost reversed. Nick had proved to be a very willing target plus there was the bonus of being able to wind his horrible wife up until she didn't know which way was up. It was becoming difficult to wait for the next session and Pheel had started to stalk Nick regardless of where he was or who he was with. The effect she was having on him was beginning to show outwardly and some of his workmates were making unseemly comments behind his back.

"Don't know who she is, but if there's any spare I'll have it."
"Not his missus, that's for sure. Heard she's gone right downhill."
"Doesn't anyone know what he's servicing then?"
"Not a clue."
"Bet she's walking around as if she's got a bit left in."
"Never mind her, have you seen the state of his eyes. That's a dead giveaway."

If he heard the chatter he was ignoring it and carried on as if everything was perfectly normal, but inside he was desperately waiting for the next visit. The frustration was building up to such a level he could hardly wait until Pheel was working on him, and sometimes he had to dash into his house and relieve himself. She seemed to find parts of his body he had never been aware of and his entire being seemed to dissolve into one erotic mass that transformed into the feeling that he had left the earth completely and had been experiencing what he thought must be heaven.

He was now making the mistake of believing that she loved him and would never leave him and if anyone had tried to tell him it would end when she was ready, he wouldn't have listened.

When he heard the news about Zoe, he was very concerned, not only for her but for Joel and had been in touch throughout the day arranging to join him to visit her that evening. Because she was still in the city hospital which would take longer to reach he arranged to leave work a bit earlier, have a quick meal and a shower then get straight round to his friend who had been at the hospital earlier in the day and was going back with him.

Emma was still at work, at least she was not at home, he didn't care but obviously had heard about her current working status. He made straight for his room to undress then walked naked to the bathroom. He was just enjoying the water running down his body when he knew he wasn't alone.

"Oh not now" he breathed.

Any other time he would have welcomed the advances but his thought was on getting to see Zoe. But what was going on? Just as he felt the familiar grip on his hampton, another sensation was caressing his back. It couldn't be the same person, not only the approach was different but it would have been physically impossible to be touching all the parts of his body at once.

He was about to try and squirm out of the position but the grip tightened and he couldn't pull against it, while simultaneously the hands coming down his back grabbed his buttocks then started to move between his legs so strongly he felt his whole manhood was in danger. As he tried to cry out, his lips were grasped in a kiss that seemed to be drawing out his air in one go.

Then he realised he was like a prize being fought over by two powerful creatures who were not about to relinquish the spoils. Why he now reacted the way he did, he would never know but something or someone was obviously on his side.

"Get your hands of my bollocks!" he screamed.

The shock must have done the trick for he felt the one behind him wrenched away at such a force the scream echoed in his ears, but the one still grasping his horn wasn't about to move. His energy seemed to drain away from him and he slumped to the floor of the shower, the water still spraying down on him and all he could think at this moment was that he never wanted to come like that again.

He was alone. Pheel had been satisfied and wasn't bothered about any after care so left feeling very smug that Phani's attempt to join in had been thwarted. But she had new found anger at the dirty tricks the other spirit was playing for if she had tried for a threesome, it probably meant she had already tasted the wine previously.

"So that's why she wanted to end the challenge." she gloated as she went in search of her opponent, but then thought "who chucked her out?"

But that was something she would learn only too soon and would wish she hadn't.

Nick finally found the strength to finish showering and made his way back to his bedroom. He had just put on some clean clothes, when the front door opening made him jump. Was it that late?

"Is that you?" he called.

"Why? Who else have you given a key to?"

He ignored the remark and, locking the door, went downstairs to get something quick to eat. Emma was sitting at the kitchen table, her bag strewn across it.

"I'm going out." he announced.

She just shrugged and took her shoes off and threw them on the floor.

"I suppose you know they're trying to get rid of me." She said not looking up.

Nick had decided to have a sandwich and was concentrating on making it. He could perhaps get a takeaway later.

"Nothing to do with me. They are making cuts across the board. I could go next."

She snorted. "Don't give me that. Joel had just about got me out on my ear but fate stepped in."

"What? Just how low can you sink? You've no heart."

She ignored him then said "And if they think that old bag can get the better of me they've got another think coming. Oh, I can handle her."

There was no good trying to have a sensible conversation but when he looked at his watch he stopped.

"Wait a minute. Shouldn't you have been on until six?"

"Told you. They can't do as they like with me."
"You've left." He nearly shouted.
"Not exactly."

He was eating his sandwich, still aware that he had to get to Joel's for them to be at the hospital ready for visiting time.

Emma was determined now that he would get her side of things.

"Well the old cow said that if I couldn't come up to scratch, I'd be out and I said that I didn't think I could possibly scratch anything, so I'd save them the trouble and went, right at the busiest time. Oh her face was a bloody picture." She sounded as though she had won a contest.

"I'm not discussing this now, I've more important things to do." He stood up and put his plate in the bowl.

"That's right 'Mr Sun shines out of his arse'. You run along and do your good deed for others."

"Wouldn't hurt you to be a bit more benevolent." he called as he left her spread over the table, then added "What a mess."

Fortunately the little scene hadn't left its mark on him and by the time he got to Joel's he had almost forgotten it, but the shower incident was still as fresh. His friend was waiting on the doorstep and got straight into the car and they were on their way. After being reassured that Zoe seemed to be doing all right, Nick broached the subject of the spiritual visits. Before long they were both describing in detail their own experiences. After relating the most recent ones, Joel said "You don't suppose they could be one and the same?"

"Never thought of that, but there's one sure way of finding out."

"If you mean what I think you mean......" Joel wasn't going to have any kind of gang bang experiment.

"I was thinking more of recording the times. Then we check if one is going round visiting, and it maybe not just us, not that we'd know of course."

"Ah, and if we put the same time, it must be different ones." Joel was happier with that.

They drove in silence for a while then Nick asked "Do you always shoot your lot?"

"Mostly. Trouble is I want to fend her off, but come on, what can you do when she's working on your cock like that, you'd have to be a eunuch or something." Then asked "You?"

Nick was quiet for a minute then answered "But you see I want it. It's different with Emma. I can't stand her near me any more but this, spirit, or whatever, I've got to have it."

They both seemed to be mulling that one over then Joel said "Danny's been a bit quiet on the subject. But he often is when he's got his teeth into something."

"Does he do a lot of this kind of stuff?"

"Never says much but I reckon so. He seems to know a lot, but you never know what he's thinking."

Nick coughed "I would be lost without mine. What I'm saying is....."

"......you don't want to be rid of her?" Joel finished it for him. Then added "Depends on what he finds out. He's come up against some bad things before so, let's wait and see before you get in to deeply." Little did either realise just how closely involved Danny had been up to now.

With Nick well out of the way, Pheel felt it was time for some more fun. She watched Emma in the kitchen for a while then transferred to the bathroom expecting this woman would need to freshen up for she looked a tired mess, and it wasn't just from work. She gave an acknowledgement of approval then went into the master bedroom to conjure up more mischief. Her plans set she moved into Nick's room to perform her own little speciality. She slid beneath the duvet and started to stroke every part of the sheet leaving not even an inch untouched so that wherever he moved he couldn't escape her presence. Then she formed an image of him and, starting at his toes slowly worked her way up his legs until she was inches from his meat and two veg. As she started to work on this area something seemed to be pushing her face away but she fought back and started grabbing roughly at anything she could make close contact with. Her being was moving over his whole body now as she fought the unseen force that was trying to remove her for she had no intention of leaving before she was satisfied, even if this was just preparation for later when he returned.

Poor Pheel, she tried her best. But she was still of the lower powers and had no way of fighting the stronger forces, especially on her own but how long would it take her to learn this? There was no option but to leave the room for now so she floated back into the kitchen to find Emma nibbling at some biscuits and drinking from a bottle of wine. Finding this very boring the spirit wandered off for a while to see what else was on offer as a back up, then returned to see Emma crawling up the stairs.

"Ah good, time for action." Pheel felt that now she may get some entertainment at last.

If she expected Emma to have even a suggestion of a wash she was wrong, for the woman had quite a bit of trouble getting her pants down and sitting on the toilet.

"Thank God she made it." Pheel thought. "She'll blame anything on the drink now. If she remembers that is, and she's got to go to work tomorrow." little knowing what the woman had said to her husband a short time before.

Although it was a sad state of affairs, Pheel was enjoying every minute of it, and as Emma tried to get off the toilet she pushed her towards the basin facing the mirror.

"What the…?" Emma was staring with her mouth hanging open for looking back at her was the most beautiful female and it copied her every move so it must be her. As she raised her hand and touched her cheek, so did the reflection, but suddenly her mouth didn't look so good and she gasped in horror. There were teeth missing! Then she noticed the dark circles under her bloodshot eyes and slowly the whole image changed until she was facing the most hideous old hag, and it was still mimicking her. She grabbed a beaker from the sink and smashed it into the glass, but it was only plastic and she hurt her hand more than do any damage. This made her angry and soon she was having a fight with herself, not knowing who the real person was anymore until suddenly she felt something warm and gentle surround her and lay her carefully on the floor.

Pheel had been despatched and reprimanded very severely as Emma's guardians took over now. This woman had been rejecting any form of spiritual help while she was enjoying herself and in command of her wishes, but now she was so drained they used the opportunity to take over, getting rid of the playful spirit and trying to restore Emma to her former self, but it would be a long journey for as soon as she regained her wits, she would be off again to her low life. She had opened the door to undesirable entities, that had got quite a hold on her and could control her actions to some extent, but the good forces were also persistent and would never give up the fight to oust them. But even with help and guidance the willpower had to come from within her, and she would have to want to change her ways.

As Joel was talking, Nick was aware of the feeling creeping up his legs and found it difficult not to react so he clenched his fists on the wheel in an effort to get it to stop, but the trouble was he liked it and wanted it to carry on, but it was impossible just at the moment.

"You ok mate? You've gone quiet." Joel cast a quick glance at him.

They were on the outskirts of the city and Nick turned into a side street and parked the car.

"God man, she's at it now." He turned to Joel almost in desperation.

"What? Not while you're driving." He was looking him up and down.

Nick rammed both hands into his groin. "What shall I do?"

"If I'd got a bucket of cold water, I'd throw it over you." Joel was at a loss.

"It's ok, it's going." The relief was obvious and Nick took a deep breath and said "It's getting out of hand isn't it?"

"Nearly was then." His friend couldn't resist the quip and they were glad of the levity to bring things back to normal.

Thankfully, Danny had been monitoring them and, seeing that Nick was being targeted, had his own way of diffusing the matter, but that was one of his own techniques and a gentleman does not divulge such skills.

Having recovered, with all his juices still in tact, they carried on to the hospital where they found Zoe had been moved to another ward where she needed less close observation and would stay until all the tests had been carried out.

As she greeted them, they were both relieved to see that she looked as though nothing had happened, for she was alert, had been eating and was now drinking a cup of tea.

"How are you feeling?" Joel kissed her.

"I'm fine." was all she answered but he felt that she would be saying more when she came home.

"Um... if you two would like to be alone I could wait in the corridor." Nick offered.

"Not at all," they both chorused and she beckoned to him to fetch a chair.

Neither wanted to ask her much about the incident and she made it easier by saying "The police have been here today, but I couldn't tell them much."

"Well don't worry about it for now, you just get better." Joel was holding her hand as if he never wanted to let her go which was quite near the truth.

She asked about work but they skirted round it just saying everything was going on as normal but everyone wished her well. Then she repeated about the police visit.

"The strange thing is, he seemed to think there had been someone else in the car."

The two men exchanged a quick glance then Joel said "Why does he think that love?"

"He didn't say, but he gave me some very strange looks and I felt he was on to something and he wouldn't let go."

"Well, we'll have to see what he comes up with." Joel was beginning to get a very uneasy feeling and didn't want to leave her. Their recent conversation was in both their minds and they were getting this feeling of combined protection sweeping over them. There was an unspoken pledge to keep it on full alert.

As they left she reassured them that as soon as the tests were done she would probably be coming home as she felt perfectly all right and they badly needed the beds.

The police officer had good reason to be following his gut instincts for Abe had been niggling at him ever since he attended the scene of the incident. He knew he had got to find some proof that someone else was involved and hoped that they would make a mistake that would lead him to them. His main concern, apart from the fact they may get away with a possible abduction, was that the woman may be investigated concerning her health as she couldn't explain what had happened and it appeared she may have passed out at the wheel. But that didn't make sense because she wasn't slumped forward in her seatbelt but sitting bolt upright and the look still on her face was one of fright.

There had been many unexplained happenings in his career and he had an open mind on spiritual matters which made him easy to guide by such as Abe, but in this case there could be no actual proof unless there was a spate of such happenings and people weren't afraid to speak out. This was the loophole Abe was looking for. The targets must be spiritually aware people who would gladly described strange happenings and then Zoe's case would fit nicely into the plan. The fact she was the first may be a problem as the following ones could be possible copycat events. But the newspapers would be invaluable here for they would build this into a talking point.

Abe quickly drew on reliable sources and gave out instructions. This was a bit underhand but they were up against an evil entity and so they often had to tweak the rules a bit to get the necessary results, so they didn't feel too bad about it, in fact it was part of the way they worked.

Immediately they selected the first victim driving his car along a country lane between two of the towns when his engine spluttered and he came to a halt. He quickly got on his phone to call out the vehicle rescue group and sat to wait. The road was completely dark but he could see the lights of one of the towns just over the fields. He wasn't a nervous man but he started to get the feeling he wasn't alone, almost as if someone was sitting next to him. After a few moments he thought about getting out of the car but decided that wasn't a sensible idea so he had no option but to sit and wait. For some reason he pressed himself up against the door as if he was trying to leave as much distance between himself and the strange feeling but it only seemed to come closer. In desperation he jumped out of the door and got into the back seat trying to face whatever it was and that seemed to work until he realised it was on the seat beside him and it was fiddling with him.

"Christ Almighty," he yelled as he jumped out of the car and stood at the front frantically looking for vehicle lights which would herald assistance approaching.

"Well close, but I'm not that good." Abe's colleague found it amusing but was well aware of the seriousness of the situation and felt sorry for this man who had innocently just been in the right place at the right time for their purpose.

When the man saw car lights in the distance he gave a sigh of relief but it was a police patrol car that had been pointed in his direction although the driver was completely unaware of it.

"Got a problem sir?" the officer approached cautiously as this could easily be a set up.

"Just waiting for the breakdown. Damn thing just died on me." The man's relief was obvious.

"How about giving it one more try? You never know."

"Sure." The driver stopped with his hand on the door handle.

This made the officer a little suspicious.

"Anything the matter?"

"No, No it's ok now you're here. Just a bit unnerving when it happens." He didn't like to admit to the experiences he'd just had and felt he'd rather say he was a bit scared. Seemed more plausible.

When he was satisfied this was a definite breakdown, the officer went to his car and put the blues on to warn any other motorist there was an unlit car parked here. As he was doing this he heard a message on his radio to say a similar thing had happened a few miles away. He rejoined the driver.

"Well it's a night for it."

"Oh?"

"Yeah, seems you're not the only one. Cars are stopping all over the place."

"But why did I have to be in the middle of nowhere?"

The officer shrugged but something rang a bell. The last one was in a similar spot too and he decided to look at all the incidents when he got back to base. But he hadn't made up his own mind, that had been done for him and he wasn't the only one with an interest.

PC Daniels, the one who had dealt with Zoe was due to go off duty at 2am but had been alerted by the casual chatter between his colleagues. His gut feeling was niggling at him and he started talking to the other lads about it. Nobody had taken any statements as there hadn't been any collisions and they all seemed to have merely stopped, made sure the drivers were safe until the recovery firms had arrived and gone on their way. He needed to know if any of them had examined the interiors of the vehicles on the chance there had been another occupant, but none had thought it necessary, although one had checked the boot as he thought he had smelled something a bit off, but it proved to be nothing.

One said the driver had seemed a bit edgy and didn't want to get into the car at first which sounded alarm bells. On further questioning it seemed they were all lone drivers of both sexes and every one had felt nervous but they had all been put down to the fact that they had broken down on lonely roads. Now that had to be a coincidence in itself.

"What, you think aliens had something to do with it?" one teased.

"Didn't see any flying saucers myself." another added

Daniels came in for a bit of stick but something was telling him to keep at it and it would pay off. Things were falling into place so well that one could have been forgiven for thinking that Abe was pulling all the strings. The next step was to make sure the doctors knew about this chain of events before they started surmising Zoe had a physical or mental problem which had caused her to run off the road. There was the problem of her being unconscious for a while which had been necessary for her spiritual safety at the time, but that would be dealt with in due course.

Now it was time for the next step. The press needed to pick up on the possible UFO sightings and of course the odd mention of abduction would creep in, but would be taken to mean something completely different to the meaning which had been applied to Zoe but could work nicely in her favour.

# Chapter 7

Vanke was not a happy being. As Katie wouldn't be available straight away without a bit of work, he toyed with the idea of scouting around for a bit and then coming back, after all she wasn't going anywhere and didn't seem interested in looking for a man. That thought made him ponder. If she really wasn't interested, was he wasting his time when it could be spent elsewhere with better results? But she had responded to his touch, even if she thought it was someone else. He kept coming back to the idea of finding a suitable host, but what if it was one she didn't like? Then he would have to start all over again.

He envied Bollik who he imagined was having a whale of a time for he was never short of action.

"Perhaps I shouldn't have concentrated on the new stuff," he chastised himself, "there's so little of it about yet there's plenty of experienced fodder."

He decided he'd leave Katie for a while and come back when he'd had some satisfaction so he went off in search of one of the smaller clubs, similar to the one Sam had found.

It was exactly the same layout and atmosphere and even in his spirit form, it took him a moment to adjust to the surroundings. He caught sight of quite a handsome man chatting up one of the girls and thought that he would do to start with so slid into his body and looked at the female at close range, as far as he could see because everything seemed to be in a sort of mist.

"I'll travel tandem for now" he thought, "and take over when the action starts."

His host steered his catch to the archway leading to the toilets and soon they were as intimate as it was possible to be, but nobody bothered. Vanke was beginning to have second thoughts. He didn't mind picking one up in a club but he liked his privacy when it came down to the bonking, and to be doing it here wasn't his way at all.

"Bloody hell" he exclaimed on deaf ears for the man was so far gone that nothing would have penetrated his mind. "I've got to get out of here."

But something was stopping him leaving the body. There was a force coming from the door to the toilets that froze him in position and he was aware of other entities streaming past him and going into the main club area.

How long he was held there he didn't know, but as soon as he could he released himself and fled from the place. Unbeknown to him he had been monitored by one of Abe's sentinels who now had some important information to pass on.

"I think I've found something." he reported and immediately was in close communication along with Danny.

"What is it?" Abe asked.

"I'm sure I've found a gateway."

"What?" Came the chorus of disbelief.

"Was watching the club where Vanke was prowling and of course he was only concentrating on a result, but in the gents' toilet there is a small slit connecting other dimensions and they're coming in."

Immediately Abe said they must have all the clubs checked but Danny picked up on the last bit.

"Hang on. Aren't they going out as well?"

The sentinel said he hadn't noticed any going back.

There was a pause then Abe said "Oh no. Not a one way, you know what that means."

"Too right." Danny was ahead of him. "They're infiltrating for a reason."

With that some of the highest scouts were sent out with this information and told to report back when they had the true facts. It didn't take long to realise what they were up against for the smaller clubs were like capillaries, letting in small dribbles of evil entities, while the larger ones in the cities were like veins with larger slits and they were then feeding the smaller ones. This meant that the veins were being fed by arteries and they would have to be traced back.

The friends had come across this operation before and now faced a problem. As the capillaries were only being fed, they were not the main gateways, likewise nor were the veins, and from their experience, neither were the arteries because they had to be supplied from one gate and that was the problem. It was easy to trace the smaller ones but the main channel was so well hidden, it often went undetected until the evil was well established and by then it had often been closed. And they were correct, it was only one way. When the evil had been distributed it was here for good and had to be destroyed, for there was no return path.

They were at the point where they now had to trace beyond the cities to at least one of the arteries but that could be anywhere in the country or even further and time would not be on their side.

Many of the arriving entities would start moving around in the area they had been planted but some quickly moved further afield attracted by strong emotions, some sexual but many by other vices especially jealousy, possession and anger. Unbeknown to her, Pheel had been stalked for a while and when they moved in to oust Phani in the shower, she hadn't realised she was now in their debt. They were way below Tule in status and knew better than to encroach on his territory, so had despatched Phani as a show of loyalty, or to put it bluntly arse licking.

They were well aware that Tule was not pleased at the moment and so they would keep their distance from him but this little staged performance should put them in his good books. The innocence of fools. Tule would have crushed them without a second thought.

At this moment, everyone would have been well advised to leave Tule alone for he was becoming angrier by the minute. He knew he would secure Zoe eventually but there seemed to be more obstacles than he planned. By now Phani should be keeping Joel occupied while the doctors should be considering that Zoe needed specialised treatment and the two should be well apart, but instead this had come to a standstill. The antics of Abe and Co were threatening the whole operation and he knew he must move now or risk having to wait an indefinite time until the next opportunity.

While the incoming surge of lower entities would steer clear of Tule, it didn't mean that the higher ones now arriving wouldn't have a go, in fact some would be only too keen to try and put him down and there was one in particular who had a score to settle, and woe betide anyone or anything that got in the way.

Sam had an uncomfortable feeling. Her physical wounds were healing but there was something she couldn't quite put her finger on and it seemed to be hovering over her like a dark cloud at all times.

"I need to go out and get drunk." she announced.

"Nothing else?" the familiar voice seemed to come from all around her.

"Annie, don't you have a home to go to?" she felt better already.

There was a little laugh. "Course I do, but I has to come and see you."

Sam knew what was coming next and sure enough it did.

"I bet you didn't see the telly last night."

"Yes I did, but I know you saw something I missed again." she was laughing now as she finished arranging the counter.

"Well, there was this monkey and you should have seen the state of his bottom."

"Oh, was it dirty?" Sam didn't want to let Annie think she knew what was coming next.

"No. It was bright red. And…." she leant forward to whisper "guess what it was doing."

"I've no idea Annie, but go on."

"It was fiddling, you know with its winkie."

"No!" Sam could hardly stop laughing.

"Ah but that's not all."

"Why, what else was he doing?"

"Well, it started with just him, and then the whole blessed cage full was at it."

"They were all wanking?"

"What dear? No they were pulling at their…….oh I see. Ha ha."

Sam couldn't stand it and was nearly crying now but as she went to answer Annie was in the distance heading for the coffee shop.

"How does she move that quickly?" she thought then realised a customer was waiting to be served. "Sorry sir."

"That's quite all right young lady." The voice was soft and very cultured.

"Oh it's a long time since I was called that." she laughed "I'm hardly young and some would say I'm far from being a lady."

She started to ring his purchases through the till.

"I'm new round here," he said quietly "perhaps you could advise me as to where one would go for entertainment."

This threw her. Just what kind of entertainment did he have in mind?

"Well, I suppose it depends on your tastes," she began "I mean if you like theatre there's one in town and..." her voice trailed off not quite knowing what to say.

"You've been very kind. I'm sure I will find what I want." As he took his change his hand brushed against hers and the contact had been made.

She watched him leave and felt a strange flutter in her stomach.

"I wouldn't throw him out on a dark night." she mused as she waited for the next customer to come to the till. "He's certainly not the club sort. Got a bit of class he has. Wonder what he's like in bed though." As it was never likely to happen she tried to push it from her mind, but it was teasing her for the rest of the day.

As the local newspapers hit the streets in the late afternoon, the first mention of UFO's became the talking point only to be followed with the national press creeping into the area. Many travellers had similar stories about what had happened during the night and more than one had suffered the same effects as Zoe by appearing to be unconscious. PC Daniels had been on duty since 2pm and was told a lady was at the police station asking to speak to him. He had just returned from a job and made his way through the building where the duty officer pointed to her.

"That's the lady. Says it's important."

Daniels introduced himself to her and asked how he could be of assistance.

"It's more a case of if I can help you." she said very quietly but looked around as if she didn't want to be overheard.

"Let me just see if one of the interview rooms is empty, then we could talk in there if you would prefer."

She seemed relieved at that and after a few moments they were seated out of earshot.

"Now," he began "what is it you want to tell me?"

"My name is Edith Soames."

She stopped as though he should recognise her, but getting no response said "I have helped the police many times. I am a psychic investigator for the want of a better description."

"Oh." This wasn't what Daniels expected and he was taken a little aback but said "Please continue."

"I know there have been some unusual events in the area and now the press are making what they will with them, but I knew you see."

"You knew?"

"Oh yes. I could feel the vibrations. There was something bad to start with but it has changed."

"Right." He wasn't quite sure where this was leading and wondered if this was some charlatan who was wasting his precious time.

"I was wondering if you could take me to the place."

"Which place in particular, there have been many you know."

She sighed. "The one that you dealt with first."

"How do you know which it was?" He was starting to feel a little uneasy about this.

"Would I have bothered to come here if I hadn't?"

An idea came to him. "If you know I had the first one, why don't you know where it is?"

"My dear man, I asked who the officer was. And as for the place, this area is covered in lonely lanes which all look very similar. I need to stand on the spot to pick up the feelings."

PC Daniels was wondering if any of his colleagues had in fact divulged his identity but would check that later. For now he felt compelled to go along with her, for what had he got to loose?

"Well all right but some time has passed you know." he said as he led her outside.

"I am aware of that." was all she would reply.

They soon came to the road where Tule had left Zoe and they parked a few yards from the gateway.

"It's over there." Daniels pointed to see if she went to the exact spot.

She got out and using his torch he followed her to the exact place the car had been. After a moment she clutched his arm and seemed about to faint.

"She was hypnotised," she breathed, he put her in a trance."

"He?"

"Of course, the man she was with, no wait."

They stood for a moment before she continued. "It wasn't a person, but it was male and there is a strong aura of evil having been here but it has left."

There seemed to be nothing more she could pick up so Daniels walked her back to the car where she slumped on the seat.

"You had better take me to some of the others," she whispered.

"Is that wise, I mean this hasn't done you a power of good has it?"

He persuaded her to return to the station for now, as he knew that he would have to get permission from his superiors before taking her properly on board. It was one thing to test her out on one place, but if it was going to get serious, he knew it had to involve higher ranks and they may not be so keen on the idea.

Nick had gone straight to his room when he returned home from dropping Joel off and didn't even bother to check whether Emma was even in the house. He needed to get some action and fast and had to admit that this was becoming a problem that was starting to rule his life. After undressing he paid a quick visit to the bathroom then almost flew back, locked the door and jumped into bed.

"I'm here" he whispered "I need you so much."

His arms and legs travelled all over the sheet soaking up the atmosphere of where Pheel had spread herself, expecting to feel the familiar caresses and nibbles all over his body and especially on his John Thomas. But something was different. He was giving his whole being to her but there seemed to be no animated action, yet he didn't feel alone.

"I'm waiting, where are you?" He called louder this time.

The reply shook him. "I can't get to you. The door is locked."

He jumped. Why should that stop his beloved getting in? It never had before.

"Someone has put a spiritual lock around you to stop me getting near to you. Only you can let me in." The voice was Pheel's and being about to erupt with frustration this was the answer to his problem. Quickly he sprang out of bed, nearly tripping himself up, and unlocked the door to be met by Emma. She pushed her way in and in seconds they were on the bed. The sight of her made him want to heave but the voice wasn't hers and suddenly it hit him. Pheel was using Emma's body to fulfil her desires.

"Oh anybody but her," he breathed, his eyes tightly closed. The sex was over in a few seconds and as he gasped with physical relief he heard laughter, not pleasant but mocking. He opened his eyes but there was no one there. Emma, or at least her body must have left immediately and he lay there in a state of utter confusion. He needed to clean up and started to sit up when the familiar presence was with him, but her pleasure turned to anger.

"Who's been here before me?" Pheel screamed. "Phani! She's done this?"

"Who is Phani?" Nick was feeling weak with all that was going on.

"Oh she's been here before, believe me." She was seething.

"In the shower? I remember there was someone else." He was racking his brains to remember the difference in touch.

"And the rest. The thieving bitch, trying to take what's mine. I knew she was up to one of her dirty tricks."

Nick tried to stop the flow. "Hang on. You'd better explain who this person is."

Quickly she related the contests the pair always had but making sure he knew that Phani had always bent the rules to suit.

"You see, she knew I was on a winner and she just couldn't accept it."

There was silence for a moment then Nick realised what had been going on.

"So she was visiting Joel, while you were working on me, for a challenge, no feelings, nothing else?" He felt drained and disappointed.

"Well yes, but I liked you and I loved shagging you so it wasn't all just to win."

"I think you had better go now, and don't bother to come back."

He wasn't sure if she was still there as the air was very calm but then she said "Did she do anything better than I do?"

"Well if you call taking over Emma merely as a body to use, yes I suppose she did."

"What?" she screamed again now but then her mood changed and she drew closer "tell me what happened."

"No. It was horrible. I want to forget it."

"I have a reason. You see I don't really think she has the ability to do that, which means......"

"Oh my God. It wasn't her."

"No. it wasn't."

"Then who the hell was it?"

Pheel lay beside him. "I'm not sure and I don't know if it's good or bad."

"Now you've got me worried." He was sitting up now. "You'd better explain."

"I don't know much, you see we aren't that high up the chain so to speak and there's been a lot of activity round here lately, but we haven't got the power to know what's going on."

"Oh you're a great help."

She waited for a moment before adding "You see your wife, well…. attracts the…um…bad sort."

"You're trying to blame it on Emma?"

"I'm not, she's brought it on herself but there's stuff going on round her, but don't worry she'll have the good guys as well to protect her. Bit of a battle you see."

"So, let me get this right, the bad ones take over her body and get me to have sex with her for their pleasures. Oh shit!"

"Look, I'm not saying it is like that, but……"

"…….it looks a lot like it." he finished for her.

"Nick."

"What?"

"I do love you, you know, and I don't want to stop having sex with you. It's the best I've known."

He thought carefully before replying. "I doubt that, and I would miss you but it's become more than just a quick session. I think we have become close."

"Let's see what happens. Can we carry on then?" She had brought her presence really close to him and it was having the usual effect and he couldn't resist her. They enjoyed the most passionate sensations until well into the early hours and when he had to get up for work he felt like a piece of chewed string.

How he got through the day was beyond him, and as he was driving home he put the car radio on to make sure he kept alert. As he listened to the news, the reports of the UFO sightings and then possible abductions made him suddenly remember his visit to Zoe. At first he had laughed off the suggestion of anything of the kind and his logical mind knew there had to be an explanation for this must be mass hysteria. But something was telling him there was a connection in some way but he didn't know what. As he was approaching the town the radio died followed by the engine and he had come to a halt.

"What the....?" He said aloud, then reaching for his mobile tried to ring Joel but his phone was also dead. Not being one to panic he sat for a moment trying to plan his next move but something was attracting his attention to the front passenger seat.

"Don't worry, there is a reason for this." There was no audible message but the words in his head were as clear as if they had been spoken aloud.

"What's going on?" He thought almost as if he knew he didn't need to speak.

"Just another one to add to the total, just to make it plausible. All part of the plan."

"What plan?"

There was a long pause then he heard very faintly "To help Zoe." And the presence had gone. Suddenly the light came back on his mobile and the car radio resumed. He reached to start the car but it was on before he could press the button.

"I don't know what that was, but I need to get home." Was all he could think as he travelled the rest of the journey without incident.

The general public had been magnificent some even elaborating on the details in the hopes they may get on the television. Abe and Danny were more than satisfied with the way the operation had gone and the press were milking it for all it was worth. The arrival of Edith Soames had been no accident either and she was the final pawn in the game to give Zoe a clean bill of health. A little push had also been given to make sure she stayed around for a while which had surprised PC Daniels who thought he would be up against more opposition but he was given a set period of time to get results, then she would be asked to leave it.

They had been to another couple of scenes but she seemed worried.

"What is it?" Daniels asked.

She never liked to divulge too much at once in case other factors came to the fore later so she just said "I have the feeling something isn't quite right."

"Such as?"

"Give me a moment please."

She knew that Zoe's scene held a very bad residue from whatever had been there, but the others didn't have this. Time for divine intervention. One of the sentinels was relaying the thought to her.

"There is a connection and it is not good. You were right. Hypnotism was used to get them to do his will."

Although she didn't understand it herself, she felt she was being forced to repeat it to the policeman and it seemed to answer his questions apart from one.

"Who is this man?"

"He is evil, and not of this world."

"You don't mean he is an alien?"

"He is not of this world." She repeated.

Daniels was a bit disappointed. He had hoped she could give a description of the offender and he could circulate it, but this hadn't given him much at all.

"There are more things than just physical bodies, and sometimes they have to complete unfinished business." She said.

"Ah, got it. You're talking ghosts now aren't you?"

"Call them what you like. But this is a bad spirit." Her eyes were shut as she spoke.

"Can't very well arrest him then. Better call an exorcist in."

"It's not a laughing matter and you would do well not to fob it off."

The job done, Abe knew she had given enough to keep the authorities happy and she could be sent packing now for there was no other explanation that would shed any further light on the matter. The UFO enthusiasts would keep that side of things going for some time and that would draw the attention to that area. Had she seen the footage at the hotel she would have had something to work on, but it was decided to keep her safe by not letting her get that involved.

Katie was having a very enjoyable evening watching one of the films she and Stefan had seen many times. The odd twinge of emotion surged through her but she drew comfort in the fact that he was safe and no one could hurt him. If she only knew he was sitting beside her, she may have been overwhelmed and it could have set her back in her recovery period, so her other guardians made sure he didn't get on the same wavelength spiritually and let her enjoy her memories.

Although many people would give anything for such a moment, the effect is not always what they expect and can be more of a torment, for it can produce the feeling of being shown something they can't have again. So in many cases loved ones are very near but it is kinder to hold back a little.

When the film ended she glanced at the clock. Nearly bedtime. She made a hot drink and sat thinking of all that had happened since he went and it didn't amount to much. She had gone back to work, stayed in the same home, and went out now and again with Sam. The thought made her sit up. She had promised to go out with her for a drink in two days' time but something felt different. No longer did she feel under the other woman's influence and she would now make her own decisions and she reminded herself that she would find new friends. But that seemed a bit daunting because how did you know who you could trust and who not? The answer was to tread very carefully and not tell anyone all the facts about her self. Her parents had warned her that a woman on her own was vulnerable and a target. So maybe she wouldn't admit to it until she got to know a person better, then if they were decent they would understand.

It was very tempting to ring Sam and put her off for some reason but Katie was such a caring soul that she felt it wasn't the thing to do when she had promised, so she would keep this arrangement but would think very carefully about making it a regular thing.

She had only been in bed a few moments when she felt as though she was being gently caressed and at first floated with the feeling as Stefan was still very much in her mind, but suddenly it was far from pleasant and she tried to push the feeling away.

"Get away from me" she yelled but didn't know what she was shouting at. As quickly as it had started the presence had gone and she lay there thinking she must have imagined it all and put it down to the grief process still cutting in.

Luckily she was ignorant of the fact that an almighty struggle had been taking place all round her, for Bollik, passing by from some recent conquest had spotted her alone and thought he would help himself to a bit of fresh, but he hadn't reckoned on her guards and apart from being unceremoniously despatched, was warned very strongly never to approach her again or suffer the consequences. As he was only here for full time enjoyment, this kind of hiccup did nothing for his ego or his reputation, so without delay he disappeared hoping word of it wouldn't get out. But the good spirits have a few tricks under their belts and before he had left the area, just about all the lower ranks knew about it, especially Vanke who knew he would get plenty of mileage out of this when Bollik started his bragging.

Sam was hoping her stranger would come into the garden centre again as he had really stirred up her juices and she was feeling well enough to appreciate a bit of enjoyment. She asked some of the other workers if they knew who he was.

"Nah, never seen him before, bit of alright though." One of the girls had wished she'd served him.

"Yes, well he's mine. Ok?"

"Who says?"

"I saw him first so hands off."

"And what makes you so sure he'll come back?"

Sam smirked, her face not hurting so much now from such an expression. "Oh he'll come, back, forwards, sideways, you name it."

"You're disgusting. He won't want you when he knows what you're like."

"Do I stand a chance?" The voice stopped their argument dead.

"Annie, might have known you'd have homed in on a bit of stuff." Sam laughed and the other girl went off giving her the filthiest look she could muster.

"And before you ask Annie, I didn't see any animals at it last night." She cut in before the old lady had chance to open her mouth again.

"Now why should I have said anything about animals?"

"'Cos you always do, you mucky old woman." Sam laughed.

Annie put her head to one side with a knowing look but didn't speak which threw her off guard for a moment. Then she said clearly "It was people!"

Sam found her voice again. "What was, if I dare ask?"

"They were all at it, they were showing you all the different positions, now let me think. What did they call that boring one? Oh I know the mission."

"Think you've got that a bit wrong Annie."

"Ah well, that one didn't do anything for me, but tell you what, wish I could have tried a few of them."

"Bet your husband would as well."

Annie laughed. "What him? He couldn't raise a gallop if his life depended on it."

Sam's mouth was dropping open. She just couldn't imagine this lady getting up to anything challenging, but there again, maybe she could.

"D'you know what he used to say?"

"Um no Annie, I never knew him."

"Well," she beckoned her to lean down so that she didn't have to shout "he used to say he thought that bit on the end was to stop his hand slipping off but then when we had a bad winter he realised it was to stop the whole damn lot disappearing completely into his body."

As Sam pulled herself back up to her full height she almost bumped into the next customer and found herself face to face with Mr Dishy himself. She gulped, partly out of surprise and partly hoping he hadn't overhead Annie's last snippet.

"Oh I'm sorry," she flustered "I was just listening to......" her finger pointed in the direction of the coffee shop where Annie was just disappearing through the door.

"Not at all." He breathed and Sam felt instantly moist.

"I had to come back for some more of these plant ties, I hadn't bought enough."

Sam heard the air come out of the cashier's mouth on the next till as she looked daggers in her direction. As the man paid for the goods he let his hand brush against hers again and she thought she would explode with desire.

"I'll see you again," he said as he left.

"Always here," the flippant reply was forced as all she wanted to do at that moment was fling him on the floor and jump on top of him.

As she turned back, Annie was just going out.

"That was quick, didn't you have a drink?" Sam asked but didn't expect the reply.

"Bet he's got a good brooch and earrings." She said without looking back, and the next moment she had gone.

Casting a smug look over to her fellow worker who ignored her, Sam was subconsciously rubbing the part of her hand the man had touched as it seemed to feel strange. It wasn't itching but there was a sensation that made her touch it to ease it, almost like a small shock that was pulsing though her and it was having a very pleasant effect. This hadn't happened the last time and she wondered why it was doing it now, but one thing was certain, she knew this was the beginning of something, and although she didn't know what, she couldn't wait for the next stage for she needed another fix and soon.

Joel had been told that Zoe could go home. The hospital had done some immediate tests which had proved to be ok and they said she could come back for some more in out patients. It was dinner time when they finally were able to leave and both were so relieved to be in each other's company in private. As soon as they got indoors they were in each other's arms and knew that when they had settled, she would be telling him all she could remember for it had become obvious that something had to be connected to their recent experiences. They were bonded again, their love feeding the protective force field around them.

Nick had been told she was coming home and was thrilled for them both, but couldn't be bothered to tell Emma, almost as if she didn't exist.

But there was one entity who was not so pleased. Tule's attempt to keep them apart had failed and he had to start again and he would use Phani to the limit to keep Joel out of the way, but this time it would be permanent. If the good forces thought they had been clever, well, let them, because next time it wouldn't be them cheering.

He was quite content for the amateurs, Bollik and Vanke to play their games as it acted like a distraction at times, but if he thought the likes of Abe and Danny were fooled by that, he should have known better.

# Chapter 8

The sentinels had been working overtime trying to trace the initial source of evil invaders into the area, and it seemed that the forces were almost working to a pattern. There was a noticeable increase of spiritual raping and sexomnia creeping out from each capillary source and as each new wave emerged, they covered a pre planned route. It was now confirmed that the veins were simply feeding them and not spreading their own little armies. Progress had been made in one area and Abe learned that they were on the brink of tracing one artery, but although this was good news, he was well aware that there could be countless of them but it was essential to try and follow even one back to the main entrance gate.

Danny wondered if anything could be gleaned from studying the actual invaders but they realised the lower ones had simply been dumped and left, and the slightly higher ones were only intent on their task seeking out their next sexual exhilaration. The likes of Tule, Bollik and Vanke had not arrived by this method and always wandered around under their own free will, but the signs were beginning to show that they weren't happy with the saturation of this place and they may move on if things didn't improve.

The one thing on their side was that the influx grabbed anything in sight and shagged it, whereas they were a little more discerning, especially Tule who thought himself way above the likes of the two clowns and while he may have been more experienced in many tactics, he still fell on his face many times. But when once he had set his target, he wasn't going to give up that easily.

The arrival of Saturday morning stirred up some very mixed emotions. Joel and Zoe were wrapped in each other's arms and had decided they wouldn't have an in depth talk until they had made up for lost time and made love until they needed to come up for air.

Nick was feeling a little low in spirits after Pheel's visit, but he still wanted her and knew he had to pull out all the stops to keep her.

When you've tasted the wine, you want another glass, and he needed the whole case of bottles.

Unbeknown to him there was an unseen fight going on in the next bedroom. Emma's guardians were doing their best to bring her back to her former self but their main enemy was her. She liked her new life but somehow she was always feeling tired now, and if she was honest, she never felt all that well. The sex she had been craving and indulging in seemed good at the time, but when the effects of the pills wore off, she started to feel dirty. So she then started the circuit again and again until it was turning her into something ugly and unclean. Now she needed an 'upper' to help her cope with the day.

"If that slag has one more go at me……"she slurred, then realised it was Saturday, she wasn't on duty, but then it hit her that she had walked out.

"Oh shit. That's alright then."

She fell back into bed and lost all sense of everything.

Katie woke with a pleasant safe warm feeling then remembered she was going to the Eagles that evening, but with her new found resolve she decided she wouldn't spoil her day by worrying about it, and soon she would be going out to other places, meeting new friends.

By contrast, Sam was the only one who had to go to work, and if it hadn't been the thought of earning extra money she would have refused. This was the week end, time to be enjoying yourself, not being surrounded with compost and plant feeds. But there was no good dwelling on it and she could leave at five.

"Big deal." She muttered as she got washed and dressed but then thought "I wonder if he will come in today. Now that would be worth going in for."

She made a quick cup of tea and some toast and Annie came into her mind.

"Ah. I wonder if she'll be there. But she doesn't know I'm working. Bet she still comes though, just for the company." Her mind started trying to think of something funny to say back to her. "Wonder where she finds all these rude things." The thought made her smile as she had quite an affection for the old dear and there had been many days when, if it hadn't been for her special little anecdotes, Sam wouldn't have coped.

"I know. I'll whisper something really naughty in her ear and see if she knows what I'm on about." She decided as she put her beaker in the bowl.

"Look out madam, I'm on to you," she said aloud then "if you do show up that is."

It didn't make any difference to the spirits as to what day, it was, what time of day or if it was raining, but it did affect the earthlings they were either guarding or attacking and so had a knock on effect. Abe and Danny worked together at night when the latter was supposed to be asleep, and although they were in constant contact throughout the day hours, they obviously hadn't the freedom of being both totally in spirit. The sentinels had not switched their attention from the hotels, especially the one where Tule had moved in on Zoe, for the cameras were not the only things to pick up on the slight movement.

One of the watchers had alerted Abe that this particular building was being used in more ways than one.

"Any definite place or room?" he was asked.

"The first floor has the most concentrated presence, and some of the guests have been molested during the nights they have been there."

"They didn't complain?" Abe wanted to know.

"Couldn't. They were all sole occupants. No proof. Put it down to their imagination because they had all been under a lot of stress lately and thought they had overdone things and it was affecting their minds."

"Very clever." Abe immediately ordered for other hotels in the area to be thoroughly checked especially business people staying there.

Danny was lying in bed and picked up on this and something struck him.

"Abe, could this be a more upper class bunch than the nightclubs?"

"Oh Christ! I imagined they had just spread to other venues, but you could be right."

"And how much higher will the next lot be?" Danny was looking ahead now.

"And how far will it go. Just who will be the targets? Celebs, government officials, anyone in the news."

They were both silent for a moment as it sunk in. Then Danny stated the obvious. "We've got to get to the main source, because that's where it all stems from."

"Yep. These little pawns playing at it may be just be doing it to keep our attention, but we've got to know what the main objective is."

"And how strong the force is."

Abe said slowly "You know, the sexual bit may seem a bit basic, but how often is it that the basic instinct has caused havoc in the past?"

"You mean sexual attachments, or people caught in compromising positions?"

"I mean exactly that. It can bring people in power down."

Danny got out of bed. "So that could be it."

"But we still can't ignore anything. We must be on our guard at all times and at all levels." Abe left him for now but both knew the battle had only just begun.

If they were worried on a high scale, Phani and Pheel had more pressing things to worry about, like was the challenge still on?

"Oh Joel's mine," Phani bragged little knowing her mistake. "Eating out of my hand."

"Well, Nick is so involved he can't bear for me to be away from him for long. Could go on for ever in fact. Now beat that."

"Scrap it, and I keep my crown then." Phani was feigning lost interest now and pushing the other one to give up the contest.

"Not on your life lady, that crown is mine."

As neither had any real intention of giving way, they argued for a bit longer then went their own ways to continue with their enjoyment.

Phani may have thought she was in charge but Tule was still manipulating her from afar not wanting to lose the hold he had on Zoe, and for that reason he must keep this sprite playing Joel at every opportunity.

While Bollik had been dipping his wick in a few places he still found this area a bit short on good talent and had made up his mind he must concentrate on finding something worth having. Not too posh but not a scrubber. Surely that couldn't be too hard a task. But if he was struggling it was nothing to what Vanke was going through. Every time he tried to secure his catch, he was chased off by either guardian spirits or other would be suitors and he was about ready to give up and move on or become celibate, but he soon put that thought right out of his mind.

Sam and Emma's antics had attracted the interest of some of the lower evil spiritual life now floating about the area, not necessarily looking for anything in particular, more a case of quantity rather than quality. Emma was reaching the point of no return and her guardians were having to strengthen their forces to stop her from being totally drawn into their clutches, and were now realising that there had to be a very powerful force behind this. On a lesser scale, Sam had merely gathered one or two followers who had since drifted off, unable to combat her protectors, but there was always the new wave creeping in that that seemed stronger than the last and once anyone had opened the door it was very difficult to be rid of them.

The latest arrivals were much more sadistic than their predecessors, not merely wanting sex with the bodily forms, but taking it to a more intense degree of satisfaction regardless of the effect it left behind when they moved on to pastures new. It was known that they created a path of sexual devastation in their wake often resulting in irreparable damage.

Two of these were hovering around Sam as she got herself ready for work, both fighting for supremacy which was normal for them, always wanting the same spoils but never willing to share, so neither would back off and now all their dirty tricks would be put into play until they had exhausted this prize.

She caught the bus and as she sat down, another passenger joined her, almost squashing her against the wall. Not one to be pushed about, she turned to give him a mouthful but he seemed to be looking away from her on purpose. That wasn't going to stop her.

"Have you got enough room?" The question was loaded with sarcasm.

Slowly he turned and stared her straight in the eye and something in his gaze held her eyes almost freezing her where she sat. After a moment he released her and she was too dumbfounded to answer so sat in the same uncomfortable position until they were nearing her stop.

"God, I've got to tell him to move." She thought, but at that moment he stood up and made his way to the door. The relief turned to concern as it meant he would be getting off at the same stop, and she held back as long as possible, hoping he would have gone on his way without noticing where she was going. She watched him alight and turn towards to the back of the bus so she made up her mind to walk the other way for a while until she was sure he was well out of the way,

When she had walked a few yards she began to feel a bit stupid. The feeling of terror had passed and she thought she must be imagining things.

"Oh come on, what's wrong with you?" she muttered, and turning back walked quickly to the staff entrance of the garden centre. She didn't know why, but it took a while for her to feel completely normal again and the idea came to her that it could have something to do with the club experience and that's why she was so nervous. As she mingled with the other workers she started to relax a little and her mind turned towards Mr Dishy.

"Oh please come in today," the thought "I could really do with a good stalking to."

They had only been open half an hour when she thought she saw the strange man from the bus and immediately a chill swept over her.

"You'll make that sore." A familiar voice said very quietly.

"What? Oh." She turned and the dishy man was standing right by the counter. "Oh, oh I'm sorry, I didn't see you there." She had that moist feeling again and her heart started pounding.

"As I said, if you keep rubbing your hand, you will make it very sore."

"I - I um, didn't realise I was." She was flustered now. She had prayed he would come and now she was acting like a jabbering idiot. What must he think of her?

"May I see please?" he held out his hand to take hers.

"Well, yes, I suppose so." She was trembling now at the mere thought of him touching her. His skin against hers. She wasn't just moist now, she was almost gushing.

"I don't think it's anything nasty." He looked back at her then stroked her hand until it felt good. "You should be careful." He warned.

"Oh, we get all sorts of things here. I'll be fine." She went to pull her hand away but he wasn't letting go of the grip which seemed to be getting tighter by the minute.

After what seemed like an eternity she realised he wasn't holding it anymore and so gave it a little shake in the air.

"Seems fine now. Are you a doctor?" she didn't know what else to say.

"Shall we say I heal."

With that he turned to go, stopped and said, "I will see you again, soon." But what he didn't say was that he had planted the virus on his last visit and now she would always need him to soothe the effects which wouldn't stop at her hand, but cover much more intimate parts of her body.

So intent had she been on this Adonis, she forgot all about the man on the bus who had witnessed every second of the encounter.

"Fancy him don't you?" the remark held a saucy note.

"Annie, you made me jump." Sam's hand went to her heart.

"You going out with him?" The tone had changed completely.

"No, of course not." Sam wished, but wasn't going to admit it.

"You mustn't."

"Annie, what are you talking about? I thought you liked him."

"Ah, he's alright to look at. But not for a bit of that, you don't know what he's got. He might have one of those venerable diseases. Clambake or whatever it is these days."

Sam was forced to laugh. "Annie, you are funny." But then noticed the old dear wasn't smiling now.

"Bet you jump in with both feet and don't even ask if they're clean do you?"

"What their feet?"

"You know very well what I mean."

Sam had to stop and serve customers, and Annie did her usual disappearing act but was there immediately afterwards. Sam looked at her quizzically

"Bet you've been around, you sly old cat."

"Oh I've had my share and a bit more besides, but I was always careful."

"What about your old man?"

"What about him? What's he got to do with the price of a condom?"

Sam didn't quite know what to say next so she whispered "You had a few besides him then?"

"What? I could tell you a few tales missy."

Sam was now going to put her plan into action.

"Did you have an orgasm every time?"

Annie thought for a minute then said. "No, he normally had a cigarette and I had a half a chocolate bar."

That did it. Sam knew she was licked. You just couldn't get one over on this lady, she always had a better answer, but she couldn't resist one more try.

"Annie."

"Yes dear."

"Did you ever perform fellatio?"

Again Annie thought and Sam couldn't wait for what might come from this one.

"Now let me see, that's Shakespeare isn't it, or is that Othello? No I don't think I ever have, although I did know someone at the Theatre Royal but I don't suppose that counts does it?"

"Annie you're a gem." Sam wanted to hug her but the manager's voice cut into her thoughts.

"You're not talking to yourself again are you? Must be the blow on the head but try and concentrate Sam, it's going to be very busy today."

"Oh, Annie was here."

He looked round and said "She must be in the coffee shop, but don't encourage her too much, there's a good girl."

If there was one thing Sam couldn't stand it was being patronised and this plonker was skating on thin ice. The look she gave him as he left was nothing to what she felt inside. Little was she aware of the forces that were so active around her, some protecting and others planting their seeds of evil.

Joel and Zoe hadn't rushed to get up and it was nearly noon when they decided to have a shower, get some brunch and have a quiet chat about events. The phone rang and Joel mouthed that it was Nick.

"How are you both?"

"We're good thanks mate, had a really good sleep and can't tell you how great it is to have her back."

"So glad to hear that. Give her my love won't you."

Zoe appeared completely nude and whispered "Ask him over for dinner tonight."

"You ask him" Joel smirked enjoying the view, as he passed to phone to her.

There was a feeling now that they would like to include him in their conversation about recent happenings but Nick seemed a bit hesitant when she suggested it.

"Oh come on, we're being perfectly open about it. Best way to fight it I think." She sounded quite elated.

"Well perhaps I don't want to fight it."

This brought her up short and she stood with her mouth open for a moment, so Joel took the phone and said "OK, just come for dinner. No chat if you don't want to."

"How can I discuss it in front of Zoe? What's she going to think of me?"

"She's not going to think anything, but it's your choice."

It was decided that he would come round but wouldn't say anything he didn't feel comfortable with. When he'd put the phone down Joel said "He's having a better time than he did with Emma. No wonder he doesn't want it to end."

"But it's not that simple is it? It doesn't stop there. And what about if she goes off?" There was nothing that could shock Zoe now. Her guardians had fed nearly all the details of her capture back to her as a warning of what could also come in the future and she knew it would be a fight to keep what they held dear to them.

When she had dressed, Joel was keen to hear of all the details surrounding the strange man that had taken Zoe but neither of them seemed to be able to come up with any answers apart from the fact that he had wanted to spiritually rape her. But when they started to discuss Joel's experiences while she was in hospital, something seemed to be warning them to stay together. Instinctively they hugged each other as if that would help but Joel suddenly shouted "That's it!"

"What is?"

"Something or someone was trying to get me on my own as if they wanted me and took the opportunity of you being away."

They sat for a moment, then almost simultaneously turned and looked at each other. Zoe spoke first.

"They succeeded." Her voice was weak.

"No they didn't." Joel looked serious. "Your attack was to get you out of the way, I'm sure of it. This Tully bloke probably didn't want you at all but why would someone clear the way for the female to get a clear run on me?"

"You mean she was in charge and he was doing her dirty work."

Joel nodded. "Seems very much that way, but it hasn't worked because we are back together and our bond is strong."

"But she will try again won't she?" Zoe looked at her husband with such a pained look it melted his heart.

Hugging her close to him he whispered "That's why we must keep our guard up at all times especially when we aren't together."

They stayed like that for a while and then she said "She must be powerful, this one that is after you."

"Don't worry, there's nothing more powerful than love."

Tule had observed this scene from his vantage point and not only found it amusing that they should have their wires well and truly crossed, but they would be keeping their guard up against the wrong source, and although his power was controlling Phani, he could play her at will and let them think they were winning until he was ready to pounce and this time he would not fail because the doting husband would be well out of the picture.

"I'm well and truly pissed off." Vanke was venting his frustration to Bollik who too was wondering if there was anything worthy of him in this area.

"For once I have to say I agree with you. Usually one of us gets the other's left off."

"Do you mind? I wouldn't sniff round anything you've licked."

Bollik was amused. "I think you mean liked."

"I know what I mean. I've seen you."

"Oh, trying to pick up some tips were you?"

Vanke took the bait. "I don't need you to teach me anything."

"Which is why you like the inexperienced is it?" Bollik scoffed. "You are a novice. You certainly didn't pick up many tricks while you were down there," he indicated to the earth "before you put the wrong meaning on that." Then added "So you're trying to make up for lost time."

"There's no need to mock." Vanke was always touchy about his last bodily form.

"A bloody monk!" Bollik always milked this for all it was worth. "Bet you never tell any of your lays. I can just imagine it. Guess what, I've just been shagged by a spirit monk! Ha ha ha."

"Some happen to like it as a matter of fact. They find it pure and sensual."

"What!" again Bollik was convulsed "Those two words just don't go in the same sentence."

There was a strained silence for a moment then Vanke said "I've decided. I need a bit of fresh."

Bollik was about to come out with an unsavoury comment but before he could answer the other one continued "I don't think women like me."

That caused another pause while the truth sank in.

"Now hang on, hold it right there man, are you telling me you're changing buses."

"It may be the answer."

Bollik visibly moved back. "Well don't look at me, go and crank someone else's shank or worse."

Vanke looked quite a sorry sight and so pathetic that his mate didn't know whether to offer his condolences or tell him to clear out of his zone. They had worked together for so long that each would have missed the other, but this seemed to make a difference.

"I never thought I'd witness a spirit coming out. Hey. How long have you known?"

Vanke didn't respond.

"You've not been looking for women have you?"

"Course I have, but I don't seem to get on very well. Bit of a failure, that's why I thought……."

"But this isn't the answer" Bollik cut in "bloody hell man, you don't just jump ship for that reason."

"But I want it."

"Of course you want it. It's no different here to down there, you still have to find the right ones. Haven't you learnt that yet?"

"No."

"Ok. Ok. Tell you what we'll do. Come with me and I'll get you a good one. Now you know I don't normally do this but I'll make an exception but promise me, for goodness sake at least try to…well, dip your bread in the gravy without me having to draw you a diagram."

"I know what to do."

"But you aren't doing it. Now, wait for the revellers to go out on the town tonight and we'll jump them, literally."

"Ok." Was the feeble reply.

As they parted Bollik admonished himself for getting involved. If the talent was about he had no trouble in finding it for himself and thought everyone did the same, but this 'fart in a colander' needed someone to hold his hand.

"Could have been worse." he laughed.

There was great excitement in Abe's camp and he called on Danny to communicate as soon as he could. As he was working from home, he was there immediately.

"We've moved up a step." Abe was elated.

"Tell me."

"The doorway in the city club, the one near the hotel where Zoe was captured was leading off to the west so we traced in that direction and we found another with the route going north, so we explored further west and….."

"You found one going east." Danny was triumphant and couldn't wait for him to finish.

"Exactly. Which means the capillaries in that area are being fed from those veins which are in turn going to lead us to an artery. We can't miss."

"That's really good but don't forget we still don't know how many arteries there could be, I doubt if it's only the one."

"True. But getting back to the hotel where Tule was working from. We now know that it is being used as a temporary base."

Danny was worried now. "What, as well as the seedy clubs?"

"No, No. Nothing like that."

"Eh?"

"There's another cell, similar to ours who are waiting for a certain entity to possibly make an appearance and our paths have crossed."

"You mean nothing to do with our problem?"

"No they've been after he or she or whatever for some time but have to keep their distance so they could be using our goings on as a bit of a cover."

"As long as they don't cock ours up in the process." Danny was a bit concerned.

That had already crossed Abe's mind. "Each of us wants a successful outcome, and you know we go to any lengths because of the extent of the evil we have to destroy, well, they have the same motivation, nothing gets in the way of any individual operation."

After a moment Danny said "Let's hope we can finalise ours first then."

"Could put someone in there," Abe suggested "someone unobtrusive but clever enough not to be detected."

"What, as a guest at the hotel?"

"Better than that, on the staff."

"Hang on a minute," Danny smelled a rat. "Why would we need to be monitoring them? Haven't we got enough on our hands already?"

Abe almost laughed "Because good buddy, that's what they are doing to us."

"But how do you know?"

"Our oldest trick."

"You never said." Danny was a bit put out to have been kept in the dark, then realised his friend's motives. "Ah, less vibes on the wires."

"Exactly."

"So which method was it this time?"

"Well let's say I was getting a bit uptight when the managers were going through the footage."

"Ah the cameras." Danny exclaimed. He had used them himself on many occasions.

"The woman picked up on the movement in the hall. The other stuff with the notice on the door was only Tule up to his tricks. They've been in all the corridors, and have spread out through most of the hotel so they must know something is afoot or they wouldn't be using so many guards."

"I know where this is going." Danny mused. "Tit for Tat. We use them as our decoy."

"That as well, but I want to send out some duff info, see where it goes."

"Not ignoring the fact there could be a connection then?"

"Don't feel as if there is, but any leads are always useful and you never know what we could pick up on the way."

"As long as we are covert. Who did you have in mind as a plant?"

"Oh just a domestic, anyone will do, someone who can move about almost unnoticed. They come and go on quite a quick turnover so no one expects to see the same one twice. That's why they don't recognise them."

"Yes?" Danny knew there was more to this, then it hit him.

"You crafty coot. You're using someone who can change their outward appearance and working there for a while, leaving and coming back as a new employee but keeping the surveillance continuity."

"It's worked before but if this other lot are good they would soon pick up the spiritual side, so again we need someone who can even alter that, and there's not many apart from you and me."

Danny knew now who Abe had in mind.

Leon got his name from his ability to change his appearance just like a chameleon. Not many knew of his true identity as he was never recognised in his own form so to plant him in the guise of various domestic servants of both sexes seemed ideal, added to which he was of a very high level in the realms of surveillance. Even the good spirits had difficulty keeping track of him and he was only used on the most important jobs when evil threatened.

But Abe's plan was not just to have him spying on the other cell, but to have him in the area ready to divert when the gateway was discovered. Although he didn't admit it to Danny at this point, he would arrange for Leon to be noticed following the other lot, as that was where the false information would be planted in order to trace where it went.

Nick had mixed feelings about going for dinner with Joel and Zoe and had reached the point that he didn't really want to discuss his sexual activities with anyone any more. Apart from feeling it was a private matter, he knew he could look rather foolish if he had to admit later that she had dumped him, and the very thought of that was enough to depress him. If his friends wanted to talk about their affairs, that was up to them, and he made up his mind that he wouldn't go and see Danny again when ever it was suggested.

He went upstairs to sort out what to wear and as a matter of habit locked himself in his room. He undressed down to his pants and started looking through his jackets when he felt Pheel behind him.

"That had better be you," he said quietly, "I'm not here for anyone else's pleasure."

"Of course it's me, can't you tell?" and her hands grabbed him by the shoulders and swung him round, then slipped to his waist and dragged his pants to the floor. He felt her lips on his red hot poker and pulled her head holding it in position. After a moment they were up against the wall, then on the bed, followed by rolling on the floor until they had covered almost every inch of the room but when he bent her over the chest of drawers it was too much and he couldn't contain himself any longer and he gave her everything he had been producing.

It took him some time to come back down to earth and at first he thought she had gone, but immediately she was on top of him again and begging for more.

"But it's all gone. You had everything." He said weakly.

It fell on deaf ears, or she was ignoring him because she carried on as though they hadn't seen each other for months, but he was too spent and his tool lay there like a defrosted sausage, fun size. After a while she seemed to just slip away with no word of farewell which didn't please him and he felt as though he had been well and truly used, and now he had nothing to offer she had gone in search of another recipient.

"It's the same as those who want guys for their money. Take it and piss off." He thought, "Only with me it's my sperm."

This left him in no mood for going out, but he wasn't one to let anybody down, so grabbing his pleasure pole he made his way to the bathroom to freshen up. It was only when he was washing it he noticed the bite marks.

"How the hell did that happen?" he screamed. It didn't make sense. Spiritual sex was one thing, but to leave actual marks?

"Sh..shut the vuck up."

The voice made him jump. He'd forgotten all about Emma and the slurred tones couldn't belong to anyone else. She pushed her way into the bathroom, took one look at him and laughed.

"God did I marry that?"

He was angry more than embarrassed. "Get out of here, I'm busy."

"Oh ho, so I see. Been banging it on the wall have you?"

"I said, get out, I have to get ready, I'm going out."

"Not like that I hope. What kind of a party is it?" She had made her way to the toilet and was sitting on it, her knees together but her feet spread apart.

"Do you have to do that while I'm washing?"

"Anyone would think you were the only one who took a piss."

This was enough for anyone, and Nick had had as much as he could stomach. He turned to face her.

"What happened to the lovely girl I married? How could anyone even touch you? I find you despicable, coarse and totally objectionable and the sooner you leave the better."

"You can't throw me out." she mocked.

"We will sit down and come to a sensible arrangement, when you are sober."

"I don't think so." She sat there smirking.

He pulled a towel round himself then leaned over to face her. "I don't like your lifestyle. I can't stand your language and you have degraded yourself beyond redemption."

"Oooo get you, all high and mighty. Well you've got nothing to brag about. You should see the studs that service me, now they know what to do with their ramrods I can tell you, and then some. Yours, pwah, barely enough to hang a doughnut on."

"I'm not listening to this." He stood above her. "First thing Monday morning I'm ringing the solicitor."

"Oh yes, this should be interesting." She farted as if to back up her comment.

"I will file for divorce on the grounds of adultery."

"Ha Ha. You make me laugh. Prove it."

He felt trapped but was determined not to show it. "Oh I can, I assure you. Pity you can't remember what you've been doing when you get drunk or drugged." It was his turn to smirk now.

"Why, what are you saying?"

"Oh nothing, except to say that when you take selfies, you shouldn't leave them on your phone for me to find and copy."

"What? You conniving bastard." She screamed. Her voice certainly wasn't slurred now.

"And what is more," he knew he had her on the run and was enjoying himself "the memory stick is already locked away in a safe."

"I don't believe you. You're lying."

"Oh yes. Why do you think I'm ringing the solicitor?"

"You haven't?"

"Oh but I have. Bet they've enjoyed looking at some of the shots."

He left her open mouthed as he went back to the bedroom, deciding to have a shower when she had vacated the place.

"Not bad for the spur of the moment he thought. That should keep her wondering for a while."

He waited until he knew she was well out of the way, then got himself ready to drive over to Joel's. He was in a happier state and when the thought of discussions came to mind he knew he could use Emma to veer any questions away from himself and keep his details private.

Sam had rushed home from work, grabbed some fish and chips on the way and was sitting eating them in front of the telly. Although the pub wasn't that exciting, she was just relieved that Katie had agreed to go and at least it would be better than staying in alone, and who knows, maybe she would be coaxed further afield at a later date.

Katie-Marie had spent the day cleaning and still going through Stefan's things. Some of the items brought back good memories but after a while she had to put them away as it kept reminding her that she wouldn't see him again. He longed to let her know he was nearby but it wasn't possible to get through to her as her hidden grief was blocking him. When she relaxed and let her love flow out to him he often felt on the point of contact but he still had to progress from his bodily state and his guardians knew that nothing must hinder that at the moment.

She wasn't sure what to wear. It could get quite warm in the Eagles but also quite chilly when she came home. It was within walking distance so she had to go prepared. In the end she settled for one of her favourite dresses with long sleeves and a heavy knit long jacket which should be enough as there was no rain forecast. She knew Sam would be in something scanty even to go for a drink, but that was up to her.

They had arranged to meet outside as neither actually wanted to go in on their own and as they came from opposite directions it wasn't worth either of them calling for the other. Katie had told Sam that she would not be standing about waiting, and if she wasn't there at the arranged time, she would go back home. Sam realised she meant it and was determined not to be late. After the club evening she couldn't wait to get back out and have a few drinks, with the possibility of a bonk thrown in and if she wanted to keep her female escort in tow to start things off, then she would have to play it very carefully. She didn't pick quite as skimpy a dress as before, but this one fitted where it touched and left nothing to the imagination.

"Wish he could see me like this instead of in that maternity smock." which was how she described her uniform "Bet he'd rub more than my hand then." She laughed out loud. "Ha, what if old Annie could see me eh? Bet she'd have something rude to say about it."

The thought of Annie often popped into her mind at the most unusual times, but the strange thing was that it seemed as if she was watching her and knew everything she did.

"Hope she bloody doesn't." she said to herself. "Wouldn't shock her though. Wonder what she's actually got up to when she was young."

The idea kept flitting through her mind as she got ready to go out and for some reason it wouldn't leave her.

Katie had timed it so that she got within sight of the Eagles to know if Sam was already there, or walking down the road towards it. It was one minute to eight and she slowed her pace to gauge it to the second. There was no sign of her friend and it seemed obvious that she would be late but Katie was not going to be lenient on this one, if she wasn't in sight by now, it was too late. Just as she was about to turn and go home, the familiar sight of the woman tearing down the road as fast as she could move in her tight dress and high heels actually filled her with disappointment.

"Trust her," she muttered "thought I might have got away with this." But she smiled as Sam joined her completely out of breath.

"Why does the bloody phone go just as you're coming out?" she gasped "always happens."

They walked into the bar which took up the whole width of the building. Years ago it had been split into two with a lounge on one side and the bar on the other but it had been revamped some time back to accommodate more customers. The bar itself was straight ahead of them, the door to the toilets to the left of it and the door leading to the function room to the right.

"Seems a bit busier than I thought," Sam looked round, "must have something on."

"As if you didn't know," Katie thought but realised there was no 'A' board outside advertising anything special, so maybe there was a private function going on.

They made their way to the bar and had to wait to be served as the crowd seemed to be increasing by the minute. Somehow they got split and immediately a man bumped into Katie knocking her against someone sitting on one of the barstools.

"Oh I'm so sorry," she said "I was pushed."

There had been no apology from the one who had put her in this position but there was something about the man she was now facing. He sat with his right hand resting on the bar holding his drink and his left one casually on his knee and she had almost ended up between his legs.

"It's quite alright. Got a bit busy suddenly." His grey blue eyes held hers with a warmth she hadn't seen for a long time. Even his voice was very gentle and soothing and she felt very safe in his company.

"Would you like a drink?" he asked..

"Oh um no thank you, that's very kind of you but I'm with my friend you see and…" she looked over her shoulder but Sam was nowhere to be seen.

"I think you'll find she has found company of her own." He nodded across the bar where the back mirrors were reflecting her flanked by several men very intent on paying her all their attention, some physically.

"I might have known." She turned in disgust to make her way out of the place but it was now so busy that she couldn't move anywhere.

"Normally happens does it?" he asked.

"All the time," she was almost having to shout to be heard, "but this is the last, I'm not doing it again."

"You might as well have a drink now you are here. What's it to be?" He reached for his money.

"No really I……" she caught sight of his look which meant he wasn't taking 'No' for an answer.

"Well just a bitter lemon would be fine, thank you." She would have liked a white wine but not knowing who this stranger was decided to keep her mind alert. "It's never this busy, what's going on?" she managed to say over the noise.

"Stag night in the other room, but they've drifted in here for a while. Be quieter when the stripper arrives."

"What in here?" she was horrified and wanted to leave now.

"No," he laughed "hope not. She'll be out there." He indicated to the function room.

As if on cue, some of the men started filtering back out of the door and Katie looked for Sam.

"Where on earth has she got to?" she started to say but thought that maybe she had gone to the loo and would be back in a minute.

"I think she has found her own entertainment." The man said then added "It's quieter now, would you like to sit over there." He nodded in the direction of the fitted lounge seating against the wall.

"Yes please, that would be better." She answered but thought "What the hell am I doing?" She could never have explained it but there was something about this person that made her feel safe and protected and when they had settled she didn't really care what Sam was doing, this was very pleasant and she might as well enjoy it.

"I'm Gary," he held out his hand to shake hers.

"Oh, Marie." She didn't feel quite ready to divulge her first name just yet as a little caution was still hovering in her mind. "I don't think I've seen you here before."

"It's my local but I don't come on a regular basis. Just when I feel like a drink and it's a nice pint here."

"We, that's my friend and I often come when there's a quiz night or something like that."

"I try and avoid those, I'm not one for a lot of noise and they can get quite rowdy."

They sat with their drinks for a moment then he said "Please don't think I'm being nosey but I see you are married."

She looked at her ring and wondered just how much she should tell him, after all they had only just met and she didn't know anything about him at all.

But he picked up her reluctance and quickly added "I'm sorry, I shouldn't have mentioned it, only…" he paused "….I wouldn't want you to think I was chatting you up or anything like that."

"Oh, right."

"You see I wouldn't anyway and especially a married lady."

"He's gay," she thought, "no wonder I felt safe. What a waste he's so lovely."

Feeling more relaxed now she said "Actually I am a widow."

"Oh I am sorry. I hope I haven't distressed you."

"No, not at all. I like to talk about him. Makes me feel as though he hasn't left me completely if you know what I mean."

"Indeed."

She was tempted to ask him about his status but didn't feel too comfy with that so just smiled.

As if he knew her thoughts he said "Never been married myself."

"I'm not surprised," she kept the thought to herself but just said "Oh, I see."

"Never found the right lass. There was one, loved her to bits but...." he had a gulp of his drink "..went off with my best friend. Guess I've never trusted anyone after that."

"Oh I'm so sorry," she felt guilty but at the same time was pleased he wasn't gay, "but don't let that put you off. There's lots of decent women around."

"At my age? Don't think so. Left it a bit too late I think."

For the first time she really looked at him. His very short fair hair was greying and his eyes seemed to hold sadness and when he smiled it was only with his mouth. He must be about her age or perhaps a little older and she felt he had just let the world slip past him which stirred up the emotion of protection in her. As she was not looking for a relationship yet, she wasn't seeing him as a prospective partner, but was being drawn to him in a very compelling way and the more she looked, the more she felt her inside churning for he was having a very interesting effect on her.

They had downed a few more drinks and she thought she ought to at least have a quick look for Sam but when she was still nowhere to be seen it was obvious she would be leaving alone.

"May I see you at least part of the way?" Gary asked.

The wary instinct raised its ugly head. "That's very kind of you but I'll be fine thanks." She didn't want to sound abrupt but she didn't really know enough about him to risk that.

"I go that way." He pointed as they stepped outside.

This was awkward. "I do too."

"Well it makes sense for us to walk together then you can go to wherever you live and I'll shoot off. I live on Bloxam Road."

As he seemed very open about his whereabouts and hadn't delved into hers, she felt she would be safe enough if they parted at the end of her road. As they approached the corner she said "I live near here, so I'll say goodnight and thank you for a lovely evening."

"Could we meet again? I've really enjoyed your company." His question was put so softly, she couldn't refuse, because she wanted to see him again and soon.

"I'd like that very much." she smiled

"I'll give you my phone number," he offered never asking for hers. "Shall I put it in for you?"

As it was quite the usual thing to save time she handed hers to him and he tapped his details in then handed it back to her.

"Want to just check?" he waited.

"Oh yes. Just a minute." She rang the number and his phone lit up. "Oh." Only then it occurred to her. By doing that he now had her contact in his mobile.

If he noticed her reaction he didn't show it but just said "Great, now we can arrange something when we are both free."

"Goodnight Gary." She smiled.

"Night Katie." He replied.

It was only when she was half way down the road she realised what he had said.

As soon as the ladies had entered the pub, Sam had eyeballed the mass of talent on view, and as usual running true to form, Katie was the last thing on her mind and any promises were forgotten.

Being a stag night, the lads were all there to enjoy themselves and the close presence of a female that was obviously up for grabs wasn't going to be ignored. The guests had all been drifting in and out of the bar as they had quite a few tricks lined up for the groom other than the usual stripper. One or two had booked themed stripper-grams and not sure which would be arriving first, they had agreed that there would be lookouts always waiting in the bar while others kept the victim busy in the function room. It didn't take Sam long to learn all this and she had attached herself one hunky chap that had undressed her several times with his eyes.

"Well if your dancer doesn't show, I'd be more than happy to oblige." She purred as she downed yet another drink bought for her.

"Might take you up on that anyway." One laughed giving her bottom a good squeeze.

"Oh yeah, and what if I did that to you?" she yelled over the din, and grabbed him straight in the gonads.

Whether the cry was from surprise or pain she didn't care and it certainly caused a laugh among his mates.

"Oh, you think that's funny do you? Who's next?" she spat on each hand and rubbed them together.

Some made a rather hasty exit as this wasn't quite what they had expected and didn't want to be in the firing line, but there were those who certainly weren't going to let an offer like that go by.

"You'd need two hands for mine sweetheart." A beery breath filled her face.

Sam was more than used to the braggers especially when the remarks were booze driven.

"Well sunshine, you put 'em on the bar and I'll decide." She didn't have to shout quite so much now as the group was thinning.

"Hey she's ok," one cut in "let's take her through with us, she can add to the fun." Then to those close to him added "and it'll only cost us a few drinks."

"Needn't have paid for any other entertainment by the looks of it." another added, his tongue almost on the floor.

"She can sit on my boner anytime, like - as soon as possible."

And so the comments went on as she was escorted from the bar.

Before Katie was even home, Sam had already lined up the first car to park in her garage.

"Now he's my kind of a meal." She pointed to one at the far end of the room.

The lads with her laughed. "He's the bloody groom."

"So?" she sniffed, "It's his stag night, why shouldn't he have the best. You can all watch if you like."

Again the audience was divided, some getting really hot now while others were starting to feel a bit uncomfortable.

"My missus would go spare if she thought I'd even looked at that, let alone touched it." One confided to his mate.

"Too right. D'you reckon it's going a bit far, well you know, I mean a laugh's a laugh but I don't like the feel of this."

"Yeah, look but don't touch like."

The others were egging her on now while others were almost standing in line waiting for their turn.

"Quick, get in there before the stripper comes."

"I'll go and waylay her in the bar until this one's finished."

"How long d'you reckon she'll keep going?"

"Who cares, this is good."

The groom was somewhat taken aback now. Hew knew the lads would have planned something, but this was a bit too sordid for his liking. Good fun was one thing, but this, no way. He wondered now if this had all been planned and took his best man on one side.

"Just get her out of here, now. I mean it."

"I'll get some of them." He indicated to where some had formed a group away from the orgy. "They don't look happy, they will perhaps help."

"Better hurry up, they look like leaving any minute."

They both went over and asked for backup from the men. Some seemed happy to assist but there were still some who didn't want to have any part in it.

"Look," one pointed, "you think I'm going into that?"

The sight was not pretty a pretty one. Sam's dress had been ripped off along with her undies and she was going from one man to another, several who were now almost naked themselves. But this was not all her doing for the evil she had attracted recently was working overtime. The male entities were riding the men enjoying banging her to the limits before being ousted by the next in line, while the female ones were in and out of Sam's body lapping up the sex as if they'd been deprived for centuries. There was an almighty tussle going on as some didn't want to leave after one humping and wanted to enjoy several male contenders, but there was such a queue that they were fighting for their time as if it was rationed and nobody was going to deprive them of a second of it.

Of course she was unaware of this other world, as were the men who were being blown out of their minds with the terrific sex going on here compared with what they got at home. Some poor beggars couldn't stand it and rushed out through the fire door to toss themselves off outside.

The door leading from the bar suddenly burst open and one of the stripper grams arrived. There were two women dressed as coppers and a huge cheer went up as they headed straight for Sam who was gasping as the latest taker had just shot his lot. It suddenly dawned on the rest of the company that these were the real thing and a few disappeared quicker than a rabbit down its hole. The poor groom looked devastated and was now surrounded by his closest mates. The manager had been alerted to the scene and tried to calm it down but had various missiles thrown at him so after calling the police, followed them into the room. Fortunately they knew this wasn't the usual kind of happening at this pub which had a good reputation, and had never had this kind of trouble before, even at stag or hen nights.

The next thing that happened stunned everyone. While others froze in horror, the two officers were forced backwards from Sam as she held her arms out with her palms facing them as if pushing them away. The male entities now had a free run and started pulling at the women's equipment and clothing until they too were naked, everything belonging to them soon lying on the floor around them. The female spirits now attacked the manager in such a vicious manner he was knocked almost unconscious. This gave them new fodder and they took every advantage of it, the females draining the manager dry while the males had two bodies to poke.

The guests were so stunned that no one moved for some time which again was no accident. This evil enjoyed an audience, and the more shocked these men looked, the more they indulged in some of the most hideous activities possible while keeping the crowd entertained

When they felt they could move, many were physically sick and felt they couldn't go home until they had recovered not knowing what they were going to tell anyone, but that would soon be taken care of, for the entities would wipe it from their minds leaving them to think they were all under the influence of drink, hence attracting no further attention to the place.

The bar staff had tried to enter the room but the door seemed to be locked. Just when they were going to approach from the fire exit, the door opened and some men just walked out looking a bit stunned. When they finally got in, the manager and police officers were fully clothed again but sitting on the floor in a daze. There seemed to be a strange mist hovering about the room and the question arose as to what could have been smoked in there to cause this. It was very nauseating and immediately the staff opened the fire door to let it escape but it seemed to hover over the centre of the room. The police and the manager looked at each other for explanations but neither could explain what had happened, so the incident would have to be recorded as sorted because what else could they put? All was quiet. There seemed to be no signs of a fight and the room was in tact. The manager tried to ask the few men that were left what had happened, but they said they couldn't remember either, so at the risk of looking silly or incompetent it was decided to say as little as possible. No other entertainers had turned up and the sad evening came to an end.

Sam was nowhere to be seen. At the moment when every bodily person seemed to be frozen, her guardians had taken over and removed her outside along with the remains of her clothes, and had steered her home with the help of a kind gentleman who had offered her a lift. She hadn't thought whether it was safe or not, because she wasn't in control of her own actions. They were being directed from a much higher force and when she was safely deposited in her own home, they left her to the care of her normal guards. As she lay on the bed wondering what she had been party to, Annie came straight into her mind.

"What would you have made of tonight my old dear?" she whispered. "Not that I've much idea, but my fanny feels as though an army as marched through it. Hope I enjoyed it, that's all."

With that she was put into a deep sleep while her mind and soul were cleansed by the protective force around her.

Nick drove home in quite a depressed mood. It hadn't been a comfortable evening although the dinner was excellent and as usual he had been made to feel very much at home, but something was different. Joel and Zoe had always been close, but he could sense the intense bond between them, almost as if it were shutting out everything else. When the subject of the spiritual visitations came up, he felt they were prying and he didn't intend to divulge any of his activities now. Again he wished he had never said anything in the first place for if he had just let things take their course it would have been private like it should be, after all he was never totally comfortable discussing any sexual activities he had experienced as that was not gentlemanly. It hadn't seemed so bad when he was just confiding in Joel but it didn't feel right to discuss anything with a woman present and somehow he had to get this pair off his back. If they had problems, that was their affair and nothing to do with him. When they had enquired about Emma, he passed it off as soon as he could and said she had her own friends now, which they knew very well. Joel didn't bring the business side of it into the conversation as previously agreed with Zoe.

As he turned into his driveway, Nick noticed the whole house was in darkness and guessed his wife was out on one of her overnight orgies. Quickly he checked the place and there was no sign of her, much to his relief. At least he could relax knowing she wouldn't surface for some time. At the thought of what could be awaiting him in his bed, his dong started to rise in anticipation and by the time he went upstairs it was almost doing a little dance of its own trying to break free as if it needed air. He was in such a hurry now he could hardly get his bedroom unlocked and when the door finally gave way he ripped his trousers and pants off and let the boy go free. He took off the rest of his clothes and flung himself on the bed giving the biggest belch as the meal said 'thank you.'

"Oh, pardon me." he said aloud.

A resounding fart followed and again he excused himself, waving the air around with the duvet as if to spread the smell evenly. He lay there waiting but the air was still.

"Phee, Filly, Pheel or whatever your name is, where are you? I need you. I'm exploding."

Again nothing. His body was getting to the point of no return and he grasped his joystick and released all the pent up fluid, yelling for his companion but when she didn't appear he lay back on the bed and burst into uncontrollable sobbing.

After a while he staggered to the bathroom to clean up and just as he was drying his tackle he felt the arms enveloping him from behind.

"Where the hell were you?" He yelled.

"No, where were you." The question was breathed into his ear.

"Were you here all the time?" He spun round now pulling her close to him.

"All evening darling, but you weren't. Now you have to realise that I am not just here to service you when you snap your fingers."

"But I had to go to friends, it was arranged." He was still put out.

"And you think I only hover around to your command?"

He threw the towel down "Oh I see, you do the rounds do you?"

"What are you saying? Are you calling me a whore?"

"Well….. not exactly, but I thought we had something special and in my book you don't go spreading yourself around while you are….well, involved so to speak."

She pressed herself to him and whispered "I don't."

"Oh. Well, I just thought….."

She didn't let him finish the sentence.

After another lengthy frantic session he found himself on the bathroom floor absolutely drained in more ways than one, and he was alone again. Slowly he pulled himself up and went to the washbasin.

"Oh God." What he saw in the mirror was a shock as it didn't look like him at all. The eyes appeared to have sunk into his face which was a pale yellowy creamy colour, and his mouth seemed to be hanging open and he was dribbling.

"Not a pretty sight is it?"

The deep voice made him jump.

"Who's that?"

He felt a strong arm on his shoulder and he was guided back to his room and gently but firmly pushed down onto his bed.

"Now Nick, I think we need a serious talk."

There was a strong and very powerful presence at his side and he knew it was male. Feeling embarrassed to be nude he grabbed at his nightwear.

"Put it on if it makes you feel more at ease," the voice continued, "but it makes no difference to me, as I am only concerned with the real you."

Nick still preferred to be physically dressed so he pulled on the shorts and vest.

"Who are you?" he whispered.

"Someone you've been ignoring dear man."

The voice was very cultured and Nick felt very much at ease.

"Are you here to protect me?" He asked.

"Have been all along."

"What? You mean you've even been here when….." his voice trailed off with embarrassment.

"Oh don't worry about that." He almost laughed. "We are not voyeurs you know."

"I don't think I fully understand."

"You of all people should. You've had your eyes closed man. Time to open them."

Nick pushed his pillows against the headboard and settled back.

"Go on, please." He felt his visitor was at the foot of the bed facing him and felt very comfortable with this.

"Let's start with your young lady friend, Phelia or Pheel as she likes to be known. You have been interacting with her for some time and now you take it for granted as though it's just the run of the mill. You don't even question it and get frustrated when she doesn't show up. Correct me if I'm wrong."

"Carry on."

"Yet, when I make myself known, you wonder what is happening." He didn't wait for an answer but continued "I am one of your guardians, it's my job to keep you from harm."

"You mean she is a malevolent spirit?" Nick was horrified.

"Not at all. She is playful and enjoys sexual interaction with those in body."

"So not just me?"

"Who am I to say? Maybe she is keeping herself to you for now, maybe she isn't, but that's not the important factor."

"What is then?" Nick wasn't too sure now where this was going.

"You are."

"That's it?"

His guardian let it sink in for a moment then said "Nick, there are always the kind of spirits that thrive on this kind of thing. Sometimes it's because they were not fulfilled whilst in body and are making up for lost time, or it's just because they can never get enough in what ever form they are in at the given time."

"But I thought the pleasure was just a physical thing, you know, when you come and that."

"Oh my dear fellow. That is the most common mistake mortals make, but I can assure you that there are many errant souls who will be forever wandering looking for their next interaction."

They were quiet for a moment then Nick remembered something.

"There was something about a contest. Oh that's right, her friend, also in spirit, um well it seems I'm part of a game to see who wins, only the other one was trying to have a go as well. It's all a bit strange."

"Yes, we know them, Phani and Pheel, they're harmless enough, nothing bad about them as such but the trouble starts when people like your good self are receptive."

"Oh," Nick was beginning to see daylight "you mean anyone who isn't on the same wavelength so to speak wouldn't be aware of them and their tricks would fall flat?"

"Now you're getting it."

"And because I did know, I mean know Pheel was there, and Phani of course, I am subject to their advances."

"Just about sums it up. But now we get to the crunch. If we step in too soon, while the newness of it and the excitement which takes over is so strong, you would have been fighting us. Only natural reaction. So we have to let things flow for a while then when the cracks start appearing we jump in then."

"Do you get anyone still tell you to clear off?"

"Oh by Jove yes. Expect nothing else. I'd probably do the same."

Nick thought for a moment. "So you feel this is the right time?"

"Couldn't have left it much longer old chap, you were going down the drain. Wha wha wha" He laughed with such a posh tone Nick couldn't help but find it amusing.

"I suppose I do look a mess." He sat up and looked in the dressing table mirror but was surprised to see he was almost back to his normal appearance.

"Sorry about the trick. Had to show you how you looked from our point of view you see."

"Clever trick indeed." But Nick had another question. "But she'll still come won't she?"

"Do you want her to?"

"Hmm. Of course I do, I've enjoyed it but I could get over it couldn't I?"

"With help, if you want to."

"How does that work then?" Nick was intrigued.

The guardian seemed to have moved nearer.

"First, you put up a spiritual block. Just concentrate on it very strongly similar to your protective force field, that's the start."

"You said with help."

"Yes we can help from this side, but only if it starts with you, because if you are willing her to make contact, you are opening the door."

"So I must close the door."

"You are a fast learner Nick but that's no surprise."

"Oh, why?"

"Don't you know?"

The was a change in the air and Nick's mind was being shown many things from his past lives and even more from his spiritual existence.

As it settled, he gasped. "Why didn't I know this before?"

"You are not made aware of all previous knowledge during your earth visits, that's where you add to your experience."

"But sometimes you almost seem to get a flashback." Nick was understanding now.

"Well you seem to be aware of your current position young man. I will always be there if you call, but I think you can handle this yourself now."

"I don't know your name."

"You don't need to. Names are not important. Just think of me and I will know."

Nick smiled. "You know, when you said that, it was as if I already knew."

"Because you did my friend."

Sitting alone in his bed, Nick felt more content than he had for some time. Even his tent pole seemed to have gone to sleep.

"Just one thing left to make my life complete now" he decided "get rid of excess baggage." And he gave a little wave in the direction of the main bedroom.

# Chapter 9

When once Leon was on a job it could be very difficult to keep up with him, even for the likes of Abe or Danny, for he was a master in his own right. He had already secured jobs at three of the hotels in the area. At the one where Tule had been active he was now an older man working on general maintenance giving him freedom of the whole building, at Joel's he had stepped in as a young female receptionist under Megan Clarke, while at the same time he was already taking on domestic duties as a young man at one situated just outside of the nearest city. Not only could he change his appearance, but unbeknown to most he could split and take on several guises simultaneously.

It was Sunday and it had been arranged that the vacancies would become available by whatever means and they were all jobs that needed to be filled immediately. Leon always did his homework and the names given at each venue were people who had a clean work record but were not in employment at present, therefore when references were requested they always came back top rate.

He (as the female) reported to Megan Clarke who was immediately impressed by the deportment and appearance of his image and couldn't but help compare this efficient 'young lady' to Emma who she had been told would not be returning.

After the introductions, Megan gave her usual briefing concerning the running of that particular establishment and updated him as to the current guests and their requirements.

"I always like to familiarise myself with any hotel before I start working, so that I can direct guests accurately and can answer any questions they may have." Leon was enjoying this role,

"Admirable," Megan began, "but as you know we are rather short staffed and I don't think there is anyone who could show you around."

"Oh that's no problem, I can take care of that myself, if that's alright with you." Leon looked her straight in the eye, unflinching.

"Well, it isn't too busy at the moment, so maybe it would be a good idea."

"I won't be long." And he was gone.

It didn't take long to cover all the floors. He could easily have done it in spirit but that may have raised suspicion so he had to appear to be carrying out a normal familiarisation of the place and let any watchers see him in his current form.

"Thank you," he said on returning, "I now know where each room is."

"Right," Megan said almost feeling that she was not completely in charge, "I have to check some things in the office. Will you be alright on your own?"

There was a slight pause as he looked at her then replied "Perfectly. Thank you."

As the older maintenance man where Zoe had been standing in, they welcomed him with open arms as there seemed to be so many little jobs that needed attention, but that was not by accident. Abe's boys had been very busy making sure he would be needed.

It was a slightly different situation at the hotel furthest away from the others. The trade was very busy being so close to the city and the domestics were changing all the time. If this was a place worth watching, he may have to concentrate his efforts on this one and drop the others. He may also have to leave as one employee and return as another if he was noticed by the other group he was supposed to be monitoring. But he had his footholds so now to start spreading the gossip and see just where it ended up.

Tule may have appeared to have lost interest in the area since his interaction with Zoe, but Abe and Danny weren't fooled as they knew him only too well and expected he would withdraw to a safe distance until his next onslaught. Things rarely fell straight into place for him, and although he could get very angry and frustrated when thwarted, he never gave up even if it took many earth years to achieve his goal. Once he considered a female was his possession he became very controlling and obsessive and would clear any lesser power out of his way, but also use them to his advantage, just as he was doing with Phani.

Keeping at a safe distance from the area, he made sure her desire to take Joel remained uppermost in her thoughts but still guiding her to attack at times when the man was alone. But he had other plans coming to the boil, then everyone would have to accept he was the master.

Zoe was keen to get back to normal as soon as possible and had arranged with the manager of the hotel where she had been filling in for absent staff to go for a few hours on Sunday afternoon, possibly until the late evening shift came on if she felt up to it. Joel was a bit apprehensive about her to returning to the very place where her trauma had started but she said that as long as she was working with familiar faces she would be fine.

"Promise me you will ring if you find it too much." He insisted.

"I will, but it will do me good."

He wasn't leaving it there. "I'd be much happier if you'd let me take you then pick you up."

"You don't have to wrap me in cotton wool." She laughed "And the sooner I get back to normal, the better."

They both knew that going back to her car in the same car park was bound to be a bit of a challenge but she promised she would park nearer to the hotel and even get someone to walk with her if that would make him happy. They both laughed and hugged but underneath there was still the nagging memory of what had happened.

Tule now had Phani lined up for her next session and instructed her by thought to make this a good one. She never queried how she could know when she had a clear run and still believed she was doing it all of her own choice. There was a very strong urge in her that was insisting he could be hers if she played the right moves and then he couldn't resist her advances but would want her above anyone else. Tule also planted the thought that Nick was about to rid himself of his wife, then gave her the idea that it could be repeated in her case.

"Could you let your friend beat you simply on that fact?" he imparted.

"Christ No!" she told herself. Pheel could use that to win the contest so she had to get even, and she must work fast and also successfully to get one step ahead. The crown must remain with her.

She floated over the house just as Joel and Zoe were planning the day round her work schedule.

"Perfect." She purred. "Got him all to myself." Then a thought hit her. "Hope the bastard isn't going out. Oh well I can cope with that."

The important thing now was to keep this to herself as she didn't want Pheel to guess what she was up to, but that was all part of her programming. Knowing she had some time to kill, she thought she would go and keep tabs on Pheel just to make sure she wasn't up to anything she wasn't bragging about. Highly unlikely, but she was becoming very distrusting now and planned to keep her senses tuned. She was not far from Nick's home and gently eased herself nearer trying to see if Pheel was in action but all seemed very still. Nick was sitting in an armchair in the lounge watching television alone. A quick scan of the house showed there was no sign of his wife so Phani decided it was a pity to waste such an opportunity and he would do as a starter to her main meal. Slowly she slid herself on top of him but there seemed to be something soft and cushiony stopping her actually making contact with him, while he carried on looking straight ahead unaware of her presence.

"What the hell is going on here?" Her thought made the air tremble.

Again she tried to get close but there was this invisible shield protecting him.

"She's done this. No wait, she wouldn't have a clue how to." Her whole being was racing. She knew something was in her way but it was far above Pheel's capabilities and this worried her. She decided to see just how strong this barrier was and so lurched herself straight at his genital region only to bounce off at high speed.

"Enjoying yourself?" The deep tones cut into her.

"Who are you?"

"You'd know that, if you are as clever as you think you are."

Phani wasn't sure now what she was up against and was trying to fathom her next approach.

"Oh don't tell me he's on the other bus? Can't you find one of your own and leave the pickings to us girls?"

"A very juvenile attitude my dear." The tone was very mocking.

"Let me see you." She thought she was being clever now.

The laughter was wrapping itself around her being.

"My dear child, if you had the capability to see me, you would have by now. No one 'lets' you see them, you just do. Is that within your meagre understanding?"

Phani was angry now. The fact that someone or something was mocking her and she didn't even know what it was, now brought her temper to the fore but by so doing, the power was making her use energy to such an extent that it wouldn't be long before she would be drained.

"Tell me who you are then."

"Just go away and think about it. Surely you are not that ignorant."

She looked at Nick who was completely unaware of the tussle going on around him.

"You haven't seen the last of me." She stormed as she made her exit.

The guardian gave the impression of a satisfied smile and said to himself while looking at Nick "I think that went jolly well don't you?"

After lunch Zoe and Joel kissed for a long time before he released her to go to work.

"You promise you will let me know how you are." He insisted.

"I promise." She laughed. "Now stop worrying."

"And you'll call me if you aren't happy with anything?"

"Yes. Now let me go. And for goodness sake stop worrying."

"Ok but do keep your guard up like we said."

She gave him a long look as much as to say 'enough' and got her things together and left.

After waving her off he went back into the house and had to admit he wouldn't settle until she was home safe and sound. At first he fidgeted, not being able to settle but then decided to watch a football match to keep his mind on something. It wasn't that he was a great follower of the sport but it was something that he could have on in the background but not bother too much if he missed any of it, whereas a film would need more concentration. He did consider giving Nick a ring, but somehow he hadn't felt they were on the same wavelength since the meal, but was that because they weren't on their own? There was always the possibility that his friend might be a bit more open if he knew Zoe wasn't there, but there was also the chance he might dwell on his own problem and Joel didn't really fancy that as his thoughts were solely on his wife

He put his feet up on the sofa and rested his head on a cushion and soon started to feel a bit sleepy. Gradually he felt Zoe's presence flowing through him and he warmed to the caresses that were creeping over his body. It didn't take long for him to react in the usual way and his desire started to become so urgent that his found himself unzipping his trousers and reaching for his ramrod. The to and fro motion was gushing through every inch of him and he was calling her name at the top of his voice.

It was only when he was gasping for breath afterwards that he realised the visitor was not Zoe but the last one he would have given in to.

"You. Get away from me." He yelled.

"Now that's not very nice is it? You are normally much nicer to me than that."

"I don't want you near me. Now clear off and don't come back. Ever."

He was shouting now. He had been so busy telling Zoe to keep her guard up that he had completely forgotten to do the same for himself. But it wasn't just Phani that he was rejecting and Tule now sent her in for the kill.

"You can't do without me. You've just proved that." She was playing with him again.

"Stop it. Go away."

"Sorry. Doesn't work like that." She breathed in his ear.

He tried to get up still clutching his crown jewels but her force pushed him backwards.

"Once we have been allotted to someone, they are yours, for good." Her tone was harsher now. "So get with it. That's how it is."

"I don't want you. I've never wanted you."

"Oh ho, now we both know that's not right don't we?"

Again he struggled to fight her off.

"I will have you exorcised. You are evil." He spat.

"I don't think so. The last cleric that tried, well shall we say I had fun with him, not that he was that well blessed, but it was a laugh."

"You disgust me."

"Where are you going, I haven't finished with you."

"Oh but you have. Can't you realise, there is no pleasure in not giving it willingly."

She seemed to shrug. "That's what you say, but believe me any man or woman for that matter will have it if it's offered."

"I'm not any man. Now leave me."

Her attention went to his groin. "Oh so you are in control. You didn't want to come all over the place, and after such a short time of me being here?"

"That was physical. Not mental or through affection."

"Oh listen to squeaky clean here. Cheats on his wife then tries to get out of it by going all pious on me."

"You are the most disgusting thing I've ever come across."

"Ha ha you came across me alright, and how."

If she had been in body he would have struck her and taken the consequences, for she had made him feel dirty and unfaithful.

"Not bad." Tule mused. "Keep that thought young man."


"Who's that? Not seen him before." Zoe nodded towards Leon as she spoke to one of the waitresses who was going off duty.

"Him, oh the new maintenance chap, just started today but pretty good by all accounts."

"Can't keep up with the turnaround sometimes." She smiled as the other girl left.

It was good to be back and Zoe was glad she had made the effort. There had been plenty to keep her occupied since she had come on shift and as there was a christening party in one of the rooms it looked as though she wouldn't be bored as there was always someone passing by or wanting information. The event turned her mind to the fact that they should think seriously about starting a family soon but there was the underlying nagging feeling that she wanted this current spiritual situation to be dealt with first. Her motherly instinct told her that nothing must threaten the physical or spiritual wellbeing of her child.

"They said you had a plug loose." The mature voice broke into her thoughts and she turned to see Leon standing smiling at her.

"Well," she laughed "I've never been told that before, but yes, there is one there that needs tightening up I think."

"Better take a look then. Ok if I come round." He nodded to the part of the counter that lifted.

"Oh of course" she said and raised the flap.

She felt safe with this man although they had only just spoken but there was an air of self assurance about him that she liked.

"Oh yes, look at this." He held the offending plug for her to see. I'll put a new one on, this looks as though it's been knocked about a bit."

"Thank you," she smiled then added "do you like it here?"

He looked around and said quietly "Not bad, not bad at all. Always plenty to do in these places and I like to be busy. Not one to sit on my…, um, well let's say I don't like to be idle. If there's nothing reported, I'll go and find something that needs doing."

"Yes, I'm a bit like that."

"I can see that," his eyes travelled over the desk "always neat and tidy." He gathered up his tool bag "Ah well, there's a light needs doing upstairs. Nice to meet you lass."

As he left, she had the strange feeling that he had said more than it appeared but didn't know why although when he was there she felt very safe.

He reached the corridor of level one where the suggestion of images had been noticed by the deputy manager. While he had been talking to Zoe he had made one of the lights start to flicker as if the bulb was about to die, so arrived with his steps. He was about to climb up when one of the doors opened and a gentleman came out. Leon pulled the steps aside and indicated for him to pass first.

"Thank you." The man didn't seem in any hurry to leave and said "Bad news about that disaster wasn't it?"

Leon's senses were alert but with his talent he kept them hidden bringing his current persona to the front for the benefit of any watchers as he never let his guard down.

"Oh it is, mind you, that's not what bothers me most."

"Why, what's that?" the man stopped and leaned against the wall as if he would like to get into a lengthy conversation.

"Well, that bio..bio warfare thing, there's been lots of it on the telly."

"Oh I think you're referring to biological warfare, or germ warfare. Yes that is always a threat to mankind."

Leon moved in a bit "But what are we doing about it? Nothing, that's what."

"It's been around for a long time you know. Nothing new really."

As if he was imparting a secret Leon beckoned him "I hear things."

This made the man take an interest and he too moved closer. "Oh yes, such as?"

"Well, it's not for me to say really, but there was one chap, had a room at one of the hotels not a hundred miles from here and he was behaving very odd."

"And that's it?"

"Shh. No. He had this small bag and he wouldn't leave it wherever he went. Now that might not mean much to you but I know he worked in one of those laboratory places."

"Well, it could have been anything." The man looked a bit uncertain but was still listening.

Leon leaned right up to him now. "Just before he left he kept a glove on one hand. Never took it off and he was worrying it, you know as if it was irritating him. Now you tell me. Wouldn't you have been suspicious?"

He stood back now like an old washerwoman chatting over the garden fence then patted his nose, nodded and said "I'm telling you, I wouldn't have touched him."

He looked up at the ceiling. "Ah well better get this light fixed before someone else reports it." and gave a little wave of his hand as if dismissing his audience and the man left, still giving him a strange look, but the end of the corridor he turned back and asked "Not this hotel then?"

"Nah, that one on the bypass."

"Oh just outside the city." The man seemed satisfied with the confirmation.

As Leon climbed the steps and started to undo the light cover he said aloud "Probably thinks I'm crackers. Ah well, people will see when it's too late, you mark my words."

His inner guard was blocking everything except the old boy going about his business and chatting to anyone that would listen so he didn't allow himself to put a proverbial tick in a box and think "now go and relate that titbit." But he knew the seed had been sown.

Danny was far away from his relaxed form in the lounge and he gave a message in code to Abe that the bait had been taken and they would wait for the next step which would be at the city hotel where Leon would be going about his domestic duties with the same detached look, not appearing to be very observant, yet missing nothing.

"That was quick." He answered.

"Expected nothing less," Danny replied

"Wonder what they're trailing?"

"I've a feeling we'll soon find out."

They spent a few moments adding up how many capillaries and veins had been located and were well on the track on one artery although had to keep their distance until the main source could be proved.

"I had thought of bunging up the capillaries and causing a blockage," Abe stated "and that in turn would give a tailback right to the source but…."

"….we wouldn't be able to trace it from the outside." Danny finished for him.

"No, but would it make them show their hand trying to clear it."

"Don't think so. I guess they've even got their own maintenance team in case of such a thing."

Abe almost sighed. "You're right. But let's see what the other team are up to, I've got a gut feeling that they are on to something to do with this, and it's a case of who gets there first."

Danny laughed "Did you read too many adventure stories when you were in body?"

"Oh, you're wondering where the two hapless villains are that are sent to spy on the enemy."

Together they chorused "Bollik and Vanke" then almost collapsed at the comical picture it conjured up before them.

"Right comedy act if you ask me." Danny smirked but then a serious mood came over him and he knew Abe had the same thoughts. His reply came out very slowly.

"That goes fumbling about and nobody takes any notice of them except to ridicule."

They both looked at each other and agreed "They mustn't leave the area. We have to find some distraction to keep them both occupied."

Sam had surfaced about her usual time for a Sunday and as usual wondered what she had been up to the night before. She was quite happy and had various flashbacks to having a good evening. Suddenly Katie flew into her mind.

"Oh God Almighty I've done it again, she won't forgive me this time."

She grabbed the phone and dialled the number. It was ringing out but no reply. Panic started to set in now and when the answer machine cut in she fumbled over what to say.

"Hello Katie this is Sam. We seem to have got split last night. I did look for you but it was so busy. Hope you are ok will talk later. Byeee."

She put the phone down. Something must be wrong, perhaps she should go round but sense said that if she didn't answer she couldn't be in.

"Well that's nice I must say, going off without telling anyone." She muttered away to herself as she fiddled around making a coffee but deep down she was uneasy. Katie-Marie was always there, she never went out, except when they went together of course, and she must go out to do shopping. Everything was racing round in her head so she sat down to have her drink and decide what to do.

She would have been unlucky if she had gone round for Katie had received a call earlier asking her to go out for Sunday lunch.

"Oh, Gary, that is a surprise, a nice one. I'd love to. Thank you." She thought of the meat she had bought but knew that could be used the next day and to have a meal cooked for her and not having to wash up after seemed like heaven.

"What time would you like to go only I can book to make sure we get a table?"

"Oh, um would about half past twelve be alright." She asked.

"Fine. Can I pick you up about twelve? It isn't far but it gets busy later and we can get a parking space then have a drink first if you like."

It suddenly occurred to her that he had a car. Somehow she imagined it would be within walking distance and all of a sudden it started to feel like a date and her stomach churned with nerves.

"Don't be so silly" she told herself but answered "Lovely, I'll be ready. Oh you don't know where I live, shall I walk to the end of the road where we said good night?"

"Certainly not." he laughed. "Just give me the number."

"Nine."

"Right, see you at twelve then."

As she hung up, she wondered if she was doing the right thing but her senses told her this was to be although she couldn't think why. Stefan watched with mixed feelings.

"She will be safe now," the other guardians said "we had to get her some physical protection with all the stuff that her friend is attracting into the area. She would have been such an easy target."

"I wish I could have gone." He felt a pang of jealousy for in his eyes she was still his wife, not his widow.

"Too soon" he was told, "not your time, that's why you have to be with a group for a while yet, you are still very much adjusting. You wouldn't have the power or knowledge to conduct yourself and the opposition would take you out straight away. No, Leave it to Gary, he knows what he's doing."

There was an uncomfortable pause as they waited for the inevitable question.

"Will he have to make love to her?"

They had to be honest with him. "Possibly, but only if she wants it."

"Oh no." He now wished he wasn't witnessing it.

"Don't worry. Doubt if it will be yet. She will have to get to know him."

"But he will want her, he is in body and he will have those desires."

The leader of the group comforted him "Stefan, she needs a show of protection, she was in a very vulnerable position and was attracting entities that prey on that but they have been warded off." Then with emphasis "For the time being, but it wouldn't have lasted. At least this is controlled."

"I know." His spiritual heart still ached, but for her sake he had to go along with the arrangement and hope that she would be treated with kindness and gentleness, at least she deserved that.

Gary always did this kind of work but in very different forms. Protection didn't always call for a big strong man, sometimes he would appear as a nun comforting those in need of succour, and even as a child supporting another one who was being bullied. It had been known for him to carry out two or more jobs concurrently and that took all his mental power to flit from one to the other. It was very rare that he was needed 24/7 and so could easily be with one person during the day and another at night. He was often called upon to see people over as they passed as he had a special way of making the passage easy for them. Many times spirits had uttered "If only Gary had been here" when they had a particularly difficult one to deal with.

He had just finished one assignment when Katie-Marie was allocated to him so he knew all about her before he established himself in a nearby street and had been waiting for the word to move in. He chose to be the kind of person she would warm to and eventually lean on and he was good at blocking unwanted advances from any sources. His current appearance was that of a middle aged kindly man on his own who liked the right sort of company but was used to being alone. That would do for a start and he would elaborate further as time progressed and play it by ear.

"I wonder if I should ring Sam." Katie thought "I bet she's still asleep though or she'd have rung me. But what if she rings when I'm out?"

The guardians guided her brain now and put the idea into her head.

"No, let her wonder for a change. This is my new beginning and she isn't going to ruin it. I am going out and it's no concern of hers."

As she cleared up her breakfast things she suddenly panicked. "What am I going to wear?" This was certainly one time she wouldn't ask Sam's advice! She looked through her wardrobe and thought "I really must get some other clothes". All her dresses now seemed boring she fancied something light and pretty. She found a pair of royal blue trousers and searched for something to go with them. There was a pale blue blouse almost hidden behind another and as she pulled it out she knew that was the one. It was long enough to wear outside and had a very subtle design on the front. Next she found a soft knitted cardigan which she would need as the weather had turned quite chilly. She sorted out some sandals and put everything ready to change into nearer the time.

He arrived on the dot and came to the door to escort her to the car. She had to look twice. Was this the man that had walked her nearly home? When she opened the door her face must have been a picture.

"Snap." He said.

"Well! I don't believe it." she had to laugh now for he was wearing navy trousers, a pale blue shirt and a smart cardigan similar in colour to hers.

"Shows we are compatible," he smiled "may I escort madam to dinner?"

"Thank you kind sir." she felt very comfortable at his relaxed manner but quite impressed with his appearance.

The journey was also very pleasant. He had a way of telling the simplest tale but making it very entertaining without hogging the whole conversation and they were soon at the eating house chain. She was glad it wasn't a posh restaurant and this seemed ideal, not too busy and a pleasant atmosphere.

He checked in at the desk and was told that the table was free now if they would like to sit there and their drinks would be brought over to them. Everything seemed to be falling into place to make this a very enjoyable meeting and as they sat and talked face to face, she realised for the first time what a very handsome man he was. It wasn't only his looks, but there was a special air about him that made her feel protected and also enable her to be her own person at last.

And so Gary was now in position.

Joel couldn't settle and must have looked at his watch at least once a minute since Zoe had left. It took all his control not to go to the hotel to check for himself but his professionalism was on his side and told him that you just didn't do that and how would he have felt if she had done the same to him.

It was about tea time and he decided he would ring Nick after all. A rather laid back "Hello" made him sit up.

"Nick?" he had to make sure this was his friend as it certainly didn't sound like him.

"Yep. Hi Joel."

"You sound good, everything going ok?" Joel was almost at a loss for words.

"Couldn't be better. Don't know when I've felt this good for a long time. How about you, and how's Zoe? Working today isn't she?"

Joel paused. Something wasn't right. It was only last night that Nick had come over for a meal and he knew how Zoe was but he decided to play along for now.

"Yes, she's good. Trying to get back into a routine." He was dying to ask about Nick's love life but somehow it would have seemed to be the wrong thing to say at that moment. Instead he said "Well you do sound more relaxed now."

"Deep meditation old man, you should try it some time."

"Old man?" Joel thought. "What's he on?" Then the thought hit him. He must be on some tranquilliser or something. But what?

He tried a new tack. "Maybe I should. What is it?" he almost flinched at the direct approach but held his breath as he waited for the reply.

"You let your mind and soul leave your body and you just float." The speech was almost slurred now.

Alarm bells were ringing in Joel's mind. "How about if I pop over and you can explain it to me. Sounds very effective."

"As you wish. There's only me here, on my own, alone, in solitude."

That did it. For a moment Zoe was out of his mind and he knew he had to get over to Nick's, the suspicion that he may have overdosed uppermost in his thoughts. He tried to keep his concentration on his driving as he made his way there and almost ran to the front door. It took a few moments for his friend to appear and as soon as Joel saw him he feared the worse.

Once they were in the lounge he came straight out with it.

"What have you taken mate?"

"Taken? It's been taken from me, I am free at last. A new man."

Joel looked around and listened for a moment.

"Where's Emma?" he asked softly.

"Who? Oh her. Who knows?" and he gave a strange laugh that made Joel even more concerned.

Joel faced him and said almost in his face. "Nick, you haven't done anything stupid have you?"

As soon as he spoke he had his answer. "What have you been drinking?"

Nick smiled again. "Not much."

There was no sign of any glasses, bottles or decanters around so Joel had another thought.

"Have you taken any pills, then had a drink?"

What happened next sent Joel backwards for Nick's face changed completely and his voice was back to normal but held a menacing tone.

"Why are you giving me a third degree? What the hell has it got to do with you? Now why don't you mind your own business and leave me alone?"

Joel composed himself and said very quietly "I thought we were friends, and friends care about one another. We are all going through a very telling time and should be supportive. It's not a case of being nosey."

For a moment they both stood facing each other, neither one giving an inch until Joel had a strange feeling that they were not alone in the room. Quickly he glanced around but there was nothing physical, then suddenly he noticed the slightest disturbance in the air on either side of Nick, and it was obvious his friend was aware of it too.

"Who is it?" Joel whispered.

The words had barely left his mouth when the attack came.

As Pheel went for Nick, Phani was pushing Joel backwards until he fell on the floor with her on top of him.

"Get off me. I told you to leave me alone," he yelled but she was already working on him in her usual way and try as he might to stay in control, he knew very well what the result would be, it always was.

He caught sight of Nick standing with his arms out in front of him, his palms to the fore as if he was commanding Pheel to leave him and the place at once, and it seemed to be working. Frantically Joel tried this with Phani but he couldn't raise his arms and was on the point of popping his champagne cork so his hands had to take immediate action to contain the out surge.

As he lay there afterwards, he felt he had never been so embarrassed in all his life. He turned to look at Nick but he was not in the room having made a hasty exit when he knew that Joel was not in control of his own actions.

"Downstairs toilet's free, there's only us here." The voice called from the kitchen.

Joel tidied himself and made his way back to the lounge where Nick was sitting with two beakers of tea in front of him on the table.

"Thought these wouldn't come amiss." He said without looking up.

"Thanks, yes much appreciated." Joel took his and sat in the chair.

After a few moments Nick said "You're having problems with yours aren't you?"

"Bit obvious isn't it. I mean for God's sake that could happen anywhere, and I can't fight her off."

"Hmm." Nick sipped his tea. "I'm not going to ask if you've tried as I could see you weren't encouraging her, that's what's puzzling."

"In what way? I was just wondering what made you say that."

"I'll come clean. I didn't want to discuss it with anyone any more because I told you I was enjoying it."

"Go on."

"But you see it takes over, and you're not you any more. They seem to get the upper hand but you really don't know what you're up against."

"Tell me what you were doing with your hand, you seemed to be holding something off." Joel remembered.

"Let's say, I've seen the light, or rather I've been shown."

"You're freaking me out now. You gone all religious?"

Nick gave a little laugh. "I wouldn't call it that but I would say that something, no, someone, a good force is looking after me, helping me to overcome this spirit that has attached itself to me."

"So how did that happen? Did you go to see someone?"

"Joel, it's not like that. It was……oh there's no other way to put it, spiritual help. This strong power was on my side and showed me that I should fight this off to avoid the consequences later."

"What consequences?" Joel was concerned now.

"Well, what seems to be having a good time at first, soon becomes possessive and you're not in control of your own actions. I could have ended up going around raping women."

"You're not serious. Bit of an exaggeration isn't it?"

"Not at all. That's why these people that dabble in what they don't know can open up all sorts of things."

"Bloody hell." Joel was sitting almost open mouthed. "But wait. Last night you seemed very distant and wouldn't discuss anything."

"No, I was a bit like that, but it was the start of this cleansing thing."

Neither spoke for a moment then Joel asked "Where does Emma fit in all of this?"

"Oh yes, Emma. Well sorry to say but we are splitting up."

"On a personal note I'm sorry to hear that." He didn't want to bring the work situation into it.

"Seems its all part of my preservation routine, she has gone beyond what anyone can reasonably expect to live with and I have to think of myself now. You'll never know what I had to put up with."

Joel sat thinking that maybe if you are married to someone you have to take everything that goes with it but who was he to judge?

"Seems a shame." Was all he could say.

"Sooner the better. Look, she's not here now is she? You've seen the state of her, well no, scrub that, you haven't, not when she's in one of her spaced out phases, when she is here of course."

"Well, there's no one can decide but you." Joel would normally have told him to think carefully but the man's mind was made up.

"Yes, I'll be glad when it's all sorted."

There was one thing Joel had to ask. "What had you been on, when I came."

"Glass of wine, nothing more. I was just in one of the relaxing states I have been taught to retreat to. Really works, you should try it. Oh and try and get in touch with your guardian angel or whatever you want to call it. Get them on your side, you'll be amazed."

What Nick didn't know was that it wasn't just Phani that was working on Joel, for she was dancing to Tule's tune and making Joel feel more and more guilty of being unfaithful to Zoe, whether or not it was in the physical sense.

The trick had worked. While he was in his own surroundings his guard was up and his wife was the only thing in his mind, but get him away and concerned about his friend and he was as easy as picking a berry off a bush. She was also delighted that Pheel had been removed from the scene for this was securing the crown she was still intent to keep, but it proved to her that she could take Joel when and where she pleased and she was going to have such a lot of fun with this.

"You stupid ignorant little fool." Tule scoffed as she withdrew, her job done for now. "You really believe you are in control don't you?"

Katie couldn't remember when she had enjoyed such a lovely day so much. After their meal, Gary had asked if she would like to go for a little run in the car and suggested the route so that she felt secure with him.

"I love the countryside." She breathed as she took in the view.

"I do." Gary agreed. "They'll be harvesting any time now."

He pulled over into to a lay-by on the top of a crest and switched off the engine.

"What more could you want than that?" he indicated to the patchwork of fields that lay before them.

"Can we get out for a minute?" her hand was already on the door.

"Absolutely, only I'd take your belt off first." He laughed.

The mood was very light and peaceful as they stood breathing in the clean air and feasting their eyes on the scene.

"Look, there." He turned her round slightly but didn't take his arm away from her shoulder. Pointing with his free hand he said "That's a kestrel isn't it?"

"Oh yes, but I don't know many birds of that family."

He pulled her slightly closer but kept his eyes on the bird.

"They hover about thirty to sixty feet above the ground like that one is doing now but watch closely."

She hadn't pulled away and seemed to be leaning towards him.

"What will it do?"

He whispered as if not to scare it, although it would have been out of earshot.

"Any minute now, when it spots something below, there it goes, straight down."

"That was so quick." Katie was enjoying this. "You'd miss it if you didn't know what to expect. Oh thank you for showing me that."

"Well," he laughed softly "I ordered it to come and perform for you."

"You are funny." She still hadn't moved from his arm and trembled slightly although she didn't know why.

"Are you cold?" he looked concerned.

"No, not at all, I was just enjoying it so much."

He smiled, his face very close to hers. "I somehow knew you would like the beautiful things of life and you can't beat nature, although it can be very harsh."

She had put her arm round his waist as if it seemed the most natural thing to do. "Yes, especially for whatever that bird just caught."

He didn't answer but his lips were now almost on hers and she didn't resist when they met. She didn't know how long they were in that position but she felt so safe and happy she didn't want it to end.

"The wind must have got up," he joked, "blew me right against you then."

They got back in the car and drove a bit further until he pulled into a small area on the edge of a local reservoir.

"Oh look at the gardens," she exclaimed "aren't they well maintained?" As she looked around there was a small shop, tearoom and all the usual facilities. "I didn't know this was here."

He was silent for a moment. Then asked "How long since you've been out, for pleasure I mean not just work and shopping?"

"Nothing like this for ages. I go out with Sam but I have to admit that's more to keep her company than for my taste."

"Thought so."

"Oh don't get me wrong, I've been quite happy staying at home, among familiar things."

"I know what you're saying," it was almost as if he already knew "but perhaps it is time to enjoy yourself a little, in your own way, not to please someone else."

She almost felt guilty when she spoke of Sam. "Well I think she needs a friend, she doesn't seem to have many."

"May I say something?" He looked straight at her.

"Of course."

"While you have been busy being such a good friend to her, how much of a friend has she been to you?"

"Oh, well, I um, I never thought of it like that."

They were quiet for a moment as he let the idea sink in then asked "Want to have a look round?"

"Oh yes," she didn't need to be asked twice and was nearly out of the door.

They wandered round the gift shop and she spied a small pair of falcons on the shelf.

"I'd like to buy those, and you keep one and I'll have the other to remind us of this beautiful afternoon and thank you for my lovely dinner." She said softly.

"I would treasure mine." He whispered.

They arrived at her home about tea time and she didn't know whether to invite him in or not, much as she wanted to. Sensing her dilemma he said "I do hope I can see you again soon."

"That would be very nice."

"May I ring you?"

She almost blushed "Of course you can, I would like that."

"Let me see you to the door." He got out before she could object.

He waited for her to get her key in the lock then said with a chuckle "I won't kiss you again, the neighbours might be looking." and turned to leave.

As she stood watching him go back to the car she couldn't help but wish he had kissed her and blow what the neighbours might think.

Something told her it wouldn't be long before he would ring and it was a very happy lady that went into her house feeling as though a new door had opened for her. She had really wanted to ask him in but she knew they had both done the right thing, after all this was the first time they had been out together although she felt she had known him much longer than that.

As she sat reliving the day's events, Sam came into her mind and she jumped.

"What if she's been trying to ring me?" she felt guilty for a moment but then as though someone had shaken her she thought "No, sorry this is the new me. The beginning of standing on my own feet and finding the new friends I wanted." Her mind immediately sprang back to Gary. "But I didn't expect that."

Slowly she reached for the phone and rang Sam. It was quite a while before there was an answer.

"Yes?"

"Hi Sam, how are you?"

"Where the bloody hell have you been? I've been worried sick."

"I doubt that very much, you've probably been asleep for most of it."

There was a pause then Sam said "I've been trying most of the day."

"Oh, my phone didn't ring."

"Well I rang."

"What number?" Katie was almost enjoying this knowing what was coming next.

"Well yours of course. What are you on about?"

"The home number?"

There was a big sigh."Yes"

"Ah well you should have tried my mobile."

"You've been out?" Sam's tone was one of shock. "All this time?"

"Why not?"
"You didn't say."
"Didn't know till today."
Another pause while Sam was trying to work this out.
"Where?"
"Oh, out for lunch then a drive."
"On your tod?"
"No."
"Oh. So….with someone."
"Obviously." Katie was trying not to laugh.
"Anyone I know?"
"Shouldn't think so."
"So, how did this all come about?"
"Met him last night at the pub."
"You picked up a bloke at the pub." Sam could just remember some pretty dishy talent being there and assumed she had got off with one of those.
"How the hell did you manage that, I mean you're not what they think of as eye candy are you?"
It was a very unkind remark but Katie could only think that neither was Sam, to the right kind of person that is.
"He is very gentlemanly." Katie kept her voice level.
"Don't remember anyone like that. Are you sure?"
"I wouldn't say so if I wasn't sure."
"Well, what's his name? I might know him."
"Oh wouldn't you just like to." Thought Katie but answered "Doubt it, not your type."
"So you're not going to tell your best friend."
"Not for now, I'll see how it goes."
Sam still tried to dig out information. "Where did he take you?"
"Oh we went for lunch then a drive around."
"That it?"
"Well what more would you expect on the first um.." she didn't want to say date "….meeting."
"You mean he didn't try it on?"
"Try what on?" Katie was getting into the swing of playing this game and she was enjoying it.
"You know. Didn't he ask you to stroke his beef stick?"

"We don't all jump at the first chance Sam. I told you he was a gentleman."

"Gay then."

"No. Everyone has to fit in a little box for you, or you can't get your head round it."

Sam tutted. "You're very naive at times. They all want the same thing, if they're straight that is."

"Well I can assure you he is."

"Oh, so he did try something. Because you certainly wouldn't have made the first move."

"We'll have to wait and see. All I'm saying is that he was very nice and I like him."

"So when are you going out again?" Sam just wasn't giving up.

"I really don't know if we are. And that's all I'm going to tell you. Like I said, wait and see."

They chatted a bit about the night before but as Sam couldn't remember much more than the fact she must have had a good time with a few men, it soon fizzled out and the call ended.

Danny was still alone at his home but now concentrating on his bodily form. He had eaten a meal and his thoughts turned to the physical happenings.

"Better give bro a ring," he decided "he must be wondering if I've found anything out after they came here last week." He reached for the phone and lay back to wait for it to be answered.

"Hmm, must have gone out." he thought but wondered why the answer machine hadn't cut in. "Unless of course they're doing the deed, lucky sods."

Any normal human being would have accepted they would ring back in due course, but not this man. Quickly he floated into his spirit state and did a quick scan of the house, not wanted to be a peeping tom, but just to satisfy himself the place was empty. He located Zoe at work, then traced Joel driving back to his home, but something was niggling at him that all was not as it seemed at Nick's house for his brother seemed to be dragging some sort of residue away with him.

Danny sensed the presence of the two female nyphos but there was more than that. Something else had been there and it felt very unhealthy. He called on Abe who soon realised that although not actually in presence, Tule had been working someone from afar which most likely had to be one of the females. Those of his level always left some sort of trace which could be detected by higher powers, but they either seemed ignorant of it or didn't have the skill to cover their tracks.

From their vast experience Abe knew the game had been raised up a notch. Whatever had been at Nick's was now part of the greater picture and somehow Joel had been drawn into it. Danny was about to call in a cleaning squad, those that can erase this kind of attachment but Abe held him back.

"If we do that, we won't find out where it's from or who's controlling it." he said.

"But it's my family." Danny was insistent.

"Only on this earth visit." Abe reminded him. "Hold off just for a while. Let's see where it leads."

Reluctantly his friend agreed "Ok, but we keep a watch."

"Certainly, because I've a feeling things are moving quicker, so we must be on extra alert no matter how small anything may seem."

They both watched as Joel neared his home.

"Look, it's fading, almost as though it's evaporating." Danny didn't know whether to be relieved or not.

"I'm hoping it's one of those that's just rubbed off but doesn't stick. You know the ones?"

"Rather. So that means he's picked it up off Nick."

"That's what it seems. But why would something of that strength be hovering round him? Thought it was just the happy band he attracted, nothing serious."

"Well something's going on." Danny agreed then said "Look he's going in, I'll get back to body and ring him as I planned, you never know what I might learn."

"Keep me informed," Abe said as he left to continue working on another area.

Knowing that another party were working in the same field, the more false leads that could be laid the better, for while their little scouts were chasing up dead ends, it gave the likes of Abe and Danny more chance to dig out the real perpetrators. Abe now had some reliable helpers planting juicy little titbits in the way of Bollik and Vanke.

The former was never one to hold back if something tasty was on offer and had been directed to the hotel near the city where a group of ladies were holding a conference. These were almost made to measure, all very smart business women who liked a bit of class when it came to the bedroom scene, but never minded throwing in a bit of rough for a change. Even at first glance he knew he wouldn't rest until he had tried everything on the menu.

"That should keep him busy for some time." The sentinels observed, then went to see what could be offered to Vanke. "Virgin convention would be suitable" was the first thought but that was too outrageous so they had to come up with something they knew he couldn't refuse.

They veered him towards a hotel some distance away but in the middle of a very busy city, hoping his presence would draw some of the opposition out of the woodwork. This was where it was suspected that one possible artery might be situated so they wanted to sneak in rather than put Bollik there who could be too much in evidence.

A very suitable target was now in place and the signals were going out. It didn't take Vanke long to home in and with the luck he had been having recently, thought it must be his birthday for this innocent looking little thing was his ultimate dream. He would wait for her to be in bed and then take her, many many times.

# Chapter 10

Zoe rang to say she was about to leave for home which put Joel's mind at rest, but he would still feel better when she had left the hotel and knew it must be a bit of an ordeal for her too.

"I'm overreacting," he thought, but when the phone rang again he jumped.

"What is it?" he almost yelled.

"Hey bro, you sound uptight."

The relief was obvious. "Oh Dan, good to hear your voice. Zoe's leaving the hotel and I was just a bit on edge."

"Sounded more like you were about to fall off." Danny joked to keep the mood light.

"Oh, yes, I see what you mean."

Without delaying Danny got right to the point. "Just thought I'd update you on the spiritual visits you and Nick have been having."

"You really are in the know on that subject aren't you? Always thought you went a bit deep but there's more to you than you like to admit."

"Doesn't do to be too open, you never know what may be around. And we have to protect our loved ones." Danny didn't want to go too much into his abilities at any time so carried on "The two that seemed to have attached themselves to both of you are harmless enough in themselves."

"What are you saying?" Joel felt there was a lot more to this than his brother wanted to impart.

"I know you and Zoe both have your guards up."

"How? You'll be saying next you've been tapping in to all our conversations."

"We don't do that, but we do monitor for your safety, and the safety of others. We have to, it's all part of a bigger picture."

"This 'we'. Who is that exactly?"

"Powers that are there to protect you."

Joel was silent for some time and Danny knew this was going to be a lot for him to take in, as it would probably be assumed that his big brother just rang someone for advice but was now learning that his own sibling was much more involved that he ever imagined.

"You ok?" Danny's calm voice cut into his reverie.

"Um, oh yes. Just trying to get my head round this."

"Let's just say, I'm a bit further advanced than you. After all you have a few tales you could tell that nobody would believe."

"I guess you're right on that."

"And Zoe is also on the same wavelength, but you must know that already or you wouldn't be working so well together, which brings me to the guarding process again."

"I'm getting just a bit confused." Joel wished Zoe was here and they could all talk about this.

"Understandable." Then after a moment "Would it be easier if I came round? Don't want to intrude but it would be nice to see Zoe as well."

"You are, aren't you? You're reading my bloody mind."

"Wavelengths bro." He laughed and waited for the reply.

"She should be here soon. That would be better I agree." The relief was obvious in his voice.

"See you soon then." And he was gone.

Joel sat almost drained. He hoped Zoe wouldn't mind but reckoned she would be alright with it as Danny was very supportive and she liked and trusted him. He didn't have long to wait before the familiar sound of her car pulling into the drive sent a wave of relief through his body.

He waited until she had settled and then slipped it into the conversation.

"Oh that's good." she smiled "I feel safe when he's around but I don't know why. Perhaps he's a guardian angel."

"You say that so matter of fact," he laughed "I think he is trying to protect us from something we aren't aware of. I feel he wants to warn us."

"Well we've done half the job for him."

"Oh?" Joel wasn't sure what she meant.

"With us both having experiences and agreeing to keep our guard up. So if that's what he's going to say, we're there already."

He took her in his arms, the relief uppermost in his mind but not wanting to ask how she coped with leaving the hotel to go to her car. That may only set her back and that was the last thing he wanted.

Phani was hovering over the house again but just as she was about to split the couple apart, a tremendous force pulled her back and threw her out of the area. Tule had felt the action along the power control line and was not only angry at the interference but he had no idea of the source for it was unlike anything he had encountered before. But one thing was certain, he intended to find out and then they would be sorry.

Zoe had just finished making some supper when Danny arrived and soon the three were relaxing in the lounge enjoying the light meal. They made general conversation then Zoe brought up the fact that she had enjoyed her first day back at work. Danny put his coffee cup on the table and looked straight at Joel.
"How about you then bro? Want to share your afternoon with us?"
The look on Joel's face couldn't have said more if he had used words so Danny continued. "Let's be open about this. There's a lot going on around you, not of your doing I might add, but we need, or shall I say it would be better for all if we could be blunt."
"Fine by me." Zoe said "Come on Joel."
"It's not that easy." He stumbled over the words.
"Ok." Danny took control. "The female spirit assaulted you again. We won't go into how I know but she attacked you against your will."
Zoe shook her husband gently by the arm "Don't worry, I know you didn't encourage her, and remember, I know what it's like to be ….used, for the want of a better word."
He smiled at her. What had he done to deserve such an understanding loving wife?
"It's true, I went over to Nick's because I thought he'd taken something and I was worried, and that's where it happened."
Zoe looked at Danny "Would that have been planned?"
"We think so."
Joel was looking from one to the other. "Am I being thick?"

Danny explained. "Not in the slightest. You see, as I think Zoe has worked out, when you are together you both put up quite a formidable defence, so anything that is trying to take over has to split you."

"But…" Joel started to say but was interrupted but his brother.

"…..why were you pulled away from this house? Think about it man. The love and protection you have built up is permeating this place and still hovering around, so you had to be removed."

"So they used Nick?"

"Hmm." Danny was not committing himself.

Something jumped into Joel's head. "Oh Zoe, I know this is wavering off the point but I have to tell you, Nick is divorcing Emma, wants to be rid of her."

"I'm not surprised, but it seems a shame." She sighed.

Danny had been watching them both during this. "You don't like it do you?" he directed the question to Joel.

"No I don't. You marry for better or worse. I'm not saying she should have carried on the way she has or that it has been easy, but you don't give up on a marriage, it's a contract."

Zoe snuggled up to him. "You're a good man, but who are we to judge. We haven't had to live through it. But I'd never leave you, no matter what." She added.

"I think that's obvious" Danny joined in now, "or you wouldn't be so understanding, and dealing with what each of you has gone through, now or in the past."

He gave them a moment to settle then came in with the bombshell.

"It's this tremendous love bond that I want you to concentrate on more than anything else, no matter what may happen." He said very quietly.

They both looked at him, sensing something serious was coming.

He leaned forward and looked at Zoe. "What started as a spiritual sex session has become something more sinister."

There was no reply from either so he continued but turned his attention to Joel.

"The female that targeted you is now in the control of a greater power who has another objective. She is being used to separate you two which is why she will take every chance she can, in fact she was here earlier but has been removed, for now."

"So she is just after Joel for herself?" Zoe whispered "but he doesn't want her."

Danny paused before delivering the final blow.

"The force is using her to get him out of the way, because he is determined to possess you."

There was a stunned silence in the room.

"Then it's me that's he's after, and Joel is just in the way?" Her words were barely audible.

Danny gave her a moment before stating "And you have some idea of his methods."

"I do?"

There was no reply but suddenly the couple realised simultaneously.

"Mr Tully!" they chorused.

You could almost hear Zoe's mind putting all the pieces into place.

"That's why they couldn't trace him. And how he moved so quickly. And when the car stopped he could have…." She didn't want to think beyond that.

Joel threw his arms round her and hugged her but looked at his brother.

"How can we stop this?"

"Well you can both do as I asked earlier, but we are already fighting this beast from our realms and that is where we will hopefully be successful, but for the time being, just make it as difficult for him as you can."

They looked at each other and nodded in agreement as Danny added one ray of hope.

"There's one thing we do have on our side, although he is quite good in his way, he isn't as powerful as he thinks, and that's our advantage."

Although they hadn't expected this, the one good thing to come out of the visit was that this pair had no secrets from each other and Danny's presence had strengthened the protective shield to a greater degree than they ever could, and he knew he must keep it topped up.

Although time meant nothing in the spirit world, they were governed by it because of the earthly habits. Pheel had been trying to seduce Nick throughout the night but each time had been thwarted by the unseen power that appeared to be protecting him. She waited until he was due to wake knowing full well that he would be fully armed with a stiffy and then she would pounce. It had always worked before, so there was no reason why it shouldn't go in her favour now.

Slowly she approached the bed almost waiting to be removed but nothing happened. She was in luck. He was lying on his side but she could squeeze herself into any position and was soon massaging his toggy to the point of bringing him off. His eyes partly opened and he moved onto his back and before he had chance to resist she had climbed aboard and finished the job for him but she hadn't been satisfied yet.

She knew he would soon go down so kept pumping away for her own benefit but it wasn't enough, she needed some reaction from him, so grabbing his hands she pulled them to her until he was rubbing every erotic part of her body. He was waking now so she had to be quick in case he rejected her, but what was he doing? He had his fingers frantically working every inch of her lady bits while he was sucking her breasts as though he was milking a cow.

If she had been in body, she couldn't have announced her orgasm better if she used a loud hailer, for she was yelling and screaming in ecstasy shouting profanities, some of her own making. When she was fulfilled, she collapsed on top of him, not from exhaustion, but to prove he wasn't pushing her away. When he did move it was only because he was desperate for a pee, but she wasn't letting him go that easily and followed him to the bathroom, smothering his body with her spiritual form.

Although Nick had been schooled in how to keep this creature away, it only worked if he really wanted it to, and he didn't want. His guardians were disappointed in him but not surprised for this was a man now intent on getting everything he wanted in whatever form, and he was about to take another step up on his ladder to success but first he had to get to work. Also today he would contact his solicitor to get rid of his excess baggage.

It was 9.30am and Leon reported for work at the hotel near the city. He had been allocated the rooms on the top floor to start with so set about his domestic duties. He had made sure he didn't look too attractive as he needed to go about almost fading into the background but he had the appearance of a tidy young man with plenty of will to work. He wanted to cover as much of this building as soon as possible as he felt there must be one of the arteries here, but they were not staring you in the face, they had to be sought out.

From the information received to date, Danny and Abe knew that the capillaries were only in the smaller venues, while the veins they had tracked were in the smaller cities or on the outskirts. The arteries may only be in the larger cities but Leon never went along with the normal train of thought, because that was often how the opposition planned at. He took each bit of knowledge and often succeeded in going to last place anyone else would have considered, so now he was following his spirit nose and it was twitching.

He had cleaned the first three rooms and was just entering the fourth when his senses pulled him into the bathroom. Cloaking his true spiritual attributes he assumed the level of a young spirit with not much awareness and started to clean the fittings. His true self noticed a disturbance in the shower and picking up his materials he started to polish the shower head, humming to himself as he studied the rest of the wall. There seemed to be nothing obvious but something told him he was in the right area, so finishing his jobs in that room he went into the adjoining one.

The layout of this chain of hotels was the same, the only difference being the size. So in the bedrooms the bathrooms were situated back to back. If you entered one the bathroom would be on your right whereas in the next one it would be on the left and so on. So when Leon had completed the right handed one, and made his way to the one next door, the bath and shower were back to back with the one he had just finished. He made that his first task and stood humming again as if his mind was far away, but his senses were on full alert. There was something different about this one but it felt as though there was a screen in front of something preventing him from seeing it. Not wanting to hang around more than was necessary, he carried on working in the same manner until he left the room, noting the number.

By the time he had finished his first shift, he knew every inch of the building from the basement to the roof. Until he was sure of what might be using the place, he decided not to report back, partly as he had nothing concrete and also he wasn't going to take the slightest risk that his communication could be picked up. He would wait until he could use the secret route.

Monday isn't often welcomed by workers as they have switched off during the weekend and have to get back into the swing of things. Sam felt that one day wasn't enough after her busy Saturday but she knew that Annie was bound to show up sometime and that would be amusing if nothing else. Although the guardians were doing their best to protect her, there seemed to be an increasing stream of no good spirits trailing her now and if they liked anyone she was in contact with, they would veer off and hang on to them, so she wasn't just putting herself at risk, but others. Katie's guard had been strengthened in order to give her as much protection as possible, but there were others who were innocently there for the taking.

As she travelled to work she suddenly remembered the strange passenger she had seen before and looked around hoping he wouldn't be there today. She breathed a sigh of relief as she got to the garden centre and there had been no sight of him.

"Wish Dishy would come in, I'd always have a bit put aside for him." She mused and immediately was in the mood for her next humping session.

They had been open for about an hour when one of the other assistants called over to her.

"Your friend not been in yet Sam." It was a statement, not a question.

"I know and I'm ready for him." She mouthed back giving a rather rude gesture to go with it.

"No, the little old lady. Usually made an appearance by now. Hope she's alright."

"Oh, Annie. You're right. Wonder where she is.

Her mind had been too full of who her next pussy visitor would be to think about her, but now she was beginning to get a bit worried.

"Penny for them." The voice made her jump.

"Annie, we were just talking about you. Where you been?"

The lady beckoned her nearer before she whispered. "I coughed and wet me knickers so I had to go back and change them."

"Ah, Annie, what you like?" she could have hugged her.

"They're not me passion killers."

"Your what?"

"Ah, you just wear those string things now, not enough stuff to carry the spuds home in, well let me tell you we didn't make ourselves that easy in my days. And you know my mother, well when she was a lass they had two sorts you know. One that tied at the sides and some that had buttons. Can you imagine getting that lot off before you started anything? Well she said you always knew the lads that had done it a bit because they could have 'em off in no time but the virgins were fiddling around all night."

"I'm beginning to get the passion killer bit now Annie." Sam laughed but whispered "I don't wear those strings as you call them."

"Well I'm very glad to hear it. They don't keep the cold out."

Sam then came in for the punch line "That's because I don't wear any."

If Annie looked shocked it was nothing to the expression on Sam's face as she looked straight into the eyes of Mr Dishy.

"Oh, my God, I mean…" she stuttered.

"Well, that was very revealing, makes it hard for me to ask you now." His eyes never left hers as the silky tones floated over her.

"Ask me? Ask me what?"

"Oh just if you would like to go out with me."

She was completely at a loss for words and what came out was anyone's guess.

"Sorry," he smiled "was that a yes?"

"Oh, definitely, I mean I'd love to, thank you."

"How about tonight? We could go for a meal if you like."

"Thank you, yes I'd like that."

"Good that's settled. I'll pick you up at eight."

It was only after he had left she thought, but I haven't given him my address.

The place was getting busy and she had little time to think much about it until dinner time.

"Perhaps he's picking you up here." her mate said and laughed.

"Get stuffed." Sam wasn't happy.

"But he must know or he wouldn't have said."

"Oh God, d'you reckon he's been stalking me?" Sam wondered now if she had done the right thing. "Well, I'll get ready and see what happens."

The other woman looked at her a bit quizzically. "Bit hit and miss if you ask me. I'd want something more definite than that."

"Well you haven't been offered it have you?"

"At least you won't have to decide which pants to wear." The tone was mocking.

"I was only winding Annie up."

"Yeah, too right." The woman scoffed as she left to get back to work.

Sam knew she would worry about this until knocking off time, but there wasn't much she could do about it. Annie kept flitting through her mind.

"Bet she'd have gone." She thought.

Nick was at his desk in good time and it appeared he looked a little smarter than usual. While everyone else was getting into the 'Monday mornings' as they called it, he was straight into his work as though he was on a time limit. At five to eleven he got up and announced "If anyone wants me, I'm in a meeting." A few heads turned as he left and as soon as the door closed behind him the speculations started.

"He wasn't surprised, almost as if he expected it."

"And why's he in his Sunday best?"

"Perhaps he's got the boot, they've talked about trimming down."

"No, not him he's too far up the department manager's arse."

The chatter died down when they ran out of possibilities and agreed they'd all have to wait and see because they would find out soon enough.

After about half an hour he returned with one of the big wigs who asked for everyone's attention.

"I'd just like to inform you all that, as from next Monday Nick will be the new manager of this section and I'm sure we all offer him our congratulations."

There was a general muttering and a few faint 'well done's' could be heard but one girl asked "Has Fred left then?"

"He's agreed to early retirement." Was the short reply with no more explanations as he turned to Nick. "You can move yourself to the manager's desk at the end of the week."

"Thank you sir." Was the polite reply.

The whole room was humming as Nick returned to his place.

"Well, that was a surprise." The statement was loaded with sarcasm.

"Came out of the blue did it?"

"Well, I think it's a good choice." One of the lads patted him on the shoulder "Well done."

That seemed to change the mood and one or two offered their congratulations and had to admit that he was obviously going to the top one day.

Although he tried not to show it, Nick felt rather satisfied. This was the start of things going his way, fantastic sex, promotion meaning a higher salary and now he would arrange his divorce and then the world would be at his feet, but one thing hadn't occurred to him. Everything comes with a price tag.

It was becoming obvious that Leon was attracting interest in the right way. More and more so called guests had stopped to pass the time of day with him in his maintenance guise and he was feeding them all sorts of interesting but useless information which was being swapped between that hotel and the one where Joel worked. The other group were obviously looking for something but it made Abe wonder if it was anything to do with the gateways as they weren't concentrating on the hotel near the city. By now they should have realised there was some sort of doorway, just as Leon did, but either they weren't high enough or their objective was more important.

"How could anything be more sinister than that?" Abe asked Danny.

"Don't know, but thank goodness Leon's on the job."

"Wonder what they're after, and more to the point what's taking them so long?"

Danny thought for a moment. "Cast your thoughts back." He reminded his friend of several incidents in their past experience. The high powers hadn't carried out the surveillance themselves but had 'hired' the spiritual equivalent of private eyes to do the ground work, thus not making the operation look important, but when the time was right had ousted the help and attacked the enemy taking them by surprise.

"Do you know, I think you've hit on it." Abe jumped.

"Which is why they are lapping up Leon's bait. A higher source wouldn't have taken it." Danny added.

"So we actually have a free run on the gateways if they're not even aware of the danger."

"At least they shouldn't get in our way, we could send them on wild goose chases when the need arose."

As the two discussed this change of events, everything seemed to take on a different meaning but one question remained. Danny was returning to his body and left the thought with Abe "I'd still like to know just what they are watching."

"I agree. You never know if it has any connection in a weird way to what we are on to. Can never dismiss anything."

And so the two parted for now, knowing it wouldn't be long before something interesting came up for them to add to the puzzle.

When something isn't quite right, one often get's a gut feeling but can't explain it. Tule was content with the way he was playing Phani and the control he had over her and Joel leaving him clear for his next attack on Zoe. He knew this one had to be successful or it could mean a long wait until he got another chance for he felt a bit trapped for some reason. He couldn't pin it down, but there were times when something seemed to be working against him and he thought it must be the bond between the husband and wife, but there were moments when he seemed to be pulled by an unknown force that wasn't emitting from them. The only way he could describe it was that he was being constantly watched. Sometimes he would put it down to frustration, but he was experienced enough to know when another entity was at work.

Although he must be on his guard he made up his mind to obtain Zoe as soon as he could for when she was his, nothing would separate them.

Bollik and Vanke were performing to perfection and although they weren't probably needed as a distraction where the other group were concerned, it was always useful to have such players around.

Although Vanke was delighting himself with this made to measure piece that had been put in his path, he was aware it may be short lived as she wouldn't be at the hotel for long. It didn't even cross his mind as to why such an inexperienced female would immediately respond to his advances without question. But why query a good thing? Whether he had been a monk in an earthly life or not didn't matter at all and he inwardly scoffed at the thought of being gay.

He was just finishing his latest session when he felt himself thrown to one side and had he been in body, would have spread a mess all over the bed such was the timing.

"What the hell was that?" he gasped.

His partner was responding in thought. "Don't know but it wasn't nice." She was already on the alert and had picked up the surge of beings rushing past them at the vinegar stroke.

"They could have let me finish." He exploded.

Her thought wave went via the roundabout route to Abe who was in presence in an instant and was just able to witness the portal closing. He left just as quickly and contacted Danny.

"She's got it. Clever lady, it was in her room."

Danny was excited. "Shower?"

"Yes. That seems to be the general point of entry." Abe said then added "Of course! It's a water power route. They have all been coming in by that method. There has to be water."

"Is Vanke still there?" Danny was wondering what the effect had been.

"It's ok. He was aware of course, but he's been in spirit long enough to know that you never are surprised"

"Are we leaving the operative in situ?"

Abe answered "Might as well, let them think we have missed it, then she can keep watch a bit longer."

"Bet he never had sex like this before."

"You thinking of charging him extra?" Abe lightened the tone but the true facts were what was important now.

Danny then asked the leading question. "Do we know what kind?"

"Think it's likely it's an artery as we suspected which is a boost. The speed is the giveaway factor here. You noticed how the capillaries seemed to just float them in and with the veins the things were quicker, they almost ran, but this was a surge."

"Wouldn't want to be in the way if we find the main gate then."

Abe was quick to correct him. "When, not if. We have to detect it."

Completely oblivious to all this going on, Bollik was bonking his way through as many females as he could. After he had sampled the willing ones, he moved on to the ones that needed a little more persuasion just for the hell of it. He was enjoying eavesdropping on their conversations as more and more started divulging their night time experiences. Soon it became the main topic of conversation and the question was who would be the lucky lady tonight?

"Must be my turn, I haven't had him yet, if there is such a man, I've only got your word for it."

"Wouldn't suit you, you're too particular."

"I've had him several times."

"How did you have it?"

"That's my business, but I'm telling you after me, none of you will come close."

"Oh, listen to her. Thought you didn't want that kind of stuff."

And so the conversations were governed by who had already, who would later, and who may never.

But what Abe needed to know now was which of their bathrooms if any may be a portal. It seemed unlikely they may hit on another artery, so it may only be a vein but would still prove the water theory.

"Keep at it Bollik, you're on overtime." Abe mused.

As if in answer to his thoughts, a message was received by one of the secret methods only known to the well tuned. Since first being suspicious of there being a portal in one of the bathrooms, Leon had returned solely in spirit to investigate, and sure enough he could make out the existence of a small exit point but it seemed to be stuck.

There was a small slit where a few entities were squeezing through but nothing like the others. This was probably only a capillary but something was blocking it although there was nothing obvious.

This confirmed the water theory but alerted Danny and Abe to a new dilemma. Was something else at work? It couldn't be the other group as they were paying no attention to this area, they had other business. But in the best laid schemes, plans can go wrong and they couldn't ignore the fact that the hiccup could be something within the evil itself. It was agreed Leon should stay on in all his capacities for now if only to cover his real motive.

Emma had crawled back home about lunchtime. She looked a fragment of her former self and appeared to have passed the point of no return. Her guardians were doing their best but for every step they seemed to lift her up she always slipped two back. Things were getting worse. She now had no job and would soon have no husband and no home, for Nick had an image to portray and he wasn't about to let her drag him down. He was upwardly mobile and he intended to keep it that way. There was no way he would be offering her any help or the suggestion of rehab as all he wanted was her out of his life. The solicitor had been contacted and soon everything would be in place to dump her, then the house would be his. No more locked rooms for he would christen every inch of the place dipping his wick with Pheel, or any other spirit for that matter who could please him the way she did. Love didn't come into it, it was pure sex, sex, and more sex and he was thriving on it.

The news of his promotion had soon gone round the establishment and Joel spoke to Zoe as soon as he could. There was still the disappointment that this friend of theirs could act in such a way concerning his wife but there was nothing they could do without interfering for he wouldn't take advice and certainly not criticism. They both were beginning to feel they didn't recognise him as the friend they once knew and loved, as he seemed to be moving away. They imagined he would only want friends of his own standing and ditch past loyal ones, but they were wrong there to a certain extent. He wouldn't pass up a good contact if it meant promotion but as far as his personal life was concerned he already had that sorted.

Zoe was still filling in at the same hotel and felt she would be sorry to go back into the offices when her stint was over. Everyone liked her and soon the episode with Tule started to fade to the back of her mind. She liked the new maintenance man and somehow always felt safe when he was around little knowing how much protection he as giving her just by being there.

Joel was equally impressed with the new receptionist who had made it quite clear she had a steady boyfriend. When the couple spoke about these two people, they little guessed it was one and the same person.

It was getting on for knocking off time and Katie had been on a cloud of happiness all day. She hadn't had such a lovely Sunday for a long time and she was hoping Gary would ring her so that she could see him again. As she tidied her desk, one of the other women stopped and said "You're glowing. Anything we should know?"

"Not really. I'm just a bit warm. Must be starting the change."

"If you say so." There was a knowing look as she went her way and Katie laughed inwardly.

"If I'd been younger, she'd have suspected I was pregnant." She smiled.

As she gathered her things together she checked her mobile which had to be on silent while she was at work. There was a message. Quickly she read it and a broad smile crept over her face. He wondered if she was free tonight. Hiding her excitement she tried to send a message back but she was trembling and somehow the words got all jumbled. Eventually she kept it short and told him she was.

It didn't take her long to get the bus home. She could drive but it wasn't pleasant in the town as there was nowhere to park and car thefts had been rife. Stefan had always taken her where she needed to go and somehow she got out of the habit. As she got off at the stop near the Eagles, she couldn't help but think that until two days ago she hadn't even known Gary and now she couldn't think of anything else.

"I wonder what he's got planned for tonight." She thought as she cooked dinner, but she didn't have to wonder for long. No sooner had she washed up than the phone rang.

"Hello." She said excitedly.

"Hi, what you doing tonight? Only there's happy hour on at the pub and I thought we could go." Sam wasn't asking a question more stating a fact and expecting Katie to jump at it. She still wasn't a hundred percent sure that Dishy would turn up and to boost her Dutch courage she fancied downing a few cheap drinks to get her ready for it. It was her intention to nip out from the pub about five to eight and leave Katie to her own resources.

"Oh, I'm sorry, I'm going out."

The reply came as a shock. "What? You can't be. Oh hang on. It's with that chap isn't it?"

"Well, what if I am. I'm a big girl now you know."

"Oh I see. You don't want your friends any more."

Katie's back was coming up at the cheek of it. How often had this so called friend dragged her along to some place she didn't want to go and then desert her? And hadn't she done that only the Saturday before?

"I know the feeling well Sam. Had plenty of experience."

"Well, where are you going?" Sam was determined to find out and she knew Katie was sidetracking the question. Giving a knowing a knowing laugh she said bluntly "So he's trying to get into your knickers. Doesn't take them long. I could have told you that."

"It's nothing of the kind. Anyway I have to go I've got another call." And she pressed the red button and switched to the incoming one.

"Thought you didn't want to speak to me." The familiar tone sent her heart racing.

"I'd rather be talking to you than the one that was on."

"Oh, well that's nice to know."

"It was Sam."

"Thought it might be."

She laughed now "And if you're asking me to the happy hour, the answer is still no."

"Aha, that's her idea of enjoyment." He laughed too then added. "Actually, I just wanted to see you."

"Oh." she felt her pulses racing and before she could think she answered "Me too."

"I was wondering, and I hope you won't think me forward, but would you like to come here and we could watch something and have a bit of supper?"

"That would be lovely." She breathed.

"Knowing how much you enjoyed yesterday, I've got some nature DVDs I think you'd appreciate, unless you'd like a film or something."

She didn't really care as long as she was with him but said "The nature would be perfect. Thank you. What time shall I come?"

"When I call for you, shall we say half an hour?"

"Call for me, but it's only walking distance." She laughed again.

"When I call," he repeated "and escort you to my humble dwelling."

Sam would have said he was smooth talking her into bed but Katie was still floating on this air of happiness and whatever he had said she'd have gone along with it.

"I will be ready."

She was buzzing. How could one person make such a difference to your general mood?

"But why ask questions, just enjoy it because you don't know how long it will last." She told herself and she didn't want to hit rock bottom if it all went pear shaped.

"Oh, what shall I wear?" she panicked suddenly and flew upstairs to rifle through her clothes. She wanted to appear feminine so took out a dress which Sam would have scoffed at, but it suited Katie's colouring and she knew she would be comfortable. She decided on a coat as it could be chilly when she came back and was ready about three minutes before he rang the bell.

"You look divine" he said and immediately she felt she had made the right choice.

"You don't look so bad yourself." She was admiring the view. He looked smart yet casual and there was nothing about his appearance she didn't like.

Before long they were in his lounge and he was going through his collection of DVDs.

"Now what do you fancy, there's birds, animals, fish, coral reefs." he was going along the line.

"I like any, but not ones where the animals kill each other."

"Got just the thing." He pulled one out, put it in the machine and sat next to her on the sofa. "Oh, would you like a drink?" he almost whispered in her ear.

"In fine for now thank you."

As she turned, her face was almost on his and the inevitable kiss followed. Not wanting to hurry things, he raised the remote and started the disc. Soon his hand had gently taken hers and put it in his and after a reasonable time his arm had pulled her close to him so that she was lying with her head on his chest feeling the gentle rhythm as it lifted up and down. The motion seemed to be stirring up something in her lower parts and she tried to ignore it. Her arm was now lying across his stomach and much as she tried to concentrate on the pair of swans that were filling the screen, she found it increasingly difficult. His hand was now on top of her arm and he was stroking it gently while still watching the picture in front of them.

As he kissed her again, her response gave her feelings away and soon neither of them were thinking of anything except each other. He knew he couldn't rush this but she seemed to want him so much that he gently let his hand slide over her breasts and she didn't complain so he became more adventurous and moved to her thighs noticing how she parted them as he moved upwards. His compass was already on north and he took the chance of guiding her hand over to it hoping she wouldn't pull away but she didn't need any guidance for as soon as she was in the area she was giving it the works.

There was no time to suggest going upstairs, for they undressed each other where they were and soon she was on the thick rug with him pumping her up as though she was an inflatable. The relief was mutual and somehow neither felt embarrassed at the speed at which they had gone for it. Now it was a case of who could reach the tissues.

There was great consternation in the upper regions. Danny had again left his body and was in conference with Abe and a few of their scouts. Leon had not only done a great job with the water routes but had picked up a snippet from one of the other group. A careless whisper had given him a clue as to the reason for their presence. They were working on the instructions of a very well known entity whose true identity was never proven so he or she had been given many pseudonyms in order refer to them. The name commonly used by Abe and co was The Black Mamba as they always thought of it as a predator that was certain to catch its prey.

As soon as this information was received a few things became clear. They knew that Tule had crossed swords with this being in the past and there had been an ongoing feud between the two of them ever since. Although he had never been caught in the act, it was recognised that Tule had attempted to secure something belonging to the Black Mamba but had failed and somehow managed to make his escape. It was thought he must have had help, as it wasn't a feat you could bring about single handed, but there again who would go against such an evil force.

Abe had often thought this was why Tule was always flitting from place to place and always keeping his distance as much as possible, therefore making it difficult to track him down. Even at this very moment no one was sure of where he was.

"You do realise," Abe was summing up the recent events "that there is the perfect trap here if Mamba decides to use it. He or she will have worked out Tule's target and will be waiting for him to step in and take it."

"Too right," Danny agreed "but does it have to be right in the middle of our patch?"

Abe was still musing "That could put Zoe in much more danger because she'll be in the middle of it."

Danny was realising this was more serious now. "She will have the battle raging around her, but will have no defence against it."

"Always the innocent one isn't it?" Abe thought for a moment and then summed up.

"So, this other group are in the pay of The Black Mamba who is gunning for Tule, who has set his sights on Zoe." He reiterated. "But we are also faced with this influx of sadistic sexual creatures that are entering by the water route but not returning. That is they are being dumped here, but who is sending them, and what are they trying to achieve?"

Danny had been going along with this but said very slowly "Can we be sure the two are not connected?"

This stopped Abe in his tracks. "Could be but I don't see how. They seem to be on two totally different paths, and we know one objective but not the other."

"Think we've got to keep our minds completely open on this so that we're not taken by surprise." Danny stated then added "Would you agree it's best to leave Leon to concentrate on the water system?"

"Absolutely. You don't know what else he may turn up, also I've been mulling this over."

"Oh?" Danny wondered "In what respect?"

"Well, think of our theory that everything is fed from the main source down through the smaller channels, as we now know, via a water route."

"With you."

"And Leon noticed slits or openings."

"Yes, go on."

"How do I put this?" Abe thought for a moment. "If say water is gushing in down the arteries, then the veins etc., how would we observe it?" He went on to explain. "If you were looking at a tube with fluid running through it, you wouldn't see it, unless it was a clear tube of course."

Danny was catching on. "But you would if it was leaking!"

"That's one possibility," Abe nodded "and that would mean they have a problem. Now, we said the fiends were only being fed out through capillaries, and I said in jest that I'd like to cause a blockage, but what if one has occurred and caused a weakness further back?"

Danny carried on with this. "It could cause a fissure and where we thought the things were squeezing through, they could have been coming out of the veins instead of going all the way to the end."

"Couldn't they just? " Abe was on full throttle now. "And what if it wasn't a vein?"

"You mean an artery?"

They were silent for a moment until Abe said "You know what we need don't you?"

Danny was there "A full blown heart attack." Then said as an afterthought, "But that would release the whole lot in one go and how would we cope with that?"

"By being ready. We'd create it but have enough forces standing by to despatch the lot to a place where they won't come back."

"A big task, but we've done worse."

They both knew there was no option, because if this wasn't nailed soon, the invasion of these annoying dirty little beings would taint mankind for a long time and take a lot of cleaning up by the good powers.

They were about to part when Abe sudden jumped.

"Oh No."

"What is it?" Danny could see it was something serious.

"Don't know but something just came to me. When Vanke and the watcher had that rush go by them, it could be thought that had to be a capillary."

"Of course because that's the only exit apart from a tear, or fracture in the pipeline. We said that. So what's your point?" Danny thought he was repeating it all again.

"Unless." Abe stopped. "The only other way you would get the rush is if you were already inside the tube."

There was a long silence while it sank into both of their reckonings. This would put a totally different view on things and meant that they had to rethink all of it.

# Chapter 11

Sam was still pretty peeved about Katie's refusal to go for a drink and as she fumbled through her clothes trying to find something suitable, the annoyance started to turn to anger. She'd always been there whenever Katie needed her, and glad of her company, and just when a man comes into her life, it didn't matter about who'd stood by her.

"Well, just wait until she wants me to go out." she fumed, little realising that that was the last thing Katie had ever wanted.

She found an outfit that most would have considered a bit tarty, but it was the one that covered the most, and as she was hopefully going for a meal, she thought she ought to dress the part.

"Don't want to be kicked out 'cos I'm not smart enough." she thought. Then laughed "Perhaps it's a transport café."

It was two minutes to eight when she heard the car pull up outside.

"Oh shit. He's here." She thought she needed another pee but decided it was only nerves so with a last glance in the hall mirror, she opened the door as he was about to knock.

"My word, you look very nice." He was eying her up and down approvingly.

"Oh, thank you, I really had nothing to wear." She sighed to herself. "I can't believe I said that."

"Well, let's go." He watched her lock the door and they made their way to the car. She was dying to look round and see if anyone was watching, and although no one seemed to be looking, she could feel the eyes peering out of the windows.

"Didn't know what you liked to eat, so I thought we'd take in a little place I know just a few miles out in the country. They do almost anything you could want there."

"Oh lovely. I eat almost anything." She said but felt "especially if you're paying."

The place was a small cosy hostelry but looked as though it might be rather expensive. They were shown to a table in an alcove which she felt was quite romantic but when her eyes became accustomed to the light she realised the whole place was designed like it. All the tables were for two people and from what she could see, each couple would feel very private.

"This is nice." She whispered.

"I think so."

"Do you come here…. oh I was going to say often." She laughed. He smiled, "Only now and again."

As they sat there with a drink there was something about him that she couldn't quite fathom. After all this was the first time she had spoken to him properly and she really didn't know anything about him. Normally it wouldn't have bothered her as long as he delivered the goods at the end. She had never expected him to ask her out and now she felt a bit cheap and out of his class wishing she had dressed a little more in keeping with the place not that she had anything of that sort.

"They'll all think he's just picked me up off the street." went through her mind and she tried to look round to see if she was being studied but they seemed to be quite private where they were.

The food was delicious and she couldn't remember when she had eaten anything so posh, but when the coffee was served she wondered if she'd either eaten something she wasn't used to, or whether one of the drinks was stronger than she imagined. Dishy was looking straight into her eyes and talking in a very soft sensual tone. Everything seemed to be slipping away, but she was aware of a door opening at the back of the alcove and him helping her through, the door closing behind them. They were in another dimly lit room and she was being lowered onto a bed but if this was what he'd brought her here for, who was she to complain?

Her senses slowly returned and Dishy was standing there completely starkers in all his glory, and what a glory!

"My god," she muttered "I couldn't eat two of those." In all her experience she'd never seen a widger like it. Her mouth opened in surprise as it seemed to be pumping away on its own without any help. The man was moving closer to her and she realised she too was naked.

"How the hell did that happen?" she gasped but she'd be a bit stupid to ignore this prize bull as he came nearer and nearer.

He was towering over her and all her juices were screaming at him to take her and he lowered himself until, with his arms held high, he inserted himself into her. But the moment he was in, his form changed and she recognised him as the strange man on the bus and tried to scream.

"What are you?" it only came out as a whisper.

"You got what you wanted," was the thought transmitted.

"Not you!" she was trying to push him away but she would have stood more chance against a concrete wall for he wasn't going anywhere.

"You wanted me. You got me."

"But you didn't look like this. How can you change like that?"

He smirked "We've been around for a while. Clever aren't we?" At which point he gave the final thrust and delivered the goods right into her with such a force she thought the knob would reach her throat.

She was nearly crying, "We? There's more of you?"

"Your sort attract us, then you complain when you are serviced. Well you're well and truly hooked now."

"I'm not. I could walk away any time."

He sneered his hot breath nearly choking her. "Stupid fool. We have hooked you and many more like you. Now you will help to spread our virus. There's no going back."

Just when she thought she would never get out, Annie flashed into her mind, all her funny sayings rushing about the air like little arrows.

"There was this programme on telly last night......did you see the animals.......I could tell you a few tales......"

They were flying all over the place filling the air and landing on Sam. Suddenly she felt she was being lifted out and she would never know how but she was on the side of the road. It was dark and deserted and although she felt afraid she knew she had been rescued. But what now? She seemed to be miles from anywhere. The sound of a car in the distance made her jump and fearing it could be her predator she tried to scramble near the hedge but there was nowhere to hide.

"You alright there?" The voice was friendly but had authority.

To her relief it was a police car and she hurried to the door.

"Please, I need to get home."

"You'd better get in."

The female officer reached for a blanket off the back seat and said "You look as though you need this."

She waited for Sam to be safely belted into her seat before driving off and called in on her radio with a code so that the control room would know what she was dealing with.

"Looks like someone dumped you." She said casually as she knew the woman may not be too forthcoming at first as to her naked state.

"You haven't told anyone." Sam was shaking and feeling very insecure.

"I just have to let them know I'm on a job so they don't send me anywhere else, that's all."

"Oh."

"Been to a hen party?" the officer said with a laugh to try and relax her.

"No."

"Why don't you tell me, in your own time. I'm here to help you, you're safe now."

Sam took a deep breath and pulled the blanket closer.

"I'm not sure but I think someone slipped me one."

"What a drink or a pill do you mean?"

"I don't know, one minute I was alright then everything went fuzzy and I'm not sure after that apart from…."

The officer gave her a quick glance.

"You being stripped have anything to do with it?"

Sam tried to piece it altogether in her mind and once the officer had enough to support her suspicions she then asked where this had taken place. As soon as she had enough information she called in for another beat officer to check out the hostelry.

"Are you taking me home?" Sam asked.

"Probably later, but for now I just need to know you are ok."

"Eh?"

"Don't worry, we just have to make sure you haven't been hurt so I have to pop you into the hospital, just to be on the safe side. There are rules you see."

"But they'll want to know why I went out with a chap I didn't really know."

The officer was trying to keep the conversation relaxed and answered "Oh, I shouldn't worry about that, people do it all the time. What was his name?"

There was silence.

"I don't know." Sam felt very foolish. "They'll think I just went out for a sex."

"Who will?"

"Your lot, they'll want to know ever bloody detail. Can't you just take me home?"

"Not allowed to. It's easiest if you just go along with it to keep them happy."

The policewoman let it sink in before asking "Do you remember if this person had sex with you?"

"It did, I mean he did."

The message had already gone through to the hospital that they were coming in and the staff were waiting for them. This wasn't how Sam thought the evening would turn out but at least she was safe for now.

PC Daniels had picked up the message to find the 'pub' near to where Sam had been found and was soon on his way. The police were aware of its existence and had never had any trouble with it before, knowing it as a place where many clandestine meetings took place away from prying eyes. If there had been an attack of any kind, others must have known, but it may be very difficult to get any witnesses as the patrons wouldn't want to come forward. But staff must have had some idea.

As he drove, a niggling feeling kept permeating his thoughts and his mind flashed back to the Zoe incident.

"No, it can't be related can it?" he mused but had learned never ignored any of his instincts.

In the meantime Abe had realised there was going to be more at this seemingly innocent venue, and had summoned up some of the most unobtrusive watchers who were observing from a safe distance. They had suspected Dishy was using several different guises and that he had already procured many females to spread the evil. The likes of Sam just walked straight into the traps he set and few got back out. But Annie had been in constant attendance although completely unrecognisable as her 'little old lady' façade and had observed all Sam's antics for some time. She had managed to dive in at the precise moment and lift the woman's spirit away followed by her body and she was now protecting her at very close range.

As she did so, the sentinels had no option but to confront the beast who was immediately joined by similar entities who sprang to his defence. But while the obvious attackers were keeping them busy, Abe and was scouring the venue and his senses took him down into the ground. Summoning his special guards, they located an underground river which was rushing in one direction and as they trailed it upstream they realised it was getting bigger and bigger until it was all they could do to prevent themselves from being dragged back with the force as it seemed to be surrounding them. The theory of being inside the arteries appeared to be frighteningly correct and it made them think that with this power they must be near the gateway. But they had to extract themselves for now and try to follow from a distance.

Abe contacted Danny to share the development. They both realised that the main source may not be in a busy area but way out in the country where no one would think of looking. But at least they had this one positive lead and if it proved to be what they were after, they needn't go searching for any more as all paths would lead to the same place.

Secretly everyone involved was grateful to Sam, because if she hadn't gone to this place, they would never have dreamt of examining it.

The only information PC Daniels was able to get, was that there had been a middle aged woman come in with a rather good looking man, but they had left. The only reason the staff remembered them was that they looked so mismatched whereas the other couples all seemed to know each other. It had been quite busy so as long as the customers were happy that was all they were bothered about.

"Would you know what they ordered?" Daniels asked,

After a bit of flicking through the slips, they found the one and let him take it.

"Have you ever seen the gentleman before?"

"No. Stranger to us but then a lot of them are." He was told.

They agreed to let him have a look at the area where Sam sat as it was empty at the moment and he felt a strange feeling come over him but couldn't describe it. He then checked outside trying to pick up any unusual movements in the atmosphere. Something was telling him this was no ordinary earthly happening and in some way it had to be connected to Zoe's kidnap. Both women had escaped in some way. Perhaps this was the same predator who was going round taking them for his own means then abandoning them.

Although he wasn't exactly on the right track, there was enough doubt in his mind for him to know that he couldn't explain his gut feelings on a report. But he knew someone who could.

Zoe was due to work the late shift on Tuesday and decided to do some clearing out in the morning. She had wanted to get rid of some clothes she'd had for a while and refresh her wardrobe, so she decided to fill one of the charity bags that were always coming through the door and leave it out the next day. Joel wasn't happy about her working late as he was always on the day shift at the moment and it meant that she would be on her own first thing and he would be during the evening. Although they were apart when working, they seemed to be safe enough from any unearthly contact, due to the presence of plenty of other people being around. In fact it was Leon's involvement that was fuelling the protection. When one of them was at home on their own, that was when they seemed to be vulnerable, also the memory of Tule's attack was still fresh and Joel didn't like his wife making the journey home late at night but she insisted that he worried too much.

She made a coffee and took it upstairs to their bedroom and stood there wondering whether to start with the drawers or the wardrobe.

"Drawers it is." She said to herself and was soon intent on whether everything ended up on the 'save' or 'throw' piles. As she bent over the bed to move a stack of jumpers she felt a strong grip on her hips and her body was being pulled to and fro in a very familiar movement. The force was so strong that she couldn't stand back up and she tried to wave her arm backward to fight off whatever this was.

Somehow she found a strength building inside her and yelled "Get from me. Go back to where you came from. Leave me alone." Although she didn't know exactly who she was addressing she kept repeating it, using all her inward fighting force to reject this being and calling on help from any protective force that could hear her. Suddenly the motion stopped and she was free and it was obvious the entity had left for the room was empty for a second then a flood of good energy swept over her as the guardians regained control.

Tule had proved one thing by this practice run. At the moment he attacked, nothing could stop him, even her so called protectors for he was stronger than all of them. He knew he could possibly have taken her for himself this time, but it had to be at precisely the right moment for it to succeed, and he had been aware of greater forces in the area. For now he had retreated to await the final onslaught when no one would get in his way. It was almost time, then there would be no going back, whatever help she called for.

He now found he had little use for Phani for he was so cock sure of himself that even if Joel had been on the scene, Tule was certain that any guardians of his would be held back in the same way as Zoe's were. She'd served her purpose so he cared little what happened to her from now on. The fact that he had been controlling her without her knowledge meant that she could have no comeback on him like a woman scorned, and would realise shortly that she had no hold on Joel and he certainly wouldn't be giving her any future pleasure.

Ignorant of this, she was bragging to Pheel about her talents and reminding her of their challenge which was only just starting its second week, so there was a long time to go yet.

"Well I don't know what you're bragging about," Pheel was very smug. "At least mine is splitting from his wife. Now beat that."

"But you're still only doing it in one position, whereas I've had mine in every one you can imagine, and then some more." Phani wasn't impressed but secretly jealous of her opponent's achievement because she didn't see how she could get Zoe to clear off.

"You just won't admit to being beaten, well I'm telling you, this one is mine. You've lost your crown."

Phani was getting angry now. "You wait. I've haven't played my trump card yet, but you're almost spent out."

Pheel smirked. "But you won't still be going until the end of next week. That's where you will loose out."

"Oh won't I?"

"Not with what I've heard." Pheel hadn't actually heard anything but was learning the art of deception.

"What?"

"Oh probably nothing."

"Come on." Phani wasn't going to let her get away without proving it.

Pheel thought quickly. "You're being made a laughing stock."

"Me?" she screamed. This was the worse thing that could happen. "Who said I am?"

"Don't take my word for it."

Phani was seething. "You'd better explain yourself, and it had better be good." She hissed.

"Oh, just that there are some who would be selling tickets for the entertainment. Seems you have quite an audience when you are trying it on." Then added "Especially when you don't get anything."

That did it. Phani flew at Pheel like a tigress protecting her young, and had they been in body, there would have been quite a lot of medical treatment needed. They split just as quickly and both went off to prove themselves in the next session

Now it seemed certain that the main artery was about to be detected, Leon checked that the path of all the veins they had found so far, followed the same direction. Some seemed to veer off for a while but connected up to another which then met others before joining to one of the smaller arteries. There was quite a pattern building up as the evil was still sex saturating the entire area and Abe knew they must act soon but they had to be sure of the exact position before attacking and at the moment this was not confirmed.

Leon agreed to stay in his watching roles in the three hotels for now but would be ready to pull out of any of them at a moments notice. He had reported that the other group seemed to be gathering strength and so The Black Mamba was getting ready to attack which meant Tule may be taken out of the picture which would leave Zoe safe, but one fact had to be considered. What if Mamba's plan didn't work?

Danny had joined Abe for a moment to recap on events.

"Tule stands no chance. He'll get taken out before he knows what hit him." Abe was certain of this.

"We don't know what tricks he may have up his sleeve." Danny was aware the fiend may have honed some skills during his absence.

"No way. It will be a push over." Abe wasn't changing his mind.

"We may have to wait and see."

"Hope it's not over here. Can leave a lot of disturbance."

"Wish he'd never come back here." Danny said.

"Well he has, so we have to cope with it."

"If I didn't know you better, I'd say you were enjoying this."

Abe paused then said very slowly "Survival my friend. We each cope in our own way."

PC Daniels had been in touch with Edith Soames, the medium who had kindly agreed to visit the pub and see if she could pick anything up. At first the landlord wasn't too happy about it but agreed that as long as it wasn't when they had customers, they could come, but be quick about it. She pointed out that this wasn't something you could be quick about but Daniels was glad to have her along. He drove her to the place before opening time and asked if she could be given the chance to wander around and see if she noticed anything.

"As long as she doesn't get in the way. I've got a business to run here." The landlord was rather sharp.

"And we have an enquiry to conduct," Daniels replied, "but of course if you would like me to get an order for you to close until we've finished our investigations I can have that arranged straight away."

With a grunt the man waved them to get on with it.

"Do you want to go about alone?" Daniels asked her.

"No, no, you can follow me, but please don't speak unless I do."

They walked towards the bar, then she suddenly turned and headed towards the alcove where Sam had been.

"She was sitting here." She pointed to the chair as she looked for the landlord.

"Is she right?" Daniels asked

The man looked up. "Don't ask me. Have to ask the waitress."

"And when will she be here?"

"Day off. Back tomorrow night."

PC Daniels asked for the name etc. while Edith carried on looking around the area. She sat on the same chair Sam had used, then seemed to be looking far away. Suddenly she stood up and moved a curtain at the back of the alcove to reveal a small door. She tried to open it but it was locked.

"I need to get through here. She was taken through this door." Edith said.

After much snorting with disgust, the man produced a set of keys and unlocked the door. Edith slowly inched her way in followed by Daniels. As far as he could see there was a bed with only a mattress on it and a chair. At first he thought someone else was in there but realised it was his reflection as he made out a mirror on the side wall.

"Can we get some light on in here please?" He called without turning round. A dim light was switched on. Edith was standing motionless a look of horror on her face and she was pointing to the bed then to the mirror.

The PC didn't speak but moved gently to the mirror, his hands round his eyes as if peering through it. Without speaking he turned round slowly and noticed another doorway on the back wall.

"Where does that go?" He whispered.

"Outside. Emergency exit." The man grunted.

That would be checked in a moment but now Daniels was watching Edith intently.

Suddenly she screamed and fell onto the bed, fighting as though she was being held there but the look of horror on her face was frightening.

Daniels wanted to pull her out but knew he mustn't interact with her and had to let this run its course. She was pulling at her clothes and, as if by an unseen force was flung against the exit door. She stopped and slowly seemed to regain her normal self. Daniels asked that she may be allowed to sit somewhere to recover and asked for her to be given a cup of tea or something she would like. The landlord seemed pleased to comply but it was noticed he seemed very on edge now.

When Edith was seated away from the alcove, Daniels pulled the man to one side and said "You probably have worked out what I'm going to want to see now."

"Oh the door."

"No. You know what I'm talking about so stop messing about. Now where is it?"

The man looked very uncomfortable so Daniels pressed the point home.

"Have it your own way, but I can get this place ripped apart. Now what's it to be?"

The keys came out again and the man led the way to an alcove adjoining the one they had just examined. He unlocked the door at the rear and stood back as though he didn't want to go in.

"After you." Daniels beckoned him in.

There was no bed in this pokey hole but there were bar stools at one side and chairs in front facing a mirror which was on the opposite side to the one in the other room.

"Right." Daniels said very precisely. "You go and make sure the light is on in the next room and sit on the bed, and I will stay here while you do it."

"Look mate, is this really necessary?" The man asked but the stare from the copper said it all.

As the man left Daniels put out the light in his room, and sure enough he had a dim but perfect view of the man entering the other room and sitting on the bed.

He left the room and called the landlord.

"And how much do you fleece your perverts to look at unsuspecting people having a shag?" he spat at him with disgust.

The conversation between the two men was held out of earshot of Edith as the language was very basic but what they both understood. Having checked the exit door and anything else he needed, PC Daniels took Edith home, but not before he had warned the landlord that other officers would be arriving at any moment and not to touch anything in the meantime. He had also taken pictures to prove the state of the place so this den of debauchery could be dealt with.

Unbeknown to him this had been one of the distribution junctions of the evil intruders. They weren't actually released here because it wasn't a capillary but it was where all the branch lines led off, hence the tremendous surge encountered by Abe.

When they were travelling back, Edith related the feelings she had picked up in the back room.

"I didn't like to say in front of that rude man," she almost apologised "but the lady was attacked by something not human, a vile spirit that would have taken over her being and her mind."

"So are you saying she might not have been drunk?" Daniels didn't want to suggest more.

"Oh no, nor pills, you know drugs. He wouldn't need to you see, he could do it without that. Very powerful, you must be careful."

"Don't know if you can help on this, but I'm puzzled as to how she escaped. I don't mean through the door, I mean if he is as powerful as you say, how in creation did she get away from him?"

"Well I didn't feel that, but it's possible her guardian angels helped there. They do you know."

"So the good forces could have overcome him long enough for her to get away?"

"My dear man. They would do more than that. They would guide her to a place where she could get help."

"But what if no one had been driving along there? It's pretty lonely as you saw."

She smiled. "Tell me again how she was found please."

"A patrol car."

"Driven by a lady officer."

"Well, yes, so I gather." He was wondering what she was getting at.

"And then you get sent to the job." She looked satisfied as if that was all she needed to say.

"You'll be telling me next that was planned."

Her silence made him exclaim. "You are. You're saying we were sent there by some,…. oh I don't know what, but that we were guided there on purpose."

"Oh they move in strange ways." Was all she would say.

"Perhaps I should trust my instincts more." He decided.

Katie had been on cloud nine all day at work and if it hadn't been for the little text messages that Gary had sent she could have thought she had imagined it all. She felt very feminine, desired and quite sexy and had made up her mind to have her hair restyled and get some more up to date clothes. Her guardians including Stefan had her well protected and any attempts from passing sex marauders were deflected.

Although Gary had been placed as her special guardian, it hadn't been expected that he would make love to her and certainly not this quickly so the powers that be were now checking that he hadn't been tainted with this current sexual trend, or in fact that an evil entity had taken over his body. But all came back clean, so it had to be assumed that the two spirits were on the same plane and had probably been close many years or even centuries before. Stefan felt many pangs of jealousy, but he was a younger spirit and hadn't experienced just how much souls were intertwined and would always find each other regardless of time and distance.

It was usual for Katie's employer to hold a gathering for the staff and partners every year and the circular had gone round saying that it was to be held this year at a local hotel, which happened to be the one on the outskirts of the city where Leon was still in situ as a domestic. The evening always consisted of a dinner followed by a little light entertainment and dancing for those who wanted to burn off the calories they'd just consumed. The boss couldn't stand discos so it didn't always attract the younger set but it was always well supported by the majority. Katie hadn't been too keen on it since Stefan had died and had only gone last year because the others persuaded her, but there was no one she wanted to take with her and felt a bit lonely. Now she felt different. But what if he didn't like that sort of thing, after all she didn't really know anything about him, but there was only one way to find out.

She was about to cook her evening meal when the phone rang.

"Have you had a good day?" the voice was instantly recognisable.

"Gary! How are you?" the excitement in her voice was obvious.

"Good, but all the better for hearing your voice."

"I found it difficult to concentrate on work today." She felt a bit silly as the words came out, but she couldn't take them back.

"Same here. Can't wait to see you again."

Here was her opportunity.

"Gary" she hesitated "I don't want to sound forward but where I work, they have this dinner dance evening and they have asked for numbers, and I just wondered if….um…"

"If you're asking me I'd be delighted." He sensed her reluctance to come out with it.

"You would? Oh that's wonderful, only I wasn't sure if you'd want to go with me. Staff take their husbands, wives friends, you know what I mean."

"I'd be honoured to go as your friend." His tone was very reassuring.

"Oh, "she laughed "I'd better tell you when it is in case you're busy."

"I will make sure I am free." He knew he would be, as his job was to protect her.

"A week on Saturday. Bit short notice I'm afraid"

She went on to explain where and what time, then said they had to choose from the menu. What he said next made her heart miss a beat.

"Wouldn't it be easier if I came over and we sorted it together? Bit difficult on the phone."

"That would be much better. Look, I'm just going to cook dinner, if you haven't eaten yet, I could do you some as well."

"If it's no trouble, I would like that very much." He assured her he ate almost anything so whatever she was having would be fine for him.

It only seemed to take minutes before he was at the door and they didn't make it past the hall before they were locked in an embrace as though they hadn't seen each other for years.

After dinner they sorted the menu and Katie couldn't explain the feeling she had, knowing they would be going out as a couple and people she knew would accept him as hers. Although she tried to quell the excitement that was taking over her whole being, it was difficult as it seemed to be growing stronger by the minute and was blocking everything else from her mind.

They were cuddled up on the sofa when the phone rang and she jumped.

"Hello."

"It's me." The voice was a bit slurred but she recognised who it was straight away and mouthed "Sam" to Gary who nodded but didn't look surprised.

"You ok Sam?" Katie didn't really know what to say and it occurred to her for the first time that she never really had anything to say to this woman.

"No I'm not. I didn't get into work until this afternoon."

"Oh you poorly again?" As Katie answered she and Gary exchanged knowing looks and he lifted his spare arm and raised it to his mouth giving the impression of having a drink.

"No. I suppose you had a good night with your bloke." She turned the tables round.

"Very nice thank you."

"Did he do anything?"

"Sam, a lady doesn't discuss that sort of thing." And she grinned at Gary who could hear most of what Sam was saying he was cuddled so close to Katie.

"Oh he didn't then. Told you he was gay."

Katie now had to clap her hand over her mouth to stop laughing and Gary was giving the thumbs up which made it worse.

"I'm sure he isn't, as I told you before he's a gentleman."

"All that means is that he takes the weight on his elbows and knees." Sam seemed to be coming to life but then Katie remembered her previous remark and used it to change the subject.

"So, why didn't you go to work this morning?" she asked.

"Well, as you refused to go out with me I had to find other entertainment."

Katie looked at Gary and raised her eyes as she whispered "Here we go."

"Are you going to tell me where?" she said aloud.

"Oh I went out with this dishy chap that's been chatting me up at work."

"Oh that's nice. So you overslept?"

"No, I didn't feel well."

Alarm bells went off in Katie's brain. "You're always going out, but you only miss work when……."

"Go on say it. When I get bladdered."

"And other reasons?" Katie wasn't going to be drawn and wanted Sam to come out with the fact she'd been in with the wrong sort again and probably got knocked about. Pity she couldn't see what she looked like but she wasn't about to ask her round.

"As if you care."

"Look Sam, if you're trying to tell me something, say so, I'm not a mind reader."

There was a long pause before the reply came.

"You can come round here if you like. My arm's going to sleep holding this phone."

And the line went dead.

Katie looked at Gary and shrugged.

"I've got to draw the line and stop this mental manipulation," she said quietly, "but what if something is wrong? I'd never forgive myself."

"That's because of the caring person that you are, you can't help it." Gary kissed her then offered "Would you like me to come along?"

"That's very sweet of you," she hugged him "but knowing Sam as I do, it will be very personal and she might not want to discuss it in front of a man she doesn't know."

"I get the impression she might enjoy it," he laughed but then said seriously "you're right of course."

Katie was deep in thought for a moment.

"You see it's the boy who cried 'wolf' isn't it? There's been so many dramas that you tend to switch off, then on the one occasion when something does happen, you ignore it. And there's the fact that she went into work this afternoon, so she can't be hurt or anything."

He pulled her close to him and said "But you won't feel easy until you've checked, will you?"

"I suppose not, but I can't let her ruin every moment I have or she will know she has me on a piece of string and can wind me in every time she snaps her fingers. I've got to put a stop to that."

He took a deep breath "How about this for a solution? You pop round and say that you can't be long because I'm picking you up.

Check she's ok and put your mind at rest. If she's got some lengthy tale to tell, you can listen but don't take it upon your own shoulders."

"But..." she started

"I will get the car and come for you, either at a prearranged time or when you ring me."

"Oh I couldn't let you do that. It's putting you out just for the likes of her. She's not worth it, I'm telling you."

"Aren't you forgetting one important thing? I will be seeing you again later and she will pick up on the fact that we are getting closer."

Katie nodded but had to say "But if I didn't go, we would be staying here so I would be seeing more of you."

He hugged her tightly and whispered "You see, that's what makes me love you so much."

They both agreed that she would visit Sam on this occasion but it would be short.

# Chapter 12

Pheel had now implanted the idea into Nick that he could have anything he wanted and achieve all his goals in life provided she was in the picture. The moment he decided to be rid of her, everything would come crashing down around him. He wasn't sure if this was correct but for now it suited his purpose for he knew his life was going forward and the spiritual sex was good and on tap at any time, so why bother to change a good thing?

But people near to him were noticing a difference that wasn't so nice. Joel who had been his friend now found him getting more distant by the day and his workmates saw an arrogance that was never there before. This didn't concern him because to him it was a sign of power and the more unpopular he became the more he would be feared. Respect never came into his reckoning. He had tried to set the wheels in motion for his divorce but Emma seemed to have disappeared from the picture and although he didn't have the problem of her hanging around, he knew he had to be rid of her.

His face was becoming set in a hard expression and he rarely smiled. The only time he let himself go was when he was indulging in the sexual acts. Then he pulled out all the stops and didn't care how he appeared, because although Pheel was real to him, he knew there could be no comeback in the physical world. She wouldn't get pregnant, he wasn't at risk of any STDs and she could never demand money or the finer things of life.

But there was a new development. It was taking over like a drug and was beginning to control him instead of him being the master. At times when he was completely spent, it would be urging him to go more and more until he was so exhausted he couldn't move. He may be on the floor, half way down the stairs, or anywhere and he would have to lay there naked until he found enough strength to get up. As soon as he entered the house, he got a hard on and that would be it for at least the next hour or so. His tent pole was always up long before he woke and it had to be attended to. It hadn't been a problem while it was confined to home but now it was catching him out at the most inconvenient times.

It was as though Pheel was becoming part of his body so that his three piece suite was always in play and he often would be needing a pee but had to wait until his todger was relaxed enough to allow it. But it wasn't only one way. He had explored more parts of her body with different bits of his anatomy than he thought possible and she wasn't going to let this man go anywhere. She owned him.

What he didn't realise was that people were beginning to notice him trying to cover his boners, and far from finding it amusing they began to wonder if he was some sort of pervert. It had happened in the supermarket when he was at the checkout so he decided not to use that store again as he may have been noticed on camera, and could be recognised.

The idea came to him to either have very tight underpants, or better still to strap it down so that it couldn't be noticed in his trousers but not only was it so uncomfortable it nearly cut off his blood supply, but the restriction was having the opposite effect and was almost bringing him off. One thing was for sure. He wouldn't be discussing this with Danny, Joel or anyone.

Tule was totally unaware of the presence of The Black Mamba and was now set for his finale. He knew Zoe had a day off on Friday this week but Joel would be working all day and that would be when he would take her.

Leon, although intent on his other task, was well aware of the other group which seemed to be concentrating just on the hotel where Zoe was filling in and he alerted Abe and Danny. They knew Tule was holding off somewhere, probably not in the same place for long, and the group was positioning near his target. But this would mean they should also be observing the area near her home and yet they seemed to be keeping away from there, which seemed odd.

"We thought Mamba would pace Tule and get him on his way to Zoe, not after he had taken her, so why isn't the group following her?" Abe was summing up again.

"Because it could be that any prey of his isn't important to Mamba, so it has just got him in its sights regardless of any innocent being that might get pulled in." Danny said.

"But that still doesn't explain why they are concentrating on the hotel where she is working. If it just wants him why not concentrate on the bigger area?"

"Not sure on that one." Danny had to admit. "Leon still on the look out?"

"Yes, he'll be the first to notice any movement."

"Guess it's best to keep him spread around, if we move him it will attract attention."

Abe agreed but added "He always works on his instincts and they haven't let us down yet. If he thought it prudent to move or concentrate on any place, he'd do it. So if he's staying put, we leave him."

As far as all the higher powers were concerned it was like waiting for a storm to break. The spiritual clouds were gathering and the air was electric and it seemed that as soon as the first flash of lightning was seen the thunder would follow and the rains would hurtle down. Many earth dwellers were going about their business totally unaware of the impending onslaught, but those who were more spiritually tuned could feel the ripples and sensed that all was not well and immediately strengthened their protective shields.

Pheel was now constantly in Nick's presence, not only for the control she had over him but, although she would never have admitted it to Phani, she was now obsessed with him, and the matter of the challenge was no longer important. He was her property and she would let no other person, whether in spirit or body, male or female come near him. For hadn't she groomed him into what he now was? There wasn't a single second when she wasn't part of him and he couldn't even take a dump without her being there to wipe his bottom. Unfortunately, this high that he was now on gave him the false feeling of self importance but wasn't shared by his colleagues who had now dubbed him 'Nick the Prick'.

It was Wednesday morning and he had been woken up in the usual way as now it would be difficult for him to function without his early humping session. He had showered, dressed and had breakfast and was just about to leave for work when the door bell rang. He grabbed it open, knowing he didn't have time to spare and came face to face with a policeman.

"Yes?" Nick said sharply.

"Mr Brent? Mr Nicholas Brent?"

"That's me. What's this about?"

"Could I come in please? I think it would be better, with what I have to say."

Nick was a bit hesitant but suddenly a chill ran through him.

"Yes, please do." He beckoned the officer to follow him into the lounge.

"Your wife is named Emma, am I correct?"

"Absolutely, now what's she been up to?"

"I'm sorry sir but it appears she has been found, dead I'm afraid."

Nick sat down in the nearest chair.

"How, I mean what happened, where was she?"

"I'll come to that, but could you tell me first when you saw her last?"

Nick put his hands to his head. "It's difficult to say, you see she's been doing her own thing lately, anyone would tell you that. She goes out and often doesn't come back at night, and recently she's been gone for a couple of days. I don't think I've seen her since last week." He was trying to rack his brains but everything seemed to be swimming in his head.

"Did she say where she was going?"

"No." Nick paused wondering how much he should say about her recent habits.

"You didn't ask?"

"Well of course I asked."

"And?" The officer had sat down now and was looking straight at him.

"Look, things hadn't been good for a while. She used to be so different but she seemed to have got in with a bad lot and I think she was often drunk and….."

"Using drugs?"

Nick nodded. "It seemed very much that way, but you couldn't communicate with her. She didn't want to know."

They both sat for a moment and the officer said quietly "We will need you to identify her I'm afraid."

"Oh God, I suppose you will." Nick was feeling quite shaky now, but said "You did say you'd tell me about.... you know."

"Oh yes, she was found by a member of the public lying at the side of the road, just outside of town near the old spinney. Thought she'd been hit with a vehicle at first but now we think she may have been dumped there."

"What?" Nick was alert now. "I knew she must have got mixed up with the wrong sort."

He then looked at the way the man was watching him and another thought hit him.

"Oh God, you don't think I had anything to do with it do you?"

The officer gave a slight shrug and said that they had to keep all avenues open at the present time, which came out as a stock reply without committing to anything.

After Nick had called into work to say he wouldn't be in, he got ready to leave with the officer but stopped at the door.

"Would I be right in thinking that she as been......murdered?"

"Like I say, it's early days. We've just got to make sure it is her first, so if you're ready, we'll get that bit out of the way."

Nick's mind was in turmoil. Although he didn't love her any more, this would have been the last thing he wanted to happen. He couldn't remember much of the journey and the widower entering hospital bore no resemblance to the cocky self opinionated man who had just been shunting his train in Pheel's tunnel.

PC Daniels had been at the station when the report came in and once again his 'nose' made him curious. He asked what had been found on the dead woman and learned that apart from her things bearing her own name there were a couple of phone numbers of friends, one of which was Zoe's. Immediately alarm bells went off. There were too many unusual events going on round here to be a coincidence.

Firstly Zoe had been waylaid in unusual circumstances which seemed to have still unexplained facts, then Sam had obviously been attacked by something not quite human from what she said, now this young lady had been found in the same area and had Zoe's number in her purse. There were too many unresolved facts but he felt that there had to be something going on, and if not directly connected, there must be a link. If only he could put the whole picture together before the next occurrence.

Abe had noticed an increased presence by the other group at Zoe's hotel.

"The Black Mamba must be getting ready to strike." he said to Danny.

"Can't understand it. Do they think Tule will go for her here again, because he's not that stupid?"

"Well it's got him lined up for something." Abe was trying to work out the plan from the other angle "If I was going to take him out, it wouldn't be somewhere like that unless the group is going to act as protection, that's why it's being strengthened."

Danny was also musing. "And why not at her home? That would be the most obvious."

"Is it though?" Abe suggested. "Don't forget Tule will know that we are watching there and he probably wouldn't succeed. But if I were he, I'd have pulled right back until we had forgotten all about it."

"Sounds a bit like Mamba knows him better than we do."

They were interrupted by a thought message from Leon.

"The main gate isn't here."

This brought their planning to a halt.

"But we thought we had it, or nearly, when we were in that underground stream." Abe was astounded. He would like to have asked more but they knew that Leon had a reason for brevity, and would communicate as soon as it was safe to do so. For now the surge of hungry sexual spirits was continuing to flood the area, but for as many that were arriving, the clean up brigade were destroying the same amount.

"You can't move without falling over the randy things." Danny said, but was corrected by his friend.

"That's if you know they are there." Abe laughed.

"Not sure if that's a plus."

Neither would rest until they had received further information from Leon who was still working all three hotels, but also observing anything else that took his attention. He was shape shifting continually and only a much higher power would have recognised him. He had the notion that this sudden sexual factor had a connection with The Black Mamba business, and wondered if it was an almighty distraction, but if that were the case, it was a bit drastic just to take out an old nemesis, especially of Tule's standing.

Phani wasn't happy. She wished she could finish this silly challenge now. She was beginning to dislike Pheel more and more and was considering ditching her altogether. Even Joel was becoming a bore, and she couldn't get anywhere near him due to the protection around him and Zoe. Seemed to be time for pastures new and she floated around the area to see what was on offer. Surely there were decent males that would welcome the company of a highly experienced lady friend, well sex partner to be honest, but the offerings around here at the moment were very disappointing. She found herself being drawn to the pub where Sam had been taken and thought she'd just check it out to see what it had to offer, not that she held out much hope.
It didn't take her long to realise the kind of business that was going on there and out of curiosity wandered around getting the layout of the place. It was closed at the moment but she made up her mind she would be back to have a look at the activities, sleazy as they may be, but she didn't have to take part she could just watch for entertainment's sake. It would be better than nothing.

One person who wouldn't be setting foot in the place again was Sam. She felt cheated by Dishy and wondered just what he really was. Although she'd been as honest as she could when questioned, she felt a fool saying he had turned into a monster and that had been interpreted that the attacker had just turned nasty to get his way, or she was under the influence of a hallucinatory drug, but as the tests had shown negative, that was dismissed. After what seemed like an endless round of questions she was told she would be taken home but then realised she hadn't got her bag. She had taken little money and some lip gloss so the loss of that didn't bother her too much but her key was in it. Fortunately she had a spare hidden under a flower pot, not a safe option, but it proved useful in this case.
She had rung in sick on the Tuesday morning saying she had a bug and it was best not to spread it around. By Wednesday she felt

able to face to world and went to work as normal, showing no signs of anything untoward. Annie was hovering around as usual and somehow it gave Sam a feeling of security. No questions were asked but the old lady gave her many knowing looks and waggled her finger at her in her own special way. They had the usual banter but Sam had no idea just what a part she had played in securing her safety.

Bollik had been enjoying himself to the limits but the ladies group were about to leave the hotel, and short of following each one, he knew he had to move on. He had learned that it was no good going after one goal when he could have all the sex he wanted with as many as he liked, but not all at the same time, that would be vulgar. So he decided to concentrate on hotels where they were holding meetings, conventions, anything that would put a congregation of desirable females in his lap. There may be a few he wouldn't want, but there would be plenty he did and he could stay satisfied for a long time. This hotel business certainly could be his provider from now on, after all there was never a shortage of guests and he could choose the ones that had the largest numbers attending, and of course staying at any venue. At the moment he could take his pick from the three in this vicinity as he had a free run with Vanke at a safe distance away in the middle of the city.
"Wonder if he's found anything yet." He thought.

Vanke's partner had been kept in place for the time being, but he was worried about what would happen when she had to leave for he didn't want this experience to end. He thought he could follow her but that was not possible due to his lower ranking and her high observation status. So there was no way that was going to happen, also she was spiritually geared not to get attached in such cases, so poor Vanke was going to be on the scrap heap at any given time as there had been no other incidents at this particular hotel apart from the one shower unit episode.

Nick had coped quite well and had identified Emma's body but had shown signs of shock when he looked at her mouth. Death hadn't done her any favours and he had been warned she may not look as he expected. He wondered what they meant but as they drew back the cloth he shuddered.

"What has she done to herself?" he pointed.

"We wondered if you had any ideas." the medical officer asked.

"But what's caused that, is it lipstick?"

Emma's lips were black and it was explained that most of the inside of her mouth was the same inky colour.

It may have confused Nick but it was explained that there could be many causes which would be determined by the necessary examination.

"You mean a post mortem?" The bare facts were beginning to hit him now.

"Afraid so. But then we should get a better idea."

It was put to him kindly but the medic was interested to get started and find out what had happened to this lady but he already had his suspicions.

Abe and Danny had already been on the scene and took a very different view. The fact that the examination would be proved to be a cocktail of alcohol and drugs paled into insignificance with the sight of the deserted body, almost as if a business card had been left. For the one creature that sported this colour on the inside of the mouth was a black mamba.

"So it's female and has been under our noses all the time." Abe felt cheated.

"We knew it was clever, but I didn't expect this." Danny was equally shocked.

But then the important question arose. Where was she now?

"Well she's left the body she was using, but she's got to be in the area." Danny continued but Abe was puzzled.

"But why leave it now? It's only Wednesday in earth time and if she isn't attacking Tule until Friday, where is she holding out?"

Danny thought for a moment then said "But we have assumed she is attacking Friday, but we don't know for sure."

"You mean," Abe was sifting this new idea, "that she may not go for him when he homes in on Zoe. It could be any time and any place."

Danny agreed but added "And does it have to be earth bound? She's free now and they will both be totally in spirit."

"You're right. But don't forget she's of a much higher power, he'll be crushed." Abe was trying to take an overview.

They were both deep in thought for a while.

"You don't think she's using the water route?" Abe wondered.

"For what purpose?"

"Either to come or go without attracting attention."

Danny jumped "So you think that's why it was put in place, not as a distraction but a means of transport. But it's a one way thing. She can't use it as an escape."

"Don't underestimate her." Abe was sifting through his past knowledge.

"Wait. Black Mambas are not water dwellers." Danny thought he had hit a problem.

Abe almost laughed. "That's where mistakes are made. You're forgetting she's only dubbed that because she is such a lethal predator, she can use any element she chooses."

"Ah yes." Danny felt he should have realised that.

Suddenly Abe yelled "We've got to find the main gate. We need Leon to search again near the same spot where we thought it was before but keep his mind open."

"Not sure I'm with you." Danny was puzzled but it didn't seem that his friend was going to impart any more, and that meant there was a good reason not to let the thought travel out where it could be detected.

It was late afternoon when Nick called Joel at work and broke the news and his friend immediately forgot any differences and offered to go round if he needed him, but Nick said he was alright and there was a lot to sort out. Joel then let Zoe know and she was so stunned as she had liked Emma before she got in with these latest friends of hers and it seemed such a waste of a good life. It didn't take long for the news to filter from Nick's office and within a very short space of time the three hotels were buzzing. In these cases, messages passed by word of mouth soon get changed and before long there were various stories as to what had actually happened.

Pheel had never left his side. She had become quite the mercenary little bitch protecting what was hers and this was just a step up for her because now no person, spirit or entity of any kind would part them.

Phani had homed in on the happenings and attempted to approach her friend but was told to clear off in no uncertain terms.

"I suppose you think I want a bit of your action." She spat at her.

"Just because you can't find your own." Pheel retorted. "It's just proved who's the top dog now. You've lost. I've won."

"There still half the time left." Phani yelled.

"Time? If you're still playing your silly little games lady, play on. I don't have to prove anything."

Phani knew she was beaten but was determined to have the last word.

"We'll see. When it all comes crashing down around you, don't come crawling back to me because I won't be there."

"Ha. I don't need you." Was Pheel's passing shot before she turned her attention back to Nick and his needs.

Joel and Zoe had arrived home about the same time on Wednesday evening and decided to have a takeaway as both had been very busy and the news of Emma had drained them a bit. They ordered a Chinese meal and until it was delivered couldn't help but discuss Nick's ordeal.

"In a way I wasn't as shocked as I would have expected." Joel said.

"Why? Because of the way she has been behaving. I mean she's not a kid. I should say 'was' I suppose." Zoe looked a bit pale and Joel guessed this was having more effect on her than she was admitting.

"I didn't agree with him divorcing her, but I don't thing he's had an easy ride." He said quite sympathetically. "But it's happened so quickly really. I keep wondering what made her suddenly get in with the wrong lot."

"Boredom?" Zoe thought. "Perhaps things weren't that good at home for a while and one partner can often look for excitement elsewhere."

"I wonder if we'll ever know." He slipped his arm round her shoulder and pulled her to him. They were still in that position when the door bell made them jump and their meal had arrived.

When bedtime came, Joel just wanted to make love to his wife to show her how much she meant to him but she didn't seem too keen and he wondered if she was coming down with a bug, but he never pushed it and they lay curled up together until they finally dropped off to sleep.

When they awoke the next morning, Zoe wasn't feeling at all good and blamed the takeaway as she was rather sick.
"Perhaps you shouldn't go in." Joel tried to persuade her to stop in bed for a while.
"No, I'll be fine. I'd rather be working, I'm off tomorrow and I'm only on reception then on Saturday then its back to the office."
"Well you know best, but look after yourself." He kissed her and reminded her that they still had to keep their guards up as they didn't know quite what was going on and after Emma's death, it made him realise how valuable time is that you have with your loved ones, and every minute counts.

Katie had seen Gary every day this week and they were already making plans for the weekend. But tonight when she left work, they were going to get the shopping done. He arranged to pick her up, go and have some dinner then face the supermarket when they were both refreshed. She always preferred to do it on a Thursday as it wasn't so busy and she hated standing in long queues at the check out.
"You could always scan it as you go." Gary told her.
"I'm not very good with those sort of things," she laughed "they seem to go wrong on me."
Even going shopping seemed enjoyable when they were together, and it had got to the point that neither wanted to say 'goodnight'. When they were in their own beds they kissed each other on the phone and, as soon as one was awake the next day, they texted the other to start the day off.

They decided to stay in on Friday evening and there were no guesses as to how that would end up and then would make their plans for the weekend. They were both so wrapped up in each other that Sam rarely came into Katie's mind and she had to admit she was living a much happier life now than when she was being dragged round the tatty places Sam like to frequent.

Katie's guardians were a bit worried for they knew that Gary had only been sent as a temporary reinforcement while the sex invaders were on the loose and he wouldn't have been there if Sam hadn't put Katie in danger by attracting the fiends. It seemed strange that he had appeared to become so much attached to her and one train of thought was that he was enjoying being back in human form with the physical pleasure that went with it, but when it was his time to be recalled, would they both accept it. The problem was that Katie was oblivious to the fact that he was an angel on a visit, not on a normal earth life span, and there was bound to be heart break.

Sam on the other hand wasn't in love and wasn't even looking for it. As long as a chap had a decent dick and knew what to do with it, that was all that mattered. Even her recent experiences didn't put her off as they would have done to most people, but it seemed to give her the urge to always find the next one. How she had never ended up in some clinic or other at the hospital was beyond anyone's understanding. Her attack by Dishy was already fading as the thought of the weekend approached and she wondered if Katie would drag herself away from her bloke long enough to go out with her, just long enough to get established, then her friend could go back to her own pleasures.

Annie wasn't one to despair and had dealt with many like Sam, so she just strengthened her presence ready for the next sexual encounter for as sure as dogs cocked their legs, there would be one and soon.

PC Daniels was still trying to make sense of all the recent happenings, but just when he thought he had made a connection, there seemed to be no proof to substantiate it. Danny felt sorry for him to a certain extent, but that was how they worked so there was no time for sentiment. Subjects such as this experienced copper proved invaluable when the spirit world needed to draw something to the earthling's attention and would direct them to a specific place but there the intervention stopped. Some people were easy to tune in to, and could be made to respond to what they thought was their gut feelings but that was all. There would be no explanations and no further communication at that particular time, until they could be used again, and while they thought they had some kind of gift to sniff out the truth, everything they learned was being very carefully stage managed. So Daniels would always wonder, until the next time.

Leon left his three physical forms for a while to contact Abe and Danny by a secure route. The conversation was electric.

"There have been so many changes," he started, "firstly the main gate is closing."

This came as a complete surprise.

"You've located it? Where?" Abe and Danny chorused.

"Let's leave that for the moment. The whole system is being frozen."

"What?" Abe was surprised. "Do you mean literally?"

"In spiritual terms, yes." He paused before saying "You were right thinking water was being used, but not earthly fluid."

"I think I get it." Danny said. "The power flows that are felt but not seen."

"Right, but they have one thing in common. They are susceptible to change."

Abe was now working overtime. "So the fluid can be changed into ice or steam?"

"You're there." Leon was grateful they were on his wavelength. "We set one of our teams to work. You were mentioning blocking the capillaries I think although you knew that was probably impossible."

Abe couldn't remember sharing that with Leon but had to agree.

"So we used one of our methods and froze them, and that in turn worked backwards until the veins were clogged and so on."

"And that is closing the gate?" Abe asked.

"As we speak."

Danny was a bit confused. "But we thought they were still coming in although it had slowed. So just when did you, or they pull this off?"

"They don't mess about. As soon as it starts it takes effect almost immediately, don't forget it's not a physical happening."

"We had no idea." Abe felt they should have been informed and his tone portrayed his feelings.

"Sorry, but that's how they work. Even I didn't know until it was well under way and I couldn't take the slightest chance of any message being intercepted."

"Damn it!" Abe exploded. "That is how I thought we would trace back to the gate but didn't think it could be done."

"Oh don't worry, they're learning new tricks all the time."

"Just who is 'they'?" Danny wanted to know but Leon just gave him a look before replying.

"Even a mystery to me."

They were all silent for a moment then Abe said quietly "That couldn't have just been a means to flood the earth with sex fanatics. It had to have another purpose."

"Well, one thing's for sure," Danny suggested, "if as you say Leon, it has been crushed, won't the instigators have to come out of the woodwork now for whatever reason to finish the job? After all, they won't be happy at being overcome."

"Possibly." Leon was thoughtful "Unless they are content with the outcome, on the other hand, if it was a distraction, what else has been festering?"

"Well it has to be the Black Mamba business, I mean there's nothing else that we know of." Abe was trying to analyse everything by repeating it through his mind.

Leon took his leave and said he felt something was still hovering and he wouldn't be satisfied until he had run it to ground.

Danny noticed Abe was doing one of his recapping sessions.

"Now what are you sifting through?" he was slightly amused but still aware that things were boiling up.

"Ok." Abe seemed pleased to be able to voice his thoughts "Something isn't sitting right and we could get caught out."

"You mean we're going up the wrong path?" Danny wasn't surprised at this comment but was eager to hear what his friend had in mind.

"Right. Let's start with Emma. Nice girl from good family, meets nice boy, gets married. Nice People. Then what goes wrong?"

Danny was trying to guess what was coming. "She goes off with some unsavoury lot and turns into a totally different person."

"But why? Why would a woman do that?"

"Wanted a bit more excitement in her life, I don't mean to be basic but Nick was a long streak of piss wasn't he?"

Abe jumped on that. "Exactly, he was, but he isn't now is he?"

"Eh?"

"What changed him?"

Danny thought it was obvious. "Emma, we've just said went off the rails."

"But why?" Abe waited but Danny didn't seem to be getting the gist of it. "What sent her?"

"Hang on, you're not saying it was Nick's fault?"

"Well….. seems he hasn't been the goody goody people took him for."

"How do you know?" Danny was wondering why nothing had been said before.

"Go and look at Emma's parents. Now I accept that they would be distraught at her death, but the accusations being hurled at Nick may hold some truth."

Danny was listening now. "Tell me."

"They are blaming him for her having to find entertainment elsewhere after the way he treated her. It appears that, behind closed doors he was an absolute swine. Treated her like shit, and always had his nose in mucky books or videos."

"Well the obvious way to find out is…"Danny thought he was one step a head now.

"Contact Emma." Abe finished. "Done it. She's still in transition poor thing, but she's had one hell of a life with him. Just because she refused to do the quirky things he demanded, he knocked her about but she didn't believe in airing your dirty washing in public and always covered it up with some excuse or other."

"Did she say why she got into drugs?"

"Was so at the end of her rope, she got in with the wrong crowd as we thought and there was no way back."

Danny was alert. "So she isn't actually the Black Mamba but was the creature using her body as a host, because if so, where is it now?"

"You're right on one thing, the black in her mouth was caused by the cocktail she was on, the medic will confirm that. And you're now going to ask where or who it is."

"That would be the next point." Danny agreed.

"But I can't tell you."

"Why not?"

"Because I don't know." Abe's reply flattened the whole atmosphere.

After a moment Danny said "So we are back to square one."

"Not entirely. Think about it. We know it's after Tule, and it is still in hiding, but it must know of his movements as soon as he shows his hand."

"I hate the thought that it could be watching everything, and we don't know."

Abe let the air settle for a minute then whispered "Unless a trap was set."

"That would be dangerous. What were you thinking?" Danny wasn't sure where this was going.

"We couldn't. But there must be some force somewhere who could do just that." He let the thought float around on the airwaves.

"What are you doing?" Danny thought his friend was having an intellectual interlude. "Mamba could pick that up."

"Yes. Couldn't it. Now it won't know who to trust will it?" Abe looked quite satisfied at that statement.

Annie had been hovering round the garden centre but not always in the same form. She didn't want to attract too much attention, so just appeared now and again with her usual innocent sexy talk, but then she would take on a variety of customers to keep passing through and evaluate the spiritual presences. There was always the usual little trail of frustrated spirits who thought they would be alright for a quickie with Sam but they soon learned that they weren't experienced enough to be able to pull it off and had to wonder off in search of relief elsewhere. There were also those who knew they were on to a sure thing so hung around waiting for the next time she let her hair down.

"You not had a bit lately dear?" Annie sidled up to Sam just before they were due to close.

"Bloody hell you could give a person a heart attack!"

Annie laughed. "Bet you're ready for the next. When is it ? Tomorrow, Saturday, both?"

"You're a wicked old woman." Sam laughed then whispered "Why? You want to come along and see if you get lucky?"

"Do I have to bring my own johnnies?"

"What are you like?" Sam laughed. "You won't need those."

"Oh you got to be careful these days, don't want to get any of those sexy downloaded sneezes."

"I think you've got that a bit wrong Annie, but don't worry, just wear two pairs of knickers."

"Oh, I never thought of that." She beckoned Sam to lean nearer "That's one thing those animals don't have to bother about isn't it? They just upend and get on with it. Can you imagine a dog having to stop and put a jiffy on?"

"Annie, go home and watch a cookery programme." Sam was crying with laughter but she felt so good with her around. Little did she realise her guardian was always at her side.

When Sam got home, she thought about calling Katie but they seemed to be drifting apart since this new boyfriend had turned up on the scene.

"It'll end in tears, you'll see, then you'll soon come running back wanting my shoulder to cry on." She consoled herself.

Putting a ready meal in the microwave, she made a cup of tea and wondered about going out on her own again. But she hadn't actually gone alone when she went out with Dishy although the experience had dampened her desires somewhat. All the recent experiences were flashing through her mind and she began to feel unsafe and very alone. Annie was feeding warnings to her, reminding her of how dangerous some of the encounters had been.

"But where can I get a good screwing, there must be some decent meat around ready for me to get my gob round."

Annie kept working on the negative side and was relieved that, for tonight anyway, Sam had no intention of going out.

Katie was getting excited about the dinner the following week, and her boss had asked her to go over to the hotel to finalise the arrangements. It was all a bit sudden but there was good reason for it. In the past when employees had been given plenty of notice, the organiser had always found it difficult to get confirmation of how many would attend, and it was forever changing even to the last minute, but rooms had to be booked and menus chosen plus deposits paid, so to avoid it this time, the date was set, and staff had to say if they were going or not. It seemed to work, because those who may have had other plans changed them so Katie was in possession of the details and those who hadn't paid by the next day, Friday, wouldn't be put on the list. There were a few grunts and groans but only from those who had always been the awkward ones. So the following afternoon she would travel over and everything would be sorted. Her main reason for looking forward to it was the fact that Gary would be with her and everyone would accept that they were a couple. This gave her a buzz just to think about it, and those around her were noticing that something was making her glow.

# Chapter 13

As Thursday slid into Friday, the higher powers were gathering awaiting Tule's attack on Zoe. It was obvious he had been holding off at a safe distance and he probably had some suspicion that he may be ambushed in his attempt to secure his prize. So he must be planning something unexpected hoping to catch them off guard.

But there was a new development. Danny had noticed something which would soon become apparent. Zoe was pregnant. This meant there were now two spirits in situ and already guardians were being placed to protect her offspring which they could tell was female.

"He won't get through the net, it's too strong." Abe assured his friend.

"She'll be on her own all day. It's got to be now, he can't afford to wait much longer, because it's weakening his cause with us on his back." Danny would still be happier when these twenty four hours had passed.

Abe reminded him of one important factor. "Unless he has been on a commando course, he is still way down on the power scale. Oh, his ego leads him to believe he can do miracles, but in fact he still isn't that clever."

"Let's hope that's his downfall." Danny stopped. "Of course!"

"What?"

"I'll go and visit in body. There will be nothing strange in that. I'll find a reason, to update or something, and be in obvious presence."

Abe nodded. "You know that might not be a bad idea at that."

"Sorted." Danny was pleased. This was where he had the slight advantage over his friend, as being in body did have its uses at times.

"I can't get near you now!" Phani was screaming at Pheel.

"Go away, you're disturbing me. Can't you see I'm occupied?" The reply was loaded with hate.

"Tell me when you're not 'occupied', you two will be fused into one the way you're going on."

Pheel sent a piercing vibe towards the other spirit. "And what has that got to do with you? Not your frigging business, now bugger off and get out of my space."

"Oh listen to Miss High and Mighty. Getting a bit above yourself aren't you lady? Well let me remind you of your lowly status. You are dirt and you only pick up dirt. Like attracts." She sounded smug now.

This got Pheel's attention. "Just because you can't get yours, don't look down on those that can. Jealous. That's what you are." And she turned to get on with the job in hand.

"Just look at you." The venom rippled through the air. "Well I'll say one thing, you two are certainly well matched. Shagging the insides out of each other and his wife not rested yet."

Nick sat up aware of both spirits. "You were here before, weren't you?"

"Oh so you do remember me?" Phani tried to sound smug.

Pheel was quick to jump in "And you got your marching orders you trollop, and that's what you've got now. So piss off."

"And is that how you feel Nick?" Phani slid her length behind him sending trembles down his spine.

"Oh déjà vu." Nick moaned. "Get rid of her, I'm bursting here."

But if a man is lying there with two desirable females working on his body in an attempt to be better than the other, it isn't easy for him to fight them off and he was reaching a pitch where he thought his very being would explode.

To the voyeur it must have looked like something from a comedy as both females seemed to be working on his totem pole to see who could bring him off first but still not ignoring the other parts of his body which stirred up the erotic sensations he had come to need.

His shout as he climaxed must have reached quite a distance because it caused such amusement among the lesser sex beasts who rushed in to see what was going on, but Pheel and Phani soon despatched them with the necessary warning to 'go away and stay away' although that wasn't exactly the way it came over.

Nick was lying there absolutely spent and still somewhere in the clouds. Phani had regained her familiar cocky 'told you so' aura, while Pheel was fuming at the intrusion upon her private area.

"Don't think you can pull this stunt again," she spat "go and play with your own, oh sorry, he doesn't want you. What a shame."

Phani was smiling as she looked down at Nick. "Just proved a point sweetheart, I can take what I want, when I want. You are stuck with that trash. Well you suit each other because you're the lowest form of depravity there is. Enjoy." And with that she was gone.

Tule knew exactly what he was going to do and had no doubt as to the success of his plan. It was too clever for any of the others to work out and yet it was simplicity itself. But there were a few hours yet and so he could sit back and wait for precisely the right moment.

Leon had been very busy. Fortunately he was able to work under his own initiative, as the likes of Abe and Danny knew that once he was on the job he wouldn't give up until he was completely satisfied. Although they could ask for his assistance, this spirit was in touch with many highly skilled groups that he could call on but their identity was never disclosed.

Apart from still holding the jobs at the three hotels, Leon was observing all that was going on in the area for he knew you had to keep your thoughts open continually. He was now aware that the other group's presence at the hotel where Zoe was covering was still as strong as ever which seemed strange as she wasn't there today and would finish on reception tomorrow. He relayed this information to Abe.

"Holy cow!" Danny yelled when told. "We've been thinking it would be when Zoe was alone, but he could be gearing up for her last stint tomorrow."

"What else has Leon noticed at that place?" Abe wondered.

"Nothing out of the ordinary, only the other group are still all there. None have gone back to either of the other hotels."

"So Mamba thinks Tule is homing in there." Abe was musing. "She or he, is going to attack him at the hotel, most likely tomorrow."

Danny was adamant "Well I'm still going to protect Zoe today, especially as she's carrying."

"Too right." Abe was still niggling at something. "You know, this Mamba is supposed to be a clever sod. Just supposing….." he trailed off.

"Now what's eating you?"

Abe paused before saying "What if that's what it wants us to think?"

Both were silent now.

"Mind games." Danny whispered. "Like I said, my guard is staying up until it shows its hand, wherever that might be."

"I'm anxious to hear from Leon again, but I'm not contacting him for obvious reasons."

"We can't." Danny agreed "Can't risk blowing it now."

Joel had been at work since 8am and it had been quite busy, but when he snatched a quick coffee, checked that Zoe was alright.

"I'm fine." She assured him. Something was different and she suspected the reason but didn't want to tell him on the phone. When they were together that evening, that would be the right time.

"Don't over do it," he laughed, "I know you. You'll be sorting out more drawers and things."

"I'll be ok. Now don't work to hard." She blew him a kiss.

"You've picked a good day to be off. There's loads coming in for the weekend, but don't worry, quite a few are arriving tomorrow, so you won't miss out."

"You cheeky thing." She laughed and they agreed to catch up later when it was convenient.

No sooner had she put the phone down when it rang again.

"Now what have you forgotten?" She asked.

"Nothing. Was wondering if I could pop over and see how things are going?" The reply wasn't from her husband.

"Danny. How good to hear from you. Of course you can. Joel's at work of course."

"Well I'm passing and thought I'd just say 'Hi'. That's what big brothers are for isn't it, and to cadge a cup of your delicious coffee."

"You come whenever you like, you're always welcome here, you know that."

Danny said his farewell and couldn't help noticing the tone of his sister-in-law's voice.

"She knows." He smiled.

Katie had been asked to go over to the hotel and finalise the room they were hiring for the dinner. She'd never been to a function there before so didn't know what to expect and her boss said he thought there had been a few alterations, so he wanted to be sure everything would be in order. He told her to use a taxi and get receipts for the journeys, as it would save him time having to sort it out.

Just after lunch she arrived at the place and one of the staff took her to see the room.

"This is where the dinner is served," she pointed to the tables at one end"and then the band or disco uses the stage in that corner, and the bar is over there. We put a few small tables down the sides for people who want to dance more and keep their drinks handy."

"It all looks very nice." Katie was taking in the whole room.

All the while she was thinking that in a week's time she and her beloved would be sharing a lovely evening here. After finalising all the details she returned to work and started looking forward to tonight with Gary.

Sam knew there was no point asking Katie to go out with her but it was Friday and she needed to go somewhere. People didn't stay in when the weekend was upon them, it was the time to enjoy yourself. There seemed to be nothing else for it but to go round to the Eagles and see if there was any talent hanging about, not that it seemed likely but you never knew if you might get lucky. Annie was trying to push images of recent events through her mind again to make her aware of the dangers, but Sam was in a rebellious mood, plus the fact that if the likes of her friend could pull, why couldn't she?

As she made her way home, she noticed there was a fun night advertised.

"Wonder what that is." She thought as she read the A board outside the pub. Being nosey she went into the bar and asked one of the staff what it was all about.

"Oh just a karaoke really, it's one of the regular's idea, not had one for a while and we've got Halloween coming up soon so we shall advertise that and if everyone's had a good time tonight, they'll come back, we hope."

"Sounds good."

"Why? You and your friend coming?" the barman's question wasn't exactly an invitation.

"Might. Well let's say I might, she's got a chap now."

"You not going to do anything daft I hope." He wished he hadn't told her anything, but the board was outside so he had little choice.

"Me? It's not me mate, it's the others." She turned to leave then said "See you later then."

"Not if I can help it." He thought.

Walking home she had a brainwave. Of course, she'd ask them both along, and they'd be so wrapped up in each other she wouldn't feel guilty about going off on her own for once.

As soon as she got in she called Katie.

"Hello."

"Katie it's me. Look there's a karaoke on at the Eagles tonight, how about it? And before you say you're out with your feller, bring him, the more the merrier." She paused for breath.

"Hello Sam. Well I'm sorry but we have already made other plans." Was the reply but Katie thought that they wouldn't want to be doing that instead of, well, getting to know each other better.

"Oh come on, it'll be a blast." Sam wasn't giving up and wasn't getting the message.

"No thank you. As I have just said…….."

"I know," Sam interrupted "you're doing something else." And threw the handset so hard it flew across the room.

"Well, I'm going," she decided. "Calls herself a friend. Pile of shit more like."

There was no way Katie would have swapped a night in Sam's company with the lovemaking session she and Gary would be enjoying to the full. Oh they would certainly be getting to know each other, but finding out more about which part of the body produced the most sensual results. And that could take a very long time.

Danny had been satisfied that the area round Zoe was more than protected, in fact it was more like a fortress and when Joel returned from work, there would be combined protection.

But the big question now was, when was Tule going to strike? Surely he would have come into the open by now for time was running short and Zoe would not be alone. Abe was wondering if they had put too much store on that. Maybe Tule would attempt to snatch her when they least expected it, tomorrow for instance because the group in presence at the hotel were going to draw him there. The ideas were being thrown to and fro but as soon as Tule did appear, so would The Black Mamba who was probably merely letting Zoe be the bait.

Everything had to stay on high alert, and to those souls who had very receptive powers, the surrounding air was electric with anticipation.

When Joel arrived home, Zoe was waiting for him with a broad smile on her face.

"You look better than you did." He kissed her as they moved from the hall to the lounge.

"I feel it." She grabbed him into her arms. "And I feel different."

"Must be in a good way, you look as though you've won the lottery."

"Better than that." She took his hand and slid it down to her tummy.

"You don't mean...?" His eyes nearly shot out of their sockets.

She nodded. "I think so. I've been sick every morning, and I just feel so different, and I'm late."

How long they stayed hugging each other they never knew, but there were tears of happiness in both their eyes.

"Oh and Danny called in," she thought suddenly "just wanted to see we were alright."

"I'm surprised he didn't guess, he seems to know things before he's told." Joel laughed.

"Funny you should say that, he did give me a funny smile."

"Well if you were grinning like a Cheshire cat, I expect he put two and two."

They didn't seem to want to let each other go, but Zoe had cooked his favourite dinner and didn't want it to spoil, so they sat down to one of the happiest meals they had shared for some time.

"And to think I told you not to overdo it." Joel said as he cleared his plate. "You must have thought I suspected."

"No, just what a surprise it would be." She thought for a moment then said wistfully "Can't announce it yet, too early."

"Absolutely, let's wait until we're sure." His hand reached across the table and stroked hers. "Thank you Mummy."

"Thank you Daddy." she whispered.

Both hoped inwardly that this may put an end to the recent spooky happenings, and they would have each other with no outside intervention.

The day had passed without any major incident. Danny had been worried since his visit that Tule, in trying to take Zoe would inevitably also lift her unborn child with her. The thought crossed his mind that if Tule had tried and realised the situation, it might have put him off striking for now.

Quickly he checked with Abe but there had been no sign of any trail so it could only mean that Tule hadn't even been in the area because he would have been forced to attempt the snatch while Zoe was alone.

"This means it has to be tomorrow." He concluded.

"Maybe." Was all Abe would offer.

"Well if not, when? Just look at that show of presence at the hotel. They wouldn't waste that amount of spirit power for nothing."

"He or she wouldn't you mean." Abe corrected him.

After a few moments Danny said "Ever had the feeling we are being taken for a ride?"

"All the time." Abe could be so casual about these things, but it didn't mean his mind wasn't still working like a machine.

Danny mused for a minute. "You know I wouldn't mind so much if it was something really sinister, But Tule isn't that much of a threat. Ok, he's a sex pest but why is Black Mamba after him at all?"

Abe joined in the thought now. "The creature always has some vendetta against another being, and if it wasn't him, it would be some other poor sod. But there must be one almighty score that has to be settled, as we've already agreed."

"Just what was it the he stole?" Danny started doing Abe's trick of summing up. "We thought it must be a person, or their soul, but it could have been anything."

Abe added "And why is it so important that he/she has to patiently lay in wait for him?"

Danny replied "You know, I almost wish they'd get on with it and clear off out."

"Been thinking that all along," Abe laughed "but at least the other business seems to have dried up."

"Nice pun. Any more where that came from?"

Their levity was interrupted by a short ping. Leon was sending a coded message that things were moving but they couldn't trace the source at the moment. Suddenly they were back on full alert scanning the area for signs of tell tale disruption in the air which could herald the onset of the confrontation.

It was almost midnight. Sam had met up with someone who she thought might fill a hole, as she put it, but just as she was about to leave the pub with him, another likely one appeared and she side tracked, leaving her original catch to disappear. This could have caused an argument but the new one simply said "If she's yours, keep her under control will you. I'm not here to pick up that kind of baggage."

"Who are you calling baggage?" Sam had screamed.

"You." Her first one shouted, his drink taking over, "Now, are we up for a poke or what?"

At this point the landlord had decided that it would be better if they left as some had now had enough to drink. Sam looked round for the second man to give him a piece of her mind and suggest that as he'd ruined her night, he had better come up with the goods himself. But he was nowhere to be seen and she had no option but to be guided out of the pub along with a few others.

So now she lay in bed alone watching the clock eat away the minutes until Saturday slipped in.

"Ah well, better luck tonight," she thought as she popped a few pills to help her to sleep.

Annie sat at her side contented that her ruse had worked to keep her safe for now. Appearing as a man, Sam would never guess her identity and it was best to keep 'Annie' for other situations. If her charge could have seen the real person guarding her at this moment, she would have been in for quite a surprise.

Katie had stayed over at Gary's and her usual guardians were happy that she was in very safe hands. The couple were very close but she realised that she didn't know all that much about him. She had been very open with him so he knew where she worked, where she lived and her likes and dislikes. But all he would divulge was that he worked for a government department which took him away sometimes and it was one of those jobs which was very important to national security so he wasn't allowed to discuss it. She would liked to have known more, but knew there was no point in pushing the matter as he wasn't going to say any more than he already had.

She was certainly being spoilt and he treated her with respect and a great deal of love and everything seemed to be too good to be true. Maybe it was because she had felt so empty and now there was someone who had bought love into her life in a way she had never known, even with Stefan and this made her feel a little guilty.

Now he was going to cook her breakfast and they would make plans for the weekend, for he wasn't going to let her out of his sight, then he could afford her all the protection she may need. He was aware that Sam hadn't scored last night so was happy in the fact that there would be no new sexual thrill seekers hovering in the vicinity.

Tule was still biding his time. He guessed that certain areas would be expecting him to go in for Zoe when she was least protected but he wasn't going to risk spoiling the one chance he may have by being hasty. It would be spontaneous, and he would be watching for any chink in the armour to take his property. Not daring to get too close himself he had used eager little scouts to keep him informed of any developments and was quite amused at the overkill of strength. He still had his simple plan on hold which he could put into play at a moment's notice.

But one thing hadn't reached him. He was totally unaware of the impending threat from The Black Mamba and that knowledge would have had a serious effect on his coming plans.

Zoe arrived for her last day as receptionist at the hotel and managed to keep her sickness to herself. She only had one bout after she arrived but everyone was too busy to notice, thinking she had just gone to the toilet. Joel was right when he said it would be busy and it was the same at his hotel. By lunchtime all three in the area were fully booked not only with guests but all the functions rooms were heaving.

To the onlooker from the spirit world, Zoe's hotel must have looked a right mess, for besides the human factor, there so many entities flooding the place, you couldn't have put a piece of paper between them.

Leon hadn't been idle. He had found out from the venue in the middle of the city that the watcher had been recalled leaving Vanke upset at being left with no explanation. The poor thing was in such a state, his tantrums were disturbing the wave patterns around the whole building. Harsh as it could sound, Abe was happy for that to continue for although it was outside the patch of the three under watch, any distraction may be useful. But Leon wasn't letting go of his hold on his current targets as something told him the concentration on the one hotel was a blind, but at the same time, that could also be false. Maybe Mamba was actually going to draw Tule into the place again and then pounce.

Danny was mulling over these conjectures, and still had the feeling that Tule couldn't show himself there a second time even in a different guise, because although Zoe wouldn't recognise him, the surrounding spirits certainly would, so his plan would be scuppered. But was Tule stupid enough to think that you didn't look in the same place twice? Or even did he consider the likes of him and Abe wouldn't take it into account?

"Well," he said to his friend "this is the last day she's on reception here, then it's back to the offices, so time is running out for Mamba."

"I've got a horrible feeling we are being held on a piece of string." Abe was serious and added "There has to be something we haven't noticed. I'm going to go over every single scrap of what has gone on. It's got to be staring at us."

Danny knew that when Abe was in this mood, nothing would budge him so it was best to leave him to himself for a while and hope that he did in fact come up with something.

When Zoe left at the end of her shift, there was almost a sigh of relief among the watching powers, but the congregation of the other group hadn't moved. This left Abe with one very important conclusion but he wasn't about to voice it just yet.

Katie and Gary had enjoyed the weekend so much, neither wanted it to end, but she reminded him that it brought the next one nearer.

"Why is that so important to you?" he laughed "We see each other every day, and we do fill every minute with the most enjoyable moments." He gave her a cheeky grin as he said it.

"I know we do, and I treasure every second but I will be able to walk in to the dinner and everyone will know you are mine."

"That really is important isn't it?"

"You know it is. Isn't it to you?" she was slightly deflated at his answer.

He took a deep breath. "You know you mean more to me than life itself but…."

She never liked the word 'but' because there was always something coming that wasn't nice.

He continued before she could say anything. "Sometimes in my work, I have to go away for a while."

"This work you can't tell me about." The hurt was in her voice.

"It's why I rarely get involved with anyone. The outcome of a whole operation relies on secrecy. If I told you of some of the things I've been involved in, things that have hit the headlines, well, you wouldn't like it."

"Is it illegal?" she was worried now.

"No. In no way. But it could affect national security. Now do you see why I have to lead a covert life?"

She still wasn't sure. "I wish you were something boring, like a banker or, well anything really. I shall worry now." It wasn't only his job she was concerned about. A nagging doubt was rearing its ugly head as to whether she was getting the truth.

"Are you saying you will have to go away soon?" her stomach churned. "Not before next Saturday, please tell me it isn't that."

He put his arm round her "I can be called at any time. I'm just praying it isn't before then."

Her heart sank. She had set so much store on this event and now it seemed to be threatened.

"And you can't refuse?" she tried.

"There is no way. You see they wouldn't class going to a dinner to be more important than saving someone from a sniper, for instance."

"Do you have to carry a gun?"

"It has been known." He wasn't being very explicit. "Look. It may not happen. I just have to warn you that's all. I do have to take off rather quickly you see. Not many people can accept it."

"I never realised." She felt she should have got to know more about him before plunging into the deep end. Then after a moment asked "Will you always have to do it?"

He thought carefully before giving his answer. "As long as I am of use."

He could always be recalled from one guarding job to go to another but usually he wasn't forced to be so close to his charge. Messages had been received that Katie was in considerable danger which was why he had been placed until the higher powers were sure she was safe.

They cuddled for a while then he said "Of course. We don't have to wait."

"What?" She wondered what he meant.

He smiled. "It's important to you for people to know we are a couple. Right?"

"Yes, I said that."

"Well then. Time doesn't matter. We don't have to leave it until the meal. Let them see now. I'll pick you up from work and I'll meet you at lunchtime. Don't worry, prying eyes will soon pick up on it."

"So by next Saturday…." she started to say but he finished it for her.

"It will be old hat. Everyone will know and think nothing about it."

"Oh, I never thought of that." She was happier now, although his previous comments still weighed heavily on her.

The next few days passed without incident and Danny was checking that the clearing up from the previous sexual invasion had been completed.

"It's as though it had never happened." He told Abe.

"Caused a fracas while it was here though. Hope there isn't another one too soon."

"You can bet there will be. It's a strong emotion and people will always be drawn to sex, basic instinct after all."

A quick flash message alerted them both.

"Forget the first hotel. There's something building at the edge of the city one." This was where Leon was still working as a domestic.

The next message followed immediately. "Keep out, no presences. Severe." This meant that any attendance could jeopardise the operation.

"We thought the group was a decoy, you watch, they'll disperse soon." Abe jumped.

Danny was alert for the next communication and he didn't have to wait long.

"Tule booked in as a woman. Unrecognisable."

"Oh shit." Danny yelled. "That's where Zoe is now working in the offices."

"The crafty bastard," Abe realised the plan now. "He didn't have to appear before because he knew that when the fuss died down, he would just walk in calm as you like."

"Well done Leon." Danny said "I knew he was hanging on in those three jobs for a reason, must have had one of his instincts something like this would happen."

"Yep, he never shuts a door before time. Bet he's been picking up all sorts of snippets."

"Wish we could get closer." Danny thought.

"Daren't. He'd sniff us out in a blink. Anyway, he won't suss Leon, and he can always call on one of his cronies."

Suddenly they both jumped as the truth hit them. The Black Mamba must have known its prey would try a trick like this, so what trap had he/she got ready for such an eventuality. That was something they would have to find out, but for now Zoe must be watched. There was sufficient protection around her now to ward off any attempt by Tule to take her, but just to be safe they would strengthen the guard where she worked.

There was another factor in the mix now. If Mamba decided to attack Tule on Saturday evening, Katie and Gary would be there. Up to now the latter had been able to sail under the radar of passing sentinels by projecting his bodily image to such an extent it covered his true self in order to afford the most protection for Katie. He must be warned to strengthen the shield as Tule may be able to detect him, in which case Mamba certainly would. However it may not be a problem if the attack didn't happen that night. There was also the point that Gary had warned he often had to leave at a moment's notice so could easily withdraw without further explanation, however sad it may leave Katie.

"Let's hope it makes its move before." Abe wished.

"If only things were that simple." Danny agreed.

Phani had been going through a period of rejection which didn't bring out her best points. She had been forced to give up on Joel altogether and had decided on a new tack. Sensing Sam's frustration, she thought she'd home in on her for a while for she was never short of a bit of entertainment, even if it did turn out to be the 'three whippets'. Whip it in, whip it out and wipe it. Obviously Phani much preferred the lengthy full blown session with all tricks of enjoyment thrown in, but at the moment she'd have anything that was being passed around. They actually made quite a good pair, the only thing was that they would be sharing the same bloke as the spirit couldn't just grab any passing male and go for it. Poor devil would probably mess his pants in fright. But if she could ride tandem for a while, who knows what it could lead to.

Sam was really pissed off with being alone and wandered down to the pub. It was only Wednesday but she couldn't wait for the weekend and had to find some fun now. Little did she know she was far from being alone and her new companion was using her talents to search the area, not just the bit Sam was occupying.

For some reason she found herself walking past the place and heading towards the bus stop. She got off near one of the smaller clubs and hovered round the entrance as though waiting for someone. Annie was doing her best to pull her away but Sam, now accompanied by Phani, was on a mission. She needed a bit of fresh.

"You going in or what?" The rough voice belonged to one of two men standing a bit closer than most would have liked.

"Waiting for a willing one to escort me." She pushed her tits towards him.

"Well get your arse in there then." They flanked her as they marched her inside.

"Bit common dear." Phani eyed them up. "Don't fancy yours." Then laughed because the which ever Sam had, Phani would too. But what was the problem? It was inevitable that they would have both before long.

"Oh well, better than nothing." Phani thought as she got her spiritual juices ready to flow.

Annie almost threw her hands up in despair but she had to stay in place, although she was going to make sure she wasn't in the firing line when push came to shove.

Nick didn't know how he would have coped with all the trauma of the last week if it hadn't been for Pheel. At least he could loose himself in her presence as well as constantly draining his tadpoles. One thing was for sure, she wasn't going anywhere and he would have a constant companion. After her, no bodily woman would do. They were now enjoying one of their 'how many positions in thirty seconds' target which was the latest amusement, but it always led to the serious stuff.

He was certain he had grown in dimensions and was very proud of the weapon he sported but he didn't realise he was becoming a victim of sexual addiction and although there was no one to tell him he was also suffering from sexomnia. His personality was changing but all he was aware of was how good life was now, and when would his next relief be?

On Thursday afternoon, Katie's boss asked if she would mind nipping over to the hotel with some table settings. She jumped at the idea and said that her friend would gladly take her later. She rang Gary who was only too pleased to help and suggested they had a drink while they were there and perhaps include a meal to test the cuisine. That seemed an excellent idea and would save them cooking so he booked a table to make sure. She was so excited and was ready long before they were due to leave. Her outfit was new and she felt as though she had cast off the tired image.

"Seems a very nice place." he said as they made their way into the foyer.

Katie left the name cards with the receptionist and they went to the bar until it was time to eat.

The meal was perfect and Gary said he hoped it would be up to that standard on Saturday because he had found that when there were a lot of people, the food didn't always seem so good. Neither wanted the evening to end so when they had finished they sat in the lounge for a while and Katie lapped up every moment of being seen out with him. She hoped it could go on for ever, whether or not he had to be called away to work. As long as she was his, that was all she wanted and she hoped and prayed that he felt exactly the same.

# Chapter 14

Leon was still warning of the rising energy levels in the area and although he had first picked them up in the hotel, they now seemed to be circulated in the surrounding area almost as if something was searching. Abe suggested they try and get Katie out as soon as possible as she could be attracting the evil because they still didn't know exactly what she was being protected from.

"Unless," Danny was hesitant "she is the source."

"Do you know what you're implying?" Abe sounded angry.

"Can we rule her out?"

"No. You're right we can't, but for now we have to act as though she is the innocent party."

This was a dilemma. The attention only seemed to be on this particular hotel since she had been visiting it, so either it was drawing her there, or it was her presence that Leon was detecting as the threat. But on the other hand both could be wrong and she could just be an innocent bystander.

"Get her out." Abe decided. "Either way, remove her from the scene."

A message went to Leon but they didn't expect a reply, and not knowing what else he may have learned, didn't even know if he could act upon it. It was the inevitable waiting game.

Nick was reaching another climax and yelling his usual profanities when Pheel stopped suddenly.

"Don't leave me like this. What are you doing you crazy bitch?" he was in agony.

"Sorry, I'm done."

"Stop arsing around. Finish me off."

"Nope.

He was so near he had no option but to do it himself and as he lay there gasping he could feel her pulling away from his presence.

"Where the hell are you going?"

"I told you," the tone was cold and unfeeling. "I'm done. Don't you understand?"

"What's got into you? Get back here."

"There's nothing else you can do for me Nick, thanks for the ride."

He was screaming mostly in temper. The nerve of her to think she could just take her leave without his permission, and what about all the love and erotic moments? But it all fell on deaf ears for she had left for good.

He was crying now, completely exhausted from his physical exertion, but more drained from this sudden rejection. His whole world collapsed round him and he had never felt so alone and deserted in his whole life. All the physical things meant nothing and as he lay there visions floated before his eyes. Emma as she was before he ruined her life. The nice house. His friends Joel and Zoe. His promotion. It seemed that all this was in the past and his soul was dying.

The guardians let him have time to adjust before they enclosed him in their comforting care. It would be a long haul back, but they would do it, as they had retrieved many before him. They were relieved this spirit had left for they knew she was no good but had no idea the evil that had been in this house. The cleaners would be sent to rid the place of every scrap of her existence so that Nick had a chance of getting himself back on the upward path.

Pheel had timed her exit to the second and was on her way to her objective. She laughed at how Phani had tried to rule her, without even guessing what she was up against but it was a good cover and no one had even the slightest suspicion of who she really was. But now it was time for revenge and nothing was going to prevent her from claiming the spoils. There was a lot to account for and it was payback time.

Her presence was now being picked up and the messages were flying around the airwaves.

"So she's The Black Mamba." Abe felt cheated. Why hadn't they suspected either her or Phani even? But it was easy to say when the truth was out.

"So she's after Tule," Danny commented "but not waiting for him to attack Zoe. We got that wrong."

"Perhaps got fed up. She knows where he is and she'll see right through his female disguise?"

They both watched as she homed in on the hotel where Katie was just leaving. Unbeknown to the mortals, this tremendous force was coming in at speed and nothing was going to stop it, so they carried on drinking and eating and enjoying themselves.

Mamba paused for a moment to take stock of the exact position of her prey then in a streak of lightning she struck, wrapping herself around Gary's neck in a strangle hold.

"You robbed me of everything, now I am going to do the same to you." she screamed indicating to Katie.

He slid from her grasp and while his body remained in the car his true being rose upwards splitting itself into small parts all around her until she didn't know which bit to attack so she took whatever was within her reach and tried to separate it permanently from his soul. He reformed some of the pieces and tried a strangle hold on her neck but her tail thrashed herself free. She now tried to dive down to grab Katie but he blocked the way. They were evenly matched in power and status and it would only be decided by who had the longest staying power.

While the battle raged around her, Katie was trying to help Gary who was slumped over the steering wheel apparently choking. Frantically she called for help and a man came rushing over, saw what was happening and pulled him from the car to try to clear his airway.

Katie was going hysterical now and one of the staff was trying to calm her but it was no use. An ambulance had been called but seemed to take for ever. When they did arrive, they moved Gary into the vehicle where they could work on him out of sight.

The battle was vicious, neither giving way to the other but suddenly a force appeared that surrounded the Mamba on all sides enclosing her in a tube and she was transported away to a place that would be very difficult for her to escape from for a very long time.

Gary was trying to reassemble his spiritual self but the scars were there making it difficult to return to his body at the moment. Abe and Danny were now in presence and had to advise him that his job was over and he ought to leave his earthly stint for a period of recuperation.

"But it's my fault she was in danger. If she hadn't been close to me Mamba wouldn't have threatened her. I can't leave her now."

"You were the target. We thought it was Tule, but she was after you. There must be a serious score to settle between you two." Abe was anxious to learn the truth.

"There was." Gary wasn't about to divulge much. "Goes back a long way, but she won't let it go. I'm not the only one. Tule did get in the way, but he's nothing."

"There's one thing that puzzles me." Danny said." That's why they sent you to guard Katie."

"That's easy." Abe answered for him. "It was only to guard against the sex fiends that Sam was attracting. Mamba only surfaced later when Gary was already in situ."

"Yes, I've had plenty of low profile jobs to keep my head down, but thank goodness I still keep my skills up or she'd have taken me out straight away." Gary added.

"So, "Abe asked "what's your decision?"

Gary looked down at his body and the state of Katie. "I wasn't supposed to be here long, but things changed."

"You saying you want an extension?" Danny smiled "Don't know if they'll allow it."

The answer was that he could go back for now, but would be needed elsewhere so to make the best of it as his time had to be limited.

"And they think it's all tickety boo in the spirit world." Gary sighed, "In fact it's a damn sight harder."

"You'd better get going and put that lady out of her misery." Danny suggested.

But Abe added "For now at least."

# About the Author

Tabbie Browne grew up in the Cotswolds in central England which is where she gets the inspiration for her novels. Her father had very strong spiritual beliefs and she feels he guides her but always with a warning to stay in control of your own mind.

Her earliest recollection of writing was at primary school and it has seemed to play a part at significant times during her life. She thinks it is only when we are forced to take step back and unclutter our minds for a while we realise our potential. This point was proved when she slipped a disc, and being very immobile had to write in pencil as the ink would not flow upwards! At this time she wrote many comical poems which, when able again, performed to many audiences. Comedy is very difficult but you know if you are a success with a live audience.

In 1991 as a collector of novelty salt and pepper shakers, she realised there was no book in the UK devoted entirely to the subject. So she wrote one. Which meant she achieved the fact that it was the first of its kind in the country and it sold well to like collectors not only in the UK but in the USA.

Another large upheaval came when she was diagnosed with breast cancer, and due to the extreme energy draining, found it difficult to work for an employer. So she took a freelance journalist course and was pleased to have articles accepted, her main joy being the piece about her father and his life in the village. Again the inspiration area.

But the novels were eating away inside and drawing on her experience at stamp and coin fairs she wrote *'A Fair Collection'* which she serialised in the magazine 'Squirrels' for people who hoard things.

When she wrote *'White Noise Is Heavenly Blue'* and its sequel *'The Spiral'* she sat at the keyboard and the titles just came to her, as did the content of the books. There is no way she could write the plot first as she never knew what was coming next, almost as if somebody was dictating, and for that reason she could never change anything.

**Loves:**
Animals,
Also performing in live theatre and working as a tv supporting artiste.

**Hates:**
Bad manners,
Insincere people.